TALES OF UNSPEAKABLE TASTE

JOHN BRUNI

© 2015 "Attitude Adjustment" in Literary Hatchet #12, © 2019 "Monster Cock 2", © 2014 "Daisy, Jeppke, and the Kid" in Hardboiled #47, © 2015 "Snipe Hunt" in Jitter #3, © 2007 "Holliday Steps Out" in Trail of Indiscretion #7, © 2012 "Party's Over" in 4 Star Stories #7, © 2005 "Clyde Nebbins Meets the Devil" in Nuthouse #77, © 2019 "JESUS WAS DEAD FOR THREE DAYS! CLICK HERE TO SEE HOW HE CAME BACK!", © 2014 "Captain Meth-Mouth on the High Seas of Chicago" in Triple Zombie, © 2014 "The Last of His Kind" in Bloodbond May 2014, © 2014 "Going Down" in M #2, © 2019 "Rumble in the Retirement Home", © 2016 "Late Start" on Flash Fiction Friday as "A Late Start", © 2015 "Piety" in Not Your Average Monster Vol. 1, © 2019 "Black Friday", © 2009 "The Worm" in Vile Things, © 2015 "Dream Quest for Dope" in Blood for You: A Literary Tribute to GG Allin, © 2014 "I Am the End" on Strange Story Saturdays, © 2019 "Dial 9 for Apocalypse", © 2019 "Butt Club", © 2009 "The Path" in Shroud #5

ISBN: 978-1-950305-64-3 (sc)
ISBN: 978-1-950305-65-0 (ebook)

First printing edition: October 26, 2020
Published by Bizarro Pulp Press in the United States of America.
Cover Design by Nicholas Day and Don Noble
Layout/Interior Layout Don Noble
Edited by Nicholas Day

Bizarro Pulp Press, an imprint of JournalStone Publishing
3052 Sassafras Trail
Carbondale, Illinois 62901

Bizarro Pulp Press may be ordered through booksellers or by contacting:
JournalStone | www.journalstone.com

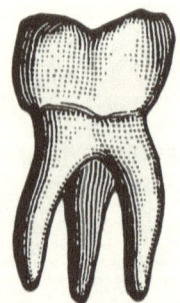

Table of Contents

Attitude Adjustment
5

Monster Cock 2
19

Daisy, Jeppke, and the Kid
24

Snipe Hunt
32

Holliday Steps Out
36

Party's Over
39

Clyde Nebbins Meets the Devil
45

JESUS WAS DEAD FOR THREE DAYS! CLICK HERE TO SEE HOW HE CAME BACK!
48

Captain Meth-Mouth on the High Seas of Chicago
56

The Last of His Kind
82

Going Down
90

Rumble in the Retirement Home
93

Late Start
104

Piety
107

Black Friday
123

The Worm
131

Dream Quest for Dope
140

I Am the End
152

Dial 9 for Apocalypse
156

Butt Club
159

The Path
180

Story Notes
190

ATTITUDE ADJUSTMENT

I never really liked Derrick. He was too much of a bro, if you get me. Drank a lot, liked sports too much, lied about hookups he'd had, things like that. I had to be nice to him—or at least polite—because we worked in the same department. Every time he talked about selling drugs when he was a kid or training boxers in college, or whenever he fist-pumped like the guido he wished he was, I had to choke back a snarky or sometimes even hateful comment. It's bad enough working with an asshole, but to be at each others' throats for eight hours a day? No thanks.

My tolerance of him got me into this mess. Because I wanted to keep the peace at work, I was stuck in the break room, listening to his macho wannabe lies. Honestly I wasn't listening. I just kept looking for a way out of the conversation. Nod in the right places, offer a polite laugh here or there, and I could hopefully get this over with and get back to work.

And then it happened. He gently tapped my arm with his hand and carefully looked back and forth, like a pedestrian about to cross the street. Just then I knew he was going to say something truly reprehensible.

"Hey, so he told me this joke, right?" A sly grin worked its way across his face. "How many black guys does it take to tar a roof?"

Ugh. Dude. Come on.

He didn't hesitate: "One, if you slice him thin enough." And he laughed, slapping his knee.

"What is *wrong* with you?" I asked.

"What?" Confused.

"What about me made you think I'd be cool with hearing a racist joke?"

"Oh, come on," he said. "It's not like I'm a racist or anything. I just thought it was kind of funny. I don't hate black people. Hey, I censored the joke. The way he told it to me, he used the n-word. I changed it."

"Oh, I'm sorry then. You're a real standup guy."

"Admit it. You thought it was funny. You just don't want to say it because of the PC police."

I couldn't take it anymore. "Oh my God. Stop talking. In fact, you're an asshole. Never talk to me again."

"But—"

I didn't give him a chance to plead his case. I stalked off to my cube, where I fumed for the rest of my break. It took a certain level of insensitivity to get to me, and Derrick hit it perfectly. It sucked that I'd blown up like that. At least he'd never talk to me again. I hoped.

Ten minutes later, he came back from lunch. Didn't even look at me. Good.

Maybe about an hour later one of the supervisors came by his desk and took him off the floor. I didn't think anything of it at the time, so I just went about my work.

Derrick came back twenty minutes later. Something about him seemed a bit off, like a slightly deflated balloon hovering low enough for its string to brush the ground.

Part of me wanted to ask what happened, but I had to remind myself of our disagreement. I figured he'd screwed up, and the boss had taken him down a peg or two.

Shortly after, my supervisor came by, a big, fake smile plastered to her face. Felicia was incapable of having a genuine, honest emotion. "Are you busy?"

Of course I was, but you can't just say that to management. Instead I offered my own phony smile. "No. What's up?"

"Got time for a quick meeting?"

As if I had a choice in the matter. "Sure."

She took me off the floor and into one of the conference rooms, where she closed the door. Uh-oh. It was going to be one of *those* meetings.

Felicia took a seat across the table from me and opened her laptop. She started typing. "How is it out there today?" Almost absently.

"You know how it is." Just like I knew all the safe answers to give.

Finally she looked over at me. "So. We heard about a little incident earlier this morning between you and Derrick Riley."

Oh. That's what this was about. She just needed to talk to witnesses for her report, or whatever. "Yeah," I said.

"I'd like to hear what happened from your perspective."

So I told her everything, from when Derrick intercepted me while getting water in the break room to when I called him out for being a racist asshole—except, I didn't say the a-word, not with management.

Felicia took notes the whole time, fingers clacking away at the keys of her laptop. Only when I finished did she look up from the screen. "That's everything?"

"Yeah."

"Good. That matches the other stories." She leaned back as if she'd just finished a filling meal and couldn't eat one more bite. "There is an issue, though."

"Hm?"

"Well, we don't like it when employees feel the need to settle issues on their own. We needed a chain of evidence, if you understand what I mean. These things need to be handled by a supervisor, especially considering how you handled it."

I asked, "What do you mean?"

"By confronting Derrick out in the open like that, it could be construed as workplace violence by some."

Had I heard that right? "It's not like I hit him or threatened him."

"We don't tolerate confrontation here," Felicia said. "You should have come to me or another available supe instead."

"But . . . he told me a joke I found offensive. I called him out on it. I don't see what the problem is."

"You shouldn't have said anything. You should have come to us instead."

I've never been a tattletale. I prefer the old playground rule about snitches getting stitches. However, even though every fiber of my being wanted to rebel against Felicia, I knew how to play the corporate game. This was just a new wrinkle, that's all. *Just tell her what she wants to hear and go back to doing whatever you want. Just ride this out.*

"Okay. Well, now I know. I'll know what to do next time."

She smiled. "Splendid! There's just one more thing. Because we have a zero-tolerance policy when it comes to workplace violence, some of those in HR wanted you to be terminated."

I almost gagged, and fear gut-stabbed me with its cold dagger. I couldn't believe what she'd just said. I had to literally bite my own tongue to stop from saying something that would surely have gotten me fired.

"We've never had a problem with you before," she continued, "and you're an invaluable member of our team. Considering the nature of the incident, I was able to talk them out of it. Instead, you'll be getting a write-up."

This couldn't be real. I forced a tight smile onto my face, as if to thank her for this stark raving bullshit.

"I want to remind you that you only get three write-ups," she said. "This is your first, okay?"

I choked back any sensible response. "Okay."

"I sent a copy of the write-up to your employee dashboard. Read it over, and if it looks good, check the box that says you agree, all right?"

I nodded.

"If you have any questions, let me know. Thank you!"

Dazed, I shambled out of the conference room, pausing by the mystery door across the hall. Nobody knew what was behind it because only the supes were allowed to go in there. A sign proclaimed in big bold letters, DO NOT ENTER. My coworkers joked about there being a torture chamber back there, but it's probably just a room for employee records.

Today that sign seemed to mock me. I ignored it and went back to my cube, where I pulled up the write-up on my screen and stared at it. A million things ran through my head—things I should have said, things I wanted to do now—but all of it would have ended in me getting fired. As much as this job sucked, I liked it better than the other jobs I'd had. Plus, the pay was good, and the benefits were better than most.

I sighed and clicked on the box. Saved it. Went about my day.

And then I went about my life, business as usual, except I was a bit more careful at work. Derrick stopped bothering me, though. He didn't talk to anyone. I was surprised they didn't fire him on the spot. You see guys on TV who say offensive things, and they get clipped off at the knees, even if they *do* apologize.

Later I heard that Derrick was on his final write-up. I guess he really wanted to keep this job. That didn't last long, though. One day I came in and found his desk cleaned out. No one ever mentioned what happened to him.

Time passed, and I forgot the whole thing, at least until I saw Kristen walking out of the conference room just after her overly cheerful supervisor had exited. Kristen looked like she'd just been told a relative died, so I asked her what happened.

"I got written up," she said.

Kristen was one of our best workers. I'd never heard of her screwing something up. A customer had never complained about her. I couldn't imagine what could have gotten her into trouble.

"It was over my Fantasy Football league. The one I do every year here. They said it wasn't a good use of company time."

Okay, I couldn't have cared less about Fantasy Football, or any sports for that matter, but this kind of thing didn't get in the way of our jobs. We had our dry seasons. The employees had to do something. Fantasy Football helped build morale, and it improved team communication, which was something our supes were always on our case about.

Kristen wasn't the only one. Every once in a while someone would come to me and start a conversation with some variation of, "Dude, you're not going to believe what just happened."

Tony got written up for looking at the internet. I asked if he was looking at porn or some other offensive thing. Nope. It was a news article. They told him that he should go on break and use his own device for something like that.

Esteban got written up for reading on the job. Just a book. Something by Steinbeck, I think. Esteban was a part-timer who went to college in the afternoons, so it was for class.

And then Paul got written up for having a friendly conversation in the break room. By then our hushed conversations ended. Message received.

Every company has down time. It's unavoidable. You can't make people look busy just to satisfy some need to keep up appearances. Employees need to cut loose sometimes. Eight hours a day is a long time. No one should be 100% business in all that time.

Things became quieter after that. Not a lot of smiles in the office. Not a lot of fun. Work quickly became unbearable, which was probably why I'd become irritable. Before long the anger had to get out.

I took that out on Ariana.

I'm not going to explain what I do for a living. No one gets it, anyway. Suffice it to say, it looks really hard, but in all actuality it's simple. Ariana had been with the company five years longer than me. I'm in for seven years, yet somehow I knew more than she did.

She screwed up something super-easy, and I saw her do it. I wanted to be kind of a dick because she should have known better, but since things in the office were a bit tense I decided to be nice about it, even though I was calling her out in front of everyone for being incompetent. I politely told her that she did something wrong and gave her advice on how to avoid the same mistake in the future. She thanked me, I you're-welcomed her, and I went back to my cube.

By close of business, Felicia called me into the dreaded conference room. The door closed. The laptop came out. Keys were tapped.

Felicia asked, "What happened between you and Ariana today?"

In that moment, I realized that I was in trouble again. I didn't waste time pretending otherwise. I spun the whole story—corporatese and all—so it appeared like I was looking out for the customer. I had recognized this as a teachable moment. I practically auditioned for a customer service award.

I finished with this: "I'm just looking out for the company. That customer brings in a lot of money. If we lost them, we'd be in trouble. I gave Ariana advice so she wouldn't make the same mistake going forward."

I thought I did a good job, but as soon as I saw that unflappable phony smile on her face, I knew I was screwed.

"We appreciate your efforts," Felicia said, "but you should have come to us instead. We need a complete record of everything that happens so we can track trends."

I wanted to argue the point—and part of me wanted to tell her how I *really* wanted to handle the situation—but my corporate sense kicked in. "Okay."

"Also, what you did could be construed as bullying."

Bullying?! Oh, if only she could have looked around inside my head when I caught Ariana messing up. If what I'd done was bullying, then I'd committed a ghastly murder in my mind.

"Because of this," she continued, "we're going to have to write you up. Just so we're clear, you're on second warning. You only have one left after that."

I bit back so many curses that Urban Dictionary yelped. "I understand. It won't happen again."

"Great!" And she gave me the usual spiel about signing the document in my dashboard.

We left the conference room, and I paused by the DO NOT ENTER door. Something back there hummed, and I could feel a headache forming.

I went back to my desk and clicked the blah blah blah. I felt so annoyed at the whole thing that I swore I would never help a coworker again, not even if I had a bucket of water and they were on fire. I even half-heartedly looked for outside employment. Anything better than this corporate bullshit. I found nothing. Good thing I didn't get caught, since that would have put me on final warning.

Work became a real drag after that. I didn't even bother to say hi to people when I arrived every day. Didn't want to put pressure on people to have a good morning, after all. That might offend someone. Or that might be considered bullying. Or whatever.

A few months passed, putting me closer to the end of the year, when my write-ups would expire, and I'd have a clean slate. Unfortunately, one of the people in the office didn't make it.

It happened to a supervisor. Of course it had to be Wallace, the one cool guy in management. He was the only one who went out with us for drinks after work, at least to the official outings, where he'd usually complain about our employer in hushed tones.

But he messed up, and a lot of people noticed. Apparently he'd been on final warning because all the supes—including Katie, the head of the department—came by his desk. Felicia said to him, "Hey, are you busy?"

Oh yeah. He was doomed.

They all spoke so quietly that none of us could hear them, even though work had ground to a halt so we could all watch this.

Wallace snapped. "You know what? I think *you* need an attitude adjustment." He cast his gaze at the supervisors. "*All* of you."

"Let's just go to the conference room and talk about it," Katie said. "It'll—"

"Why bullshit me? I know what you're going to do to me. Why not let it happen out here?"

"Calm down," Felicia said.

"No! These people have a right to know the truth about this place! Morale is at an all-time low because you're trying to mold their behavior—"

"Stop," Katie said. The warning stood out clearly in her voice.

"—You're brainwashing them! Trying to get them to become safe little people in a safe little world! Well, I won't have it! I—"

Two very large men in uniforms showed up, and they displayed their tasers, ready and waiting.

"You think this scares me?! I know what's going to happen! You're going to—"

One of the guards fired and ran five thousand volts through Wallace's body, immobilizing him instantly. They moved quickly after that. While the remaining supervisors tried to give us the old nothing-to-see-here speech, Katie and the office goons picked up Wallace and took him away. Not to the conference room, by the way. Not even to the onsite medical facility, either.

They took him past the DO NOT ENTER door and in.

We all tried to go back to work, but none of us could completely ignore the remaining supervisor cleaning out Wallace's desk.

The next week went rough because Wallace did so many important things. It was New Year's, though, our driest time, so it didn't get too bad. And then my warnings expired, giving me a fresh start. I didn't take it as an opportunity to get lazy in my vigilance, but I relaxed a bit.

A few days after that, Katie pulled me into her office. My danger sense didn't go off, even though she closed the door. If I'd done something worthy of a write-up, Felicia would have handled it. No, the vibe I got was that Katie wanted to ask me for a favor.

I sat down across the desk from her, and she asked me how it was going out there. I gave the stock response. Only then could we get down to business.

"I know things have been hectic since Wallace left the company," she said. "We're still making some adjustments in this period of transition."

Right. He'd "left the company." As if he'd had any choice in the matter.

"We're looking to get someone to fill the position," she continued. "The company doesn't like to hire outside for such an important position, so we're looking at personnel within the department."

A chill wormed its way through my stomach, and I knew why she'd called me into this meeting. I kept quiet, though.

"We've taken an interest in you. Your work is impeccable. You're never late. You always commit to your projects. It helps that you have so much experience, so you have an excellent level of knowledge."

Dear God! I never wanted to be management. I could never handle that kind of position. I didn't have that kind of mindset. I couldn't cope with betraying my close-lipped rebellious nature. I'd be selling out if I agreed to this lunacy.

"We've had our issues in the past," Katie said, "but they seem to have been resolved. You've learned from your mistakes. When we needed you to become better in your relationship with your coworkers, you stepped up and fell into line. We appreciate your effort and loyalty. We would like to offer the position to you."

My heart nearly stopped. I knew if I stayed true to myself and said no, they'd find an excuse to get rid of me. Lack of ambition was *not* rewarded by the company, especially since they were asking me for such help in a desperate time of need. I had bills, in particular monthly payments for my new car. I couldn't afford the risk.

"Wallace worked the same shift as you," Katie said, "so you won't have to change your schedule. Plus, you'll be salaried. You'll make sixty thousand dollars a year. How does that sound?"

Compared to my fourteen bucks an hour? With the OT I got last year, I barely cracked forty thousand before taxes.

Greed made my heart swell. "I'll do it," I told her.

"Great! Welcome to management!"

I didn't like the way that sounded. My guts churned as we

started filling out paperwork. On the one hand, I couldn't have been happier with the raise. Suddenly, my bills didn't seem quite so daunting. Yet . . . I just couldn't bring myself to look forward to the job. The bullshit I had to deal with on a regular basis was bad enough, but now I had to *become* bullshit. I knew I could do that for a while, but after a few years? I'd break just like Wallace.

After I signed everything I went back to my desk, my head clouded with the haze of disbelief. Had I really just been promoted to management? What had I gotten myself into?

I didn't have time to ponder it. Felicia popped up over the top of my cubicle like a whack-a-mole, all smiles. "I just heard the news," she said. "Congratulations!" As if there had never been trouble between us. As if we were lifelong friends.

Then she did something odd: she reached over the wall and offered me her hand to shake. I didn't think we'd ever done that, not even on my first day. It kind of creeped me out, actually.

We shook hands, and she passed me a tightly folded piece of paper like it was some kind of a drug deal going down. She didn't acknowledge it. Instead she just congratulated me again before walking away.

I unfolded the paper, which tried to close back in on itself like a dead spider. Given Felicia's secretive attitude, I hunched over the note to hide it from anyone who might walk up behind me, the only way into my cube.

The handwriting was nothing like hers. She wrote clearly in elegant cursive, pretty to the point of calligraphy. This note, however, was in block letters, all caps, like someone wanted to hide their penmanship.

It said, "YOU AND I NEED TO TALK. IT IS URGENT. MEET ME TONIGHT AT 10:00. THE STONEWOOD HOUND. I'LL BE AT THE CORNER BOOTH IN THE BACK, FAR LEFT. DO *NOT* TELL ANYONE."

Then, almost as an afterthought, "BURN THIS NOTE."

In all my years of dealing with corporate craziness—in particular Felicia's corporate craziness—I'd never encountered anything like this. It had to be a joke. I wanted to show it to friends—after hours, of course, far away from the office—because it struck me as hilarious.

But it couldn't have been a joke. Felicia, the company woman of all company women, did not have a sense of humor.

I took a break and went outside for some fresh air. I don't smoke, but I carry a lighter, mostly because all of my friends smoke and they constantly lose theirs. It drives me crazy because we have to stop everything—*everything*—until they find it. I don't mind carrying it, though. It's a useful tool to have on hand.

It came in handy that day. I burned Felicia's note and watched until nothing remained of it but ash in the wind.

After work, I went home and got a good workout in before taking a shower and heading out to the Stonewood Hound. It was a great little bar and grill a couple of blocks from the office. A lot of my coworkers liked to have unofficial outings there, where we could maybe have a couple drinks too many and bitch about our jobs without having to whisper.

In that moment I realized my days of going to those get-togethers were over. Management never got invited to them, not even Wallace, as cool and laid back as he was.

I got there early, which I usually did in all things. Felicia knew me well; I arrived at 9:40, and it looked like she'd been sitting there for a while. She wore a t-shirt and jeans. Odd. Could it be that outside the office, she was kind of a slob?

I could almost like her for that.

I sat down on the other side of the booth. We were beyond pleasantries at this point, so I didn't bother with a greeting. "What's all this about?"

Felicia opened her mouth but paused when the waitress stopped by, asking us if we needed anything to drink. I ordered a beer, and Felicia had water.

The waitress left. I said, "Not drinking anything?"

"I don't drink," Felicia said. "I quit a while ago. I recommend you do the same. You should also quit all of your other bad habits, anything that lessens your control over yourself. You can't get sloppy around Katie and upper management. They'll be watching you like a hawk, making sure you're a good fit with the company."

I had to restrain a laugh. The whole thing struck me as absurd. Had I stumbled into a spy movie? If I'd known how crazy Felicia was . . .

"You should also kill any social media you might have. Anything you say there will get back to the company. And watch what you say to whom. The company has spies everywhere.

Some of them have been here, drinking with you while you complained very loudly about the company. In case you thought we didn't know about your unofficial outings . . ."

Our drinks arrived, and I took a healthy swig from mine. I couldn't wrap my mind around this surreal meeting. But part of what she said made a little sense. My write-ups had happened surprisingly close to these unofficial parties, particularly if I'd said something really bad about the company. Could one of my friends have snitched me out?

Felicia sipped daintily at her water. "I know you sense something's wrong at work. That's why you pretend so much. I'm not stupid. I know you don't like me, no matter how pleasant you seem. I don't like you much, either. But we have to keep our phony faces on. It's a matter of survival."

Something about the way she said that made me look up from my beer. In a fleeting moment I caught something unusual in her eyes.

Fear.

Felicia was afraid of upper management.

"I just wanted to give you a word of warning. Now that you're a supe, their eyes—" She pointed up. "—will be on you more than ever. You don't want to mess with them. They won't take a lie to their face as graciously as I would."

I couldn't take it anymore. I had to say something. "You can't possibly be serious. This sounds too crazy."

She nodded. "That's what I thought at first, but I've been here for twenty years. I've seen things."

"Well, if you hate the job so much, why don't you quit?"

"You don't get it. It isn't just our company. It's *all* of them, going back to the One True Corporation."

A part of me wanted to laugh. The bigger part was too shocked for humor, though. "Come on," I said. "That's just ridiculous."

"You'll see."

"Okay, if that's how things really are, then why? Why do they do all of this? What's the conspiracy?"

"Mind control," Felicia said. "They expect all of us to obey them at all times. The government can't do that, but your employers? They're the real Big Brother. They know how to hurt you—in your wages. You get three chances to be manipulated into behavior of your own free will. After that they give you an attitude adjustment."

Despite her insane rambling, that phrase sounded familiar. "What's that?"

"It's . . . unpleasant. But it's the craziest thing I *can't* tell you about. Instead I'm going to let you find out for yourself. If you can accept that, then everything else will make sense to you."

She slid out of the booth and stood, dropping enough money on the table to cover my drink and the tip.

"You can't just lay all this loony tunes shit on me and then walk away," I said.

"I've warned you as best as I can." And then she started for the door. She got two steps before she turned around. "If you want proof, stop by the convenience store on your way home. The one by the ramp onto the expressway. Be there at—" She took her phone out of her purse to check the time. "—eleven."

"And then what?"

"Take a look around." This time, she headed to the door and left me alone with my drink as I tried to sort through everything she'd told me.

I had a while to go before eleven, so I ordered another drink and tried to figure out if tonight had been a hallucination. I couldn't work through it, so I paid up and headed for the convenience store. I needed some caffeine for the drive home, anyway.

Once there, I headed back to the freezer and made my selection. As I started toward the counter, I saw a janitor mopping the same spot on the floor. I thought back to when I walked in and realized he hadn't mopped anything else in all that time.

Maybe he had a mental problem. Stores in the area tended to hire such people to help them out, get them some real-world experience. Yet this guy seemed familiar. Had I seen him before?

I stepped around the cleanest tile in the world, and when I saw his face, I couldn't help but gasp. I know that sounds melodramatic, but it happened because . . .

Well, I *did* know the janitor.

"Wallace?" I asked. "You all right?"

He didn't even acknowledge me. He continued mopping, and a single strand of drool ran from his lips.

I had to try again. "Wallace? It's me, John. What happened to you?"

I waved my hand in front of his face and got no reaction.

"There a problem?" The clerk.

"Uh . . . no." I couldn't take my eyes from the thing that had once been Wallace. "I just thought I knew this guy."

The next day at work Felicia greeted me as cheerfully as she usually did with no indication of our talk from last night. I treated her the same.

On my way to my new desk I passed the DO NOT ENTER door. I thought about Wallace and his attitude adjustment, and I suddenly no longer cared to find out what was really in this room.

In short I settled into my new job, and I made zero waves at work. I did what I was told, no matter how stupid it was. And it was often stupid. I just got along to get along.

I guess I wasn't the rebel I thought I was, but then again, with that kind of threat hanging over us, who could be?

Sometimes I think about taking down the system from the inside, especially whenever I have to write someone up or—God help me—send someone for an attitude adjustment, but I know I never will. Just like when I sent out those half-hearted job applications. I knew I'd fallen into my rut. I'd never leave here, and I'd never rebel.

It's safer that way.

MONSTER COCK 2

Once upon a time there was a young man named Cobra McClane. He was just as cool as his name suggested. A lifelong bodybuilder, he drove the hottest cars and banged the hottest chicks, or at least that's what he did when he wasn't working his job as a cop on the edge who played by his own rules.

But there was one thing that wasn't cool about him: he had a micro penis. At his hardest, it was no longer—or thicker—than his pinky finger. He boned so many hot chicks because none of them would fuck him a second time. Every one of them went away disappointed and unsatisfied. It depressed the hell out of him. On the few occasions he masturbated, the tip of his dick wouldn't even poke out the end of his fist. He barely had anything to jerk. To make it worse, whenever he sat down his little acorn would turn inside out and hide in his body. Nothing embarrassed him more than digging in to retrieve it.

Cobra had to do something about it. Not surgery, though. That scared him. Besides, he'd heard that he could only get an extra half-inch that way. That left all the pills and creams. Instinctively he knew it was all horseshit, never mind the so-called money back guarantees.

But there was something different about Monster Cock™. They didn't advertise, and Cobra only found out about them because he discovered a bottle of the stuff at a crime scene. While his methods were always unorthodox, he was an honest cop. He'd never stolen anything, and he'd never taken a bribe.

But he took that dick cream instead of bagging it as evidence.

When he got home, he read the instruction label. It said to smear a dollop on his peter and let it air dry. The next day he'd be hung like Ron Jeremy. It warned not to use more than a dollop

—whatever *that* was—and that it would burn.

He squeezed the entire bottle out into his hand and rubbed it all over his tiny piece. It set his genitals on fire so badly he screamed and almost blacked out. It reminded him of the time he'd put cologne down there in his teenage years. He desperately wanted to wipe off the Monster Cock™, but he was afraid it wouldn't work if he did.

Cobra suffered through the night, and when he got up to take his morning whiz, his boxers felt different. Fuller. He whipped himself out—holy shit!—to discover that he now had a six-inch softie.

He called in sick and played with himself all day. Posed himself in the mirror. Took dick pics for his next chick. Tried Puppetry of the Penis. He couldn't wait to use it on a woman, so he hooked up that night with a femme fatale who was a suspect in a homicide case he was working.

He made her cum. That was a first for him. She also stayed the night; another first.

The next morning his cock hung out the bottom of his boxers, almost to his knees. Excited, he stripped down and stroked himself, eager to see what it looked like hard. Blood rushed from one head to the other, and he passed out, falling backwards into the bathtub. His guest from last night heard the clamor and ran in to his aid. When she saw how much bigger his dick had grown, she slapped his face until he came to and demanded that he refuck her.

Cobra liked that kind of demand. This time he carefully stroked himself until he was hard enough that his glans rested on his chest. She took it from there.

Later she went home bowlegged. Alone, Cobra decided to try sucking his own cock. When he was in high school, it sounded like the best thing anyone could do. When he actually did it, though, it felt wrong in his guts. He didn't like the taste, and he suddenly realized that cumming in his own mouth sounded absolutely disgusting. So he stopped.

He promised himself he'd go back to work tomorrow, but on the third day his dick almost dragged on the floor. He had to tuck the head into his sock so it wouldn't be visible. But when he looked at himself in the mirror, he could see the obvious shape of his penis through his pants. He couldn't hide that. Worse, what woman would want to have that thing inside of her?

Suddenly having a big dick wasn't fun anymore.

Day four. He had to lift his cock so the carpet wouldn't tickle the head. How much bigger could it get?

Day five. He found it much harder to walk with such a heavy member.

Day six. It was too big to walk at all. Time to call the doctor...

Day seven. Cobra was confined to a hospital bed, and he needed another one for his penis. No one knew what to do with him. He cursed himself for using the whole bottle.

Days passed, and his dick got bigger, to the point where it nearly filled his hospital room. The doctors pleaded with him to amputate, but having no dick was scarier to him than this situation.

By the time it broke through the window and hung down ten stories, Cobra McClane didn't even know who he was anymore. Fear and shock drove him into catatonic madness. The doctors tried to remove the ever-growing monster cock as if it was a tumor, but the skin had grown too thick to be penetrated. They tried lasers, but all they did was cook him a little.

Administrators, worried that the floor wouldn't be able to sustain the weight of Cobra's cock, arranged to have him and his mass cut out of his room and lowered by several helicopters to three wide load trucks. One of the choppers zigged when it should have zagged, and the cock fell onto the trucks, busting all their suspensions.

It also broke Cobra's skull. Not badly enough to kill him. Just badly enough to change his catatonic state to a blithering, laughing, screaming type of insanity. The doctors sedated him and built a tent for him while they tried to figure out how to move his massive appendage.

They didn't figure it out in time. The street collapsed the next day, and when they couldn't get Cobra out, they realized it didn't matter; the dick got even bigger and cracked the entire street down the middle.

By the end of the week the city had been evacuated, and the military moved in. No one considered Cobra McClane a patient or victim anymore. He was a threat, and his cock needed to be neutralized. A cigar-chomping commander named Duke Slater—who had a fairly sized dick himself, but not as cool a name as

Cobra McClane—ordered his men to throw everything they had at the giant dick. Bullets, bombs, artillery. They tried it, and the dick seemed only to eat it up and get bigger.

Cobra was unconscious at the time, so scholars thought the action might have stirred his dreams into a nocturnal emission, for by the time the military was done, he came. A lot. So much that he flooded and drowned the entire county, including Duke Slater, who never thought he'd die choking on a giant sperm. This event also created Semen Creek, which emptied into the Mississippi.

The president of the United States had no choice but to call in the Broken Arrow gambit. It pained him to be the first president in history to order a nuclear strike on American soil, but he felt sure that this would finally put an end to this horror. He really wanted to evacuate anyone still unfortunate enough to be alive from the area, but time was of the essence. He stabbed his finger down on the button.

When the mushroom cloud cleared, the world was dismayed to find that the monster cock was bigger than ever. Shockingly, Cobra still lived, although he seethed with blisters and couldn't stop laughing.

The next time he had a wet dream, it flooded the entire Midwest, and his leavings overcame the Mississippi. It rolled down the US until everything from Green Bay to New Orleans was covered in a blanket of warm jizz.

The president cut his own throat after that. His vice president gave up and moved to France. A rag-tag team of scientists and military men tried a lot of unorthodox plans—ranging from kooky to abso-fucking-lutely insane—but nothing worked. They all died. Hollywood was working on making it into a movie—but to get an R rating, they changed the dick to a finger and the cum to blood—but everyone involved drowned and died in the semen of what was called the Third Cumming. They hadn't even moved past pre-production.

Shortly after, the dick covered all of North America with a laughing, gibbering Cobra McClane at the center. Earthquakes tore at the planet. Cum storms killed the coastal cities. The shell-shocked survivors wailed and gnashed their teeth, knowing they could do nothing to stop the world from ending beneath the ever-growing cock.

Then one day the astronauts on the International Space Station watched on in horror as the earth cracked and imploded. The sudden displacement of gravity sucked the station and the moon into it, and so the world ended.

Not even Cobra McClane survived this time. The sudden absence of air froze his lungs, and the last of humanity asphyxiated as the remnants of the debris formed a new asteroid belt in the solar system.

But the monster cock did not die.

It kept growing.

And it never stopped.

DAISY, JEPPKE, AND THE KID

Daisy looked at herself in the mirror, took in the flaking skin, the thinning hair, the bruises and the gap where her front teeth had been. She wondered if Jeppke could be right. The reflection offered nothing appetizing, and she knew it would only get worse. The tremor she felt down to her bones reinforced the idea.

Tears wet her cheeks, and she squeezed her eyes. Though she had done many questionable things in her time, she never considered herself to be a bad person . . . until now. That she even considered Jeppke's proposal spoke poorly of her character. And now that she'd actually made a decision in *his* favor?

She wanted to break every mirror in her apartment. In the *world*. Break every window, anything that might reflect herself. And it still wouldn't be enough.

"Hey, sugar tits! You takin' a shit or somethin'?"

"Gimme a minute, Jeppke!"

"I gotta' piss, babe! Chop-chop!"

She sniffed and wiped a hand across her eyes. The wetness remained. "Just use the kitchen sink, like you always do!"

"I don't always." The response was sulky, but he went away.

Daisy yanked a swath of toilet paper from the roll and dried her face as much as possible. The sweat continued to bead up, but it always did, especially when she hadn't used for a while. This was her seventh day, and pain gnawed at her insides like a dog at a bone.

They had no money. They had no *choice*. If they did this, they'd have less responsibility, more money and more time to use.

She tried to work some make-up on her face, but it just made the blotches and bruises worse. She gave up, plumped up her cleavage and stepped out of the bathroom. Shortly thereafter Jeppke left the kitchen, zipping up his pants. He didn't look much better than her. His rotten complexion gave his condition away. He shook as if he had Parkinson's, and his mouth looked like an abandoned cemetery. The bandana he wore over the bald spot at the front of his head bore a circular wet spot as sweat worked its way through.

"Okay," Daisy said. "Let's do it."

"Really?" His dead eyes shone as much as they could.

"Yeah."

"Aw, baby." He stepped forward and encircled her with his bony arms. When he hugged her, it felt like he barely existed. "You know I don't like to hit you. Sometimes I gotta'."

"I know."

"You piss me off sometimes. I just wish you'd let me do the thinking for us. You know I can take care of you, right?"

"Right." All these words came on their own. She felt none of them.

Jeppke pulled back. "Good. Go get the kid and all his shit."

—

While they drove Daisy said, "How much are we going to make?"

Jeppke, who had been hammering a tune out on the steering wheel with his knobby hands, paused. "Shit, I don't know. Let's highball 'em for a couple grand. Prob'ly get halfa' that, which is cool. That's still enough for an ounce, right? That'll keep us good for a while."

"For an ounce?"

"Well, it won't be the best, but it'll do the job, babe."

"Fine. No lower, though."

"No shit. My kid ain't worth less than that."

"So, what do we do? How do we . . . do this?"

"What's with the questions, yo? I never done this before. I guess we stand around and proposition folks. The *right* folks. I mean, the pigs can't fuck with us that way, right? The spics do practically the same thing at Home Depot. We can do all right at Wal-Mart."

"What if we sell him to the wrong people? What if they want

to do sex things to him?"

"Daisy, darling, *we're* the wrong people. We can't raise this kid. We can barely stay alive on our own. Besides, the real creeps hang out online. We'll probably wind up selling him to a Wall Street broker, or something."

In Nebraska? she wanted to say. And she wanted to remind him that "the kid" had a name, but what good would it do, this late in the game?

"Believe me, babe. This kid's going to thank us someday. We're not gonna' be around to fuck it up. That scores us cool points, right?"

Jesus, how did she become like this? When she was ten and daydreaming about her Prince Charming, she never would have guessed she'd wind up with a guy like Jeppke. Still, he hadn't always been like this. A long time ago, before they'd discovered meth, he'd been kind of handsome and cool. Hell, even after they'd had their initial meth send-off, things had still been pretty keen. Fun still existed. They still had faces worth looking at. They still had full sets of teeth.

And then baby Richard had come along. Was that the turning point? When had meth taken over their lives? And how deep was the cost to their child? The doctors said he was healthy, which defied everyone's expectations.

But what would happen to him if he stayed with them? What would happen when he grew old enough to understand things? What if he, too, became a meth-head?

Suddenly Daisy felt glad that they'd never find out.

—

Even though the sun shone hard, Daisy felt a chill shudder in her guts. She wore a heavy flannel shirt, but the cold still managed to find her core.

She sat in the back seat of their beat-up station wagon while Jeppke paced around outside, smoking their second-to-last cigarette. They had been here for hours, but he hadn't gotten up the nerve to approach anyone. He said he wanted to shop for the right people, but his nervousness spoke out from his wild eyes and his trembling hands.

Daisy looked up and saw he was halfway through the Basic.

"Hey. It's my turn."

Jeppke took another drag and pretended not to hear.

"Come on, Jeppke! You promised!"

"Shit." He held out the remains of the cigarette to her. She got out of the car and took it, inhaling as deeply as she could. There was some warmth there, and it made her feel better.

Jeppke continued to pace, casting his gaze about.

"Keep Richard company," Daisy said.

"Fuck that. Too muggy in there."

"It's your turn. You've got to watch him."

"It don't matter anymore. We're getting rid of him. The less he sees of us, the better."

Daisy wanted to say something, but she knew not to. Jeppke's fast speech meant he wanted to hit something. She didn't want to be his target, at least not until she had some meth in her. She'd be able to take the pain, then.

"What about him?" Jeppke asked. "He looks shady enough."

Daisy saw the fat, greasy man and nearly choked. "We don't want shady. Richard's going to a good home."

"If I approached decent people, they'd call the cops on us."

"Then why don't we take him to the agency?"

Jeppke bit his lip and shook his head. "You stupid bitch. They won't *buy* him. We need *money*."

A year ago, this would have angered her. Now the need in her saw his wisdom. She sucked on the Basic one final time and flicked it away.

—

When Daisy got back into the car, the baby started crying. One whiff of the air explained it all. "Jeppke. Richard went poopie."

He shrugged. "And?"

"Where's the diaper bag?"

"That's your department, babe."

She found it under some food wrappers. There was one diaper left. Fitting. "Never mind. I have it."

Jeppke ignored her as she put the bag on the roof of the car, then leaned back in to unstrap Richard from his chair. She straightened up, holding the baby on one arm while she slung the bag onto her other.

"Where you goin'?" he asked.

"Bathroom. They have a changing station there."

"Do it here."

"It's a poopie."

"Nobody cares."

"I'm not changing him in a Wal-Mart parking lot." Her voice had just enough edge to startle him.

He sighed. "Whatever."

As she walked to the automatic doors, she wondered if Jeppke would just up and leave them. He would definitely do it—and she wished he would—but she thought he'd stick around to sell the baby. He had his own Need to tend to.

Inside, as she used a wipe on Richard's bottom, she felt sadness overcome her. She'd never change his diaper again. Her fingers would never again smell like shit, cream and powder.

Daisy dropped the used diaper into the trash, and she felt a part of her go with it. Jeppke couldn't sell smack to a junkie, but she knew that today he would succeed at selling their child . . . and she'd be just as guilty for letting it happen.

Richard—fresh as clean bedsheets—looked up at her with a blank face. Would he even remember them? She hoped not.

Daisy picked him up and caught a glimpse of herself in the mirror. No, she couldn't be evil. But she knew right from wrong, and this was awful. Unforgivable.

On the way back to the parking lot, she saw a pay phone, and she knew she couldn't go through with this. The Need clawed at her belly and screamed inside her bones, cried that her drug would make her forget about this, forget about Richard, but she knew better.

Jeppke would kill her for this, but she could no longer ignore the proverbial moral compass. She searched her pockets only to find a dime and three pennies. Forty-two cents short.

And then she remembered that she didn't need money for the call she was going to make.

—

When Daisy found her way back to the car, Jeppke stubbed out the remains of their last cigarette. He didn't notice her approach; he spoke animatedly with a fat man in overalls and a trucker hat. The newcomer's shirt said, "Wrecked her? I hardly knew her!" Jeppke's hands flew everywhere as he talked with this guy.

"Nah. Can't help you, man. I gots three kids already. Don't need another mouth to feed."

"Okay," Jeppke said. "I'll go as low as a thousand."

"Ain't the cost, bubba. Jest can't do it. Good luck, fella."

Jeppke grimaced. "Yeah, fuck you, too. Go buy yer fuckin' chaw! You redneck tubba' lard!"

Wrecked Her just shrugged and went on his way. Daisy wondered if the guy would call the cops, but he didn't seem to give too much of a damn.

Jeppke finally saw her. "Where the fuck you been? That guy woulda' bought Richard if he coulda' seen him. I'm busting my ass off here, Daisy. What the hell?"

Daisy put the baby back in his chair. "Been changing him. I told you."

"You cost us a sale."

"He wouldn't have bought Richard. You saw him."

He rubbed his face. "Yeah, well, there was another guy. Had on a suit and shit. Said his wife couldn't have children. Offered five thousand. We would've been set, Daisy."

Daisy recognized the lie, but she didn't feel like saying anything. "Sorry."

"Fuckin' oughta' be."

Daisy smiled. "You got that last cigarette?"

"Shit, babe. We already had it, before you went in to change the kid."

She nodded. "Right. Of course."

———

About ten minutes later Daisy noticed two cop cars pull into the parking lot. Neither used their sirens, but they seemed to be in a hurry. This, she knew, was it.

She'd been chewing her nails ever since she'd gotten back in the car. Playing with Richard helped keep her mind off things, but it couldn't calm her; her foot tapped, and her teeth ground against each other.

"Shit." Jeppke leaned in the open window. "Be cool. It's

probably nothing."

Daisy couldn't meet his eyes. "Sure."

Jeppke looked at his watch, but it hadn't worked for a week. Still he studied it, pretending to wait for someone.

The cops blocked their car in, front and back. How had they known where to find them? She didn't remember giving them a description of the wagon. Then again her memory usually had holes in it.

She almost laughed. When she'd been a kid, her memory had been perfect.

Two cops came out and approached Jeppke, saying his name.

"I ain't done shit, man. I don't have any papers out for me, neither."

One of them casually touched his gun. "I hear you're trying to sell a baby out here. Mind if I check your car?"

"This is bullshit! You know I have a record! You're just harassing me! I been clean for a month! Ain't been in the system for a year!"

"We received a call—"

"An anonymous call, huh? Fuck that! You're scaring my wife and kid!" He gestured to the car.

"Please step out of the vehicle, ma'am."

"But, my baby—" Daisy said.

"It's okay. It'll only be for a moment."

She kissed Richard's forehead, then followed orders. Outside, Jeppke still yelled at the officer. "So I got a kid! So what? You can't prove shit! Did that fat hick tell you something? Let me tell you, I made fun of him, so he's getting his revenge on me, the chubby fuck!"

"Calm down, sir," one cop said.

The other asked, "Are you Daisy Carpenter?"

Did she really give them her name? She hadn't meant to. She didn't want Jeppke to find out. Sometimes she hated her memory. This seemed important, so why couldn't she recall the phone conversation?

Wait, what phone conversation? She hadn't called 911, had she? She'd dreamed about it, sure, but did she actually *do* it?

She couldn't have. The Need would never have allowed her.

"What's your name, ma'am?"

"Uh . . . Daisy."

"Have you ingested any substances today?"

In the background Jeppke no longer yelled. He stared at Daisy, shocked.

"No, sir," she said.

"Is this your child?"

"Yes. His name is Richard."

"Did you fuckin' call these guys?" Jeppke asked.

"No, Jeppke, I—"

"I'm not going back inside, not for a cunt like you!"

"Calm down, sir."

Jeppke yelled, and though mostly incoherent one of his words got through: "Bitch!"

Daisy cringed, and she didn't see the blade in Jeppke's hand, not even when it slid into her throat. She grimaced, waiting for Jeppke to start hitting her. Instead she choked on her own blood.

Two gunshots. Daisy tried to scream, but a red ribbon poured out of her mouth instead. The world tilted, and everything went foggy. How did she fall over to the ground? When?

She stared at Jeppke's lifeless body, into his empty eyes. He wore the grimace he'd died with. The police stood over him, guns drawn. Voices tangled with each other in the air above her.

A cop turned her over and jammed a handkerchief against her throat. She barely felt it. His mouth moved, but she couldn't hear anything. The thunder of her blood flow was too loud in her head.

Then she saw another cop holding Richard, rocking him back and forth, keeping his face away from the gory scene.

And then she knew: *They'll find a good home for him.*

SNIPE HUNT

"Heads up, Teddy. Here comes your kid."

I don't even waste time looking up. While I've already had a few to drink, my reflexes are still good. My fingers automatically flick the cigarette into the campfire, where it turns brown and starts to shrivel. I promised Philly that I'd stop smoking, and I don't want to be caught in the act.

Mark keeps puffing away. "The kid looks kind of excited. Think they found one?" He winks.

I utter a laugh. I had never fallen for the snipe hunt ruse when I was a child. Even then I knew such an exercise was only an excuse for fathers to get their Cub Scout sons out of their hair so they can engage in adult stuff, like smoking, drinking and talking about women who aren't their wives. This is the third night of our outing, and I'd been looking forward to sending the young 'uns out into the wilderness.

Three days without nicotine . . . that first cigarette tasted so good. It nearly got me high. After having cast the fourth into the fire, though, I am much more relaxed.

"Hey, Dad!" Philly says.

I finish off my Schlitz and pop open another. "What's up, Philly?"

"We found one, Dad! A real live snipe!"

I exchange a glance with my fellow fathers. All of them wear a yeah-right grin, and it takes me a moment to realize that I have one, too. "Are you sure?" I ask.

"It looks just like you said, only it's bigger! We'd'a brought it back, but we couldn't even *drag* it!"

The amused faces around the fire melt away, replaced by worry. It's as if we are thinking with the same mind. We are now certain that our sons have captured something, maybe a *dangerous* something. What is the scariest animal out here? There are no bears, but maybe they caught a baby coyote.

What if the mother wants her offspring back? Images of the other boys being mauled by a pack of vicious animals start to form in my—

"What's it look like?" Don asks.

"Just like you guys said. It's kind of a big bird with a beak as big as my arm. It has rainbow colored feathers and long spindly legs with claws like hands."

That is exactly how we described it to the kids about an hour ago. It's perfect, almost as if they're trying to prank us. When I was a kid I did the same thing to my old man. Practically gave him a heart attack. We just picked the smallest of us, put him in the sack and lured our parents into the trap.

Is this what Philly has in mind? Like father, like son? The sad thing is, I don't know him enough to make such a judgment. I never married his mom. I keep up the child support, and I see him once a month, but I don't really know him. His favorite movie is *The Sandlot*, he likes to read old science fiction books and he's a passingly fair softball player, but we never talk. It's not like I don't try, but he's quiet around me. With his friends he's boisterous and full of laughter, but with me he always seems distracted.

I don't think he likes me very much.

At home he's not allowed to watch horror movies, so I let him when he's with me. And if a booby makes an appearance, I don't tell him to close his eyes. It's not going to kill him, and besides, it makes him smile.

"What do you think, Teddy?" Don asks. "Should we see their snipe?" The way he says "snipe" is so patronizing that not even a baby would miss it.

Even Philly catches it. "We *do* have a snipe! See for yourselves!"

I shrug. "Okay, Philly. Take us there."

We grab our flashlights and beer, and we follow my son into the woods. As we walk I take a hefty gulp from my beer, and I try to ignore the dirty look Philly gives me. He's in some kind of substance abuse class in school. Just say no. After having learned the ills of vice, he has gone out into the world to convert us sinners. Last month he demanded that I quit smoking and drinking. I told him I'd only do one at a time because adults need *some* bad habits in order to have fun. I told him I'd stop smoking.

The truth: I can do without cigarettes. They're kind of nasty. My fingers are yellow, and my clothes stink. I can't even indulge this habit in public, so really I don't like smoking all that much anymore. It makes me feel good, especially after a hard day. Besides, I'm addicted. It would be nice to quit, but it's damned near impossible.

Drinking, on the other hand, isn't so bad. It helps me unwind, and it's not like I drink the hard stuff. Maybe a couple of beers after work, or three on the weekend with some friends. I'm not an alcoholic. It just helps me maintain a social life.

Philly can have smoking, but drinking? I'll keep that one.

"So, Philly," says Mark, "how'd you boys catch the snipe?"

"Brent saw it first," Philly says. "It was pecking at a dead squirrel's guts. When it saw us, it froze. Steve came up with the plan for some of us to flank it and scare it toward the others, who were holding the sack."

"Did you hurt it?" Mark asks.

"No, sir. But it doesn't like being in the sack. It's real mad."

Again, the fathers look at each other. "Will the sack hold it?" I ask.

"Sure! The beak and claws aren't too sharp."

Ahead, through the motes of fireflies, I see a group of boys holding flashlights. Philly leads us up to them, and I get my first look at the sack.

Steve's the biggest of the kids at five-seven and a hundred and forty pounds, so it's no surprise to see his meaty hands holding the sack shut. Whatever's inside is big and it's writhing like a pit of snakes. A high-pitched squawk comes from the sack, but it's brief and clipped.

I look around the group of boys and start to count faces. It takes a minute to match them all up to their fathers in my mind before I realize that everyone is accounted for.

Unless they found another kid—a co-conspirator—this is not a trick. They really found something out there and captured it.

The other fathers have deduced this, too, and once again we glance at each other. "What should we do?" Mark asks.

I make the decision. "Stand back, everyone. Steve, you, too."

"But it'll get out if I let go."

"Okay. Let go when I say." I kneel down to grab the bottom of the sack, and my cigarettes and lighter fall from my shirt pocket. I hurry to rescue them from the dirt, but it's too late. Philly has seen them, and his mouth is as thin as a paper cut.

"I haven't had any," I tell him. "I just have them, well, you know. Just in case."

"I can vouch for him," Don says.

Philly says nothing. His face says it all.

Why does this upset me so much? I can smoke if I want to. Philly's just a kid. He can't make me do anything. I jam the pack into my pants pocket. When I look at my hands, I see they're trembling.

"Give me the sack," I say. Steve hands over the bunched opening, and I bend down to grab the bottom. I meant to turn the sack upside down, but it is heavier than I thought it would be.

"What the fuck is in this thing?" I say this before I remember I'm surrounded by kids. None of the fathers seem to care about my loose lips, though; all eyes are on the sack.

"Open it up, Teddy," Mark says.

To hell with it. I pull the sack over to its side, and the thing within topples over with a squawk. It struggles harder, and I can feel it pushing at the opening with something long and hard, like a blade.

The boys back away a little, and so do their fathers. Only Philly stands with me.

"It's okay, Dad," he says. "You can let go."

I let out my breath, and my fingers drop the opening of the sack. I tense up, waiting to see what will crawl out.

HOLLIDAY STEPS OUT

I knew he'd come, and sure enough, when I glanced up from the dime novel I was reading—it was about me, naturally, and filled with enough lies to give me a chuckle (laughter hurts too much to be the best medicine)—there he was, dressed in his finest. God damn! Wyatt Earp never seemed to age. He looked the same as he had when I'd first met him back in Kansas. Tall, steely-eyed and in possession of a most impressive mustache, he hardly had any wrinkles, and he still had all his hair. Though most had a difficult time telling the Brothers Earp apart, I never had trouble singling out Wyatt. He was the nerviest son of a bitch I'd ever known, and it was etched in the stone of his face for the world to respect and fear.

I'd always admired him, and on some level he was my hero. I don't mean that in a hokey, dime novel way. Wyatt was the kind of man I wanted to grow up to be when I was a child dreaming of the adult world, playing John Law 'N' Injuns during the simmering summers of Savannah. How I became more villain than bawcock is beyond me, and it was *my* life. Blaming consumption was too easy. Human nature sounded like a more reasonable culprit. I was one of the haves, and I was well on my way to having more. A perfect gentleman, the talk of all social circles. Potential wives lined up at my front door, not a whore among them. A thriving practice. Dear friends. My lovely cousin. I had everything to live for until I found out I was very mortal and would die sooner than later. It's funny, how that changes a man, or maybe it just makes him less likely to hide who he really is. Like most, I tend to romanticize my past, but not even *I* can deny the terrible thoughts that had hounded my younger brain, back when I was just John.

There I was, at the end of my life, with many years of drinking, gambling, womanizing and killing in me, and somehow I'd lasted longer than anyone had expected. For a while I thought I really *would* live forever, despite the blood I kept hacking out. But my body was done, so it didn't matter anymore.

"Doc," Wyatt said through his fine, waxed mustache. "You look like hell."

"You're an absolute peach," I said. "Thank you for coming to see me, Wyatt. I hear you're fairly busy in California. Have you bought your way into the upper class yet?"

"Workin' on it, Doc. Why'd you ask for me?"

I could tell he suspected, but he was too polite to say it himself. "This is it, Wyatt. This time next week, I probably won't be here." I laughed, hoping he didn't understand my joke.

Wyatt seemed less than comfortable, and his sharp blue eyes slicked over a bit, but they didn't start pouring. Such a manly fellow. Very solid and static of him. He was everything legend had made him. "You're leaving us?" His voice cracked slightly, betraying the humanity he hid so well. He may have been a walking myth, but he was no cardboard cut-out from a dime novel.

"Shuffling off the mortal coil," I said. "The Bard had a way with words, did he not?"

"Who?" Wyatt asked.

Maybe he wasn't well-read, but I was literate enough for the both of us. "Forget it. I'm just babbling, as is a dying gentleman's right. I feel spent, Wyatt. I've been living off pure willpower, and as egotistical as I am, I've finally run out."

"Hell, Doc, you're invincible."

"Maybe," I said. "You know, after all the times I've tried to commit suicide by throwing myself into danger, I started to believe you were all products of my imagination, that I really was the only person in the Universe. It was my stage, and I was the omnipotent director. What do you think of that, Wyatt?"

"I think dyin's done something to your brain."

I remembered what the Indian had told me two weeks ago, and I thought perhaps Wyatt was right. I'd committed many deplorable acts in my time, but I'd always been loyal to my friends. I was never one for Bible talk, but if it was all true, then my fidelity would be the only good quality on which St. Peter could compliment me.

Until now.

"Wyatt, could you reach in the drawer on my night table? There's something in there I want you to have."

He didn't question me, which was for the best. Wyatt went to retrieve the medicine bag the Indian had fashioned for me from my blood, some of the usual tidbits of savage magic and a handkerchief Wyatt had forgotten lending to me back in Tombstone. All he had to do was touch the enchanted object, and my worries would be over.

And there it was in his bare left hand.

I felt electricity crackle in the lobes of my brain, and the world spun around me like water going down a drain. Wyatt cursed wildly, and it was my damned name he uttered.

Or rather, *my body* uttered, as it was now occupied by Mama Earp's noblest son. I now had Wyatt's hardy and hale body, and for the first time in years, I knew what it was like to be healthy. I took a deep breath, and my chest didn't even hitch.

Wyatt, in my old body, was trying to speak, but he wasn't used to being a lunger, and all that came out was blood.

"I'm sorry," I said. "Really, Wyatt, I am. But I have to go."

And I did, without so much as looking back at my old confederate. I'm not proud of what I did, but what can I say? I'm a Darwinist.

-

Two days later a nurse overheard what she thought was Doc Holliday speaking his final words. "This is funny." And he was gone. Miles away, when Wyatt Earp was notified, he had many good things to say about the tubercular gambler and wept more than a few tears for a dead friend.

PARTY'S OVER

I see the younger version of myself hanging out with all of my dead friends in the front yard of my building, and I think I've finally died. Then, I wonder *how* I died. Can't be the drugs. Been off 'em for years. And I remember getting home safely last night. No way I croaked in my sleep. Rock stars just don't do that.

My knees feel a bit watery, so I sit on the steps and watch the 22-year-old me walking with my old band mates. Ronny, who died in a car wreck in '82. Jeff, who got too drunk at a party and choked on his own puke, died in '76. Freddy, who . . . as far as I know is still alive. I think he's a used car salesman in Decatur. What the hell's he doing here?

And why's King James here in that stupid Sgt. Pepper get-up? He OD-ed in '72. And Jenny, the lead singer of "Peace 'Copter," didn't she get murdered in '79? And there's that moody acid freak, Timmy Franks, prancing around behind her. Poor bastard slipped in the tub and cracked his skull in '86.

But here's the thing: none of them looks like they did when they died. They all look like we did back in '69. Hell, some of us still have pimples on our faces.

It's got to be a prank. Even though I haven't cut an album in five years, I'm still touring annually. *Rolling Stone* just named me the best old man in the biz. I have a few good years ahead of me. My point being, I usually have at least some fans or paparazzi camped out on my lawn.

Where are they today?

I catch a glimpse of myself reflected in the window. Pitch black long hair. I have to dye it, but it's all still mine. Skinny, craggy face from all the years of wear and tear, but I'm still swimming in chicks. Both *People* and *Us* magazines still think

39

I'm sexy. I'm dressed in a fedora and leather jacket, tight jeans and boots. The feathered boa might be a bit much, but the fans expect it.

So I'm really here. I'm not dead. I should take this as good news.

And then, Young Me approaches. "Guys! It's really him! See? I told you so!"

Good. These are just fans. I can deal with this.

Jenny lifts a hairy eyebrow. "You sure? He looks kind of . . . old."

That little barb digs in more than I'd care to admit. I'm about to retort when Young Me says, "Come on. It's to be expected. We received the transmission years ago."

I don't quite know what to make of that one, so I ask if they want autographs. They exchange glances, and I wonder if they heard me. I open my mouth to repeat myself when King James says, "What's an autograph?"

"Never mind that," Timmy says. "What I want to know is, how did Vietnam end? It did end, right?"

Young Me slaps him on the chest. "Knock it off. If you'd watched their TV transmissions like I told you . . ."

"Hey, don't hassle me, man. I had other things going on."

They argue back and forth, and I get this cold, shuddering feeling in my belly. "Who are you guys?"

Young Me grins like a kid. "Sorry. We're big fans of you, but we live so far away, it took decades to get here."

"That's, um, some trip."

"No," Timmy says, "we're here *for* the trip. We saw, like, Woodstock, and we figured you guys knew how to have fun."

"Well, some of us do." I think back to my drunk and disorderly charge in Alabama, back in '77. The sheriff of that county had a decidedly different idea of fun, and I still have the scars to prove it.

Young Me takes over again. "Look, we really like your music. We don't have rock 'n' roll in our part of the galaxy. We're just here for the party."

"Galaxy?" Didn't Timmy think he was a space cowboy back in '72?

"We know times have changed, sir. Like I said, we've come a long way. But we just want to hang out on this planet for a while.

You know, party."

I sigh. "There is no party, guys. It's been over for years. The drugs aren't even good anymore. You should go home."

King James shook his head. "We've come too far."

"But he's old," Jenny said. "He might break if we breathe on him wrong."

"He practically looks the same!" Young Me says. "He's almost sixty-five, and he's not frail at all! He still tours!"

I must really be crazy, because I find myself thinking about letting these loonies into my condo. I think it's boredom that makes up my mind for me. Too many people I meet on a day-to-day basis are the same these days. So what if these guys think they're from outer space? This could be fun, and it's been a while since I've hung out with fans. Besides, I want to know how they got their costumes done so well.

"Come inside for a bit," I say. "We'll talk about the old days, but then you have to go."

—

Three years ago I would have had a fridge full of beer for them, or a bunch of top-shelf liquor. Now I give my visitors Sierra Mist. At my age—and in this business—good vices are hard to hold on to, especially if you have people who care about you. My daughters made me quit drinking. Probably for the best, but sobriety puts a crimp on being social.

I flop down in an easy chair and watch as my fans wander around my trophy room. They marvel at the platinum and gold. They finger the instruments. They gawk at my Grammy.

"Okay," I say. "How did you get the costumes right?"

Young Me beams. "They're holograms. We scanned them from the Woodstock footage."

"Funny. But how'd you *really* do it?"

Timmy holds up a finger, both eyebrows raised. "Check it out, man." He places the finger behind his ear, and his body shimmers. Timmy's gone, replaced by a mass of yellow and green . . . things. I can see arms that aren't really arms, not even tentacles, and there is a head with vague features. Gray veins seem to pulse all over the body.

Maybe it's the strange life I've led, or maybe decades of

drugs, but this doesn't startle me as much as it should. Perhaps I actually find comfort in knowing these cats really are aliens. I nod my head. "Far out."

Timmy switches back.

"What's this?" Freddy touches a turntable.

I explain what it is, and then say, "It's from the old days. No one uses them anymore, really. We have this now." I pull my iPod from my pocket and tell them what it does.

Jenny grunts. "You guys are so primitive. Why don't you have music that plays in your head?"

"Um." Well, what can I say?

"Man," Young Me says, "are those books?" He points to a corner shelf where I keep biographies about me and the band.

"Yep," I say. After the thing with the turntable, I think it best to keep my mouth shut.

Young Me flips through some pages while Freddy peers over his shoulder. "What's all this white stuff? I get the words, but what are they on?"

"Paper," Young Me says. "Didn't you pay *any* attention in school?"

Once again Jenny scoffs. "What's wrong? Didn't kill enough trees?"

Contrary to the rumors, I never slept with Jenny. I wanted to, Lord knows, but we never got together. I always regretted this, but as much as the alien *looks* like her, she *isn't* her. She's pissing me off, so I defend our culture: "We have e-readers now. Most of us read books digitally." I show her my Kindle.

She yawns. "A new novel comes out, we jack it into our heads. It's fast and easy. How do you think we learned English?"

"Cool it, Jenny," Young Me says.

"No wonder the Emperor marked this place for death."

A hush falls over my visitors, and all I can hear is the beat of my own heart. "Emperor? Death?"

Young Me grimaces. "Sorry. You weren't supposed to know that. Our version of your president also saw the TV transmissions. News stories about Vietnam. He thought you guys were too dangerous for the rest of the galaxy, and when you made it to your moon, that made up his mind to send warships here."

This makes no sense, and I stammer for a moment. "That's . . .

that's just stupid! Vietnam was decades ago! We're not like that anymore! The technology I showed you means we're getting better!"

Young Me nods. "You guys are a lot less violent, at least. And if given enough time, maybe you can work through the garbage your leaders feed you."

"That's why we rebelled," Timmy says. "Just like you and Vietnam."

"Most of these guys are related to me," Young Me says, "and I'm the Emperor's son. I came up with the plan to steal a starship and come here, mostly because I thought Father wouldn't blow up a planet with us on it."

"Boy, were *we* wrong," Timmy says. "We received word that shortly after we left, he launched warships anyway."

My heart savages my ribcage. I pray this is some kind of acid flashback. "They're on their way here?!"

"Yeah," Young Me says. "But don't worry. You still have another year to go before they arrive."

"But . . . " I gag on my own words. It takes a moment to clear my throat. "You guys don't have rock 'n' roll. We could export it. We're valuable."

"Not to everyone. Father thinks people like you are too subversive."

"We like it, though," Jenny says. She smiles for the first time, and all of a sudden, she's my Jenny. I'm twenty-two again.

"I'm sorry we missed the party," King James says. "But we can still make our own, right?"

I feel like I should tell someone, but who? My agent? I met the president once, but would he take a call from me? And would he listen to my crazy ramblings? What about the press? They'd crucify me. I'd be lucky if a tinfoil hat-wearing podcaster broadcasting from his mom's basement would take me seriously.

I've been thinking about writing new songs. Maybe I can get an album out before the warships arrive. Get all the bile out of me. My swan song. I know the end is coming, and I know I can go out on top.

But we can save that for tomorrow. Tonight I want to remember what fun is like. I send out for booze and coke and some weed to help chill us out later. I search around my studio for a stale pack of smokes, which I always kept around when I'd first quit . . . just in case.

I don't invite anyone else, though. This is my party. My past.

I consider the iPod for a moment, and then I toss it out the window. I turn up the volume on one of my old records and dance with my dead friends. Even though the rush of youth floods my system, I feel like an outsider because there is Young Me, singing along and using all of my old moves, the ones my hamstrings can't handle anymore.

My band mates surround me, and the illusion is banished. We all do shots, and the fear I feel for the end of the world dulls.

After decades of fantasies I finally bang Jenny. I don't know how we do it, since her body *is* an illusion, but we manage. With the party still roaring in my living room, I hold Jenny with one hand, a joint with the other, and stare up through my skylight, to the stars above.

One year to go, and there's nothing I can do. Or is there? Maybe it's just because I'm feeling younger, but optimism creeps back into the folds of my drug-addled, age-feebled brain.

When I was younger, a lot of people thought I was a waste, that I offered nothing to the world. But I do: rock 'n' roll. And now, I'm critically acclaimed.

HA! If only my high school music teacher, the one who told me I'd never amount to anything, can see me now. I wonder what Officer Carney, who arrested me at least a half-dozen times before I dropped out of school, would think of my unique position in this situation. Not even my own mother thought much of me.

I can save the world. Never underestimate the power of music. To top it all off, I have the Emperor's son on my side. How can I lose?

CLYDE NEBBINS MEETS THE DEVIL

"Look, I know I'm the Devil and all, and I'm supposed to strike the hardest bargains in the business, but are you sure about this? Even I'm kind of thrown by your offer."

Clyde Nebbins nodded. He was sure.

"This has got to be a joke," the Devil said. "Tell me it's a put-on. Did Mammon put you up to this?"

Clyde thought back to last week, when his perfect record was forever shattered. There he was, clad in a neon-orange reflector vest, a stop sign clutched in his hand like a ping pong paddle. His other hand he held aloft, in case a wayward motorist didn't see everything else. A gaggle of prepubescent children ambled and hopped across the street as one, babbling as if they spoke a language only ten-year-olds could understand.

When they'd passed him, he dropped both arms and turned to follow them. He failed to see, behind him, a lone child who had seemingly materialized out of nowhere. The boy did not notice the crossing guard was no longer paying attention; all he saw were his friends getting farther ahead.

The driver of the H2 saw only Clyde lowering the stop sign. He waited until the crossing guard was back on the sidewalk before he gunned his suburban assault vehicle. He never saw the boy; his "car" was too big. Only when his tires smashed the boy to a waffle did he know something was amiss.

Clyde heard the flesh tear and the bones crunch and turned in time to see one of the boys—a child under his protection—get rolled over by a tank-like machine. It was this sight that haunted his dreams, reminding him that he'd failed in his life's mission.

Even worse, he was fired by a bureaucrat who could never understand the artistry in being a crossing guard.

"No put-on," he told the Devil. "I want to be the greatest crossing guard in history."

The devil had to restrain a laugh. It was so absurd it would be criminal to do business with him. "Okay, Mr. Nebbins. Just sign on the dotted line."

Clyde considered the levity of selling his soul for something an ordinary man would find a piddling sum, but he knew it was for a good cause. He pricked his finger with the Devil's quill pen and scratched his John Hancock on the parchment.

"Great doing business with you," the Devil said.

—

The Devil was true to his contract. In the course of the next five years, Clyde not only got his job back, he received frequent raises, was featured in several articles printed in local newspapers, won a couple of community awards and, most importantly, was adored by the children he protected. They never made fun of him, not even to his back.

The part that surprised him most, however, was the sudden lack of memory on the town's part. No one had any recollection of the dead child, not even the kid's parents. Clyde visited the cemetery to see if the gravestone was still there, but no one ever mentioned the accident.

Clyde lost no sleep over it. As long as he was the best at his chosen profession, nothing else mattered.

On the fifth anniversary of his deal with the Devil, Clyde found himself in the middle of the street, performing his duties as usual, the stop sign held high and proud, with a group of children crossing like a family of ducks, all laughing and babbling and being kids.

And then Clyde saw the oncoming pick-up. Despite the stop sign and Clyde's apparel, the driver didn't seem ready to pause long enough to let the children pass.

"Hey!" Clyde shouted.

Everyone looked up to see what was happening. There were five kids left on the street, and the pick-up was aimed directly at them.

Clyde had to think quickly. Could the Devil really renege on the deal? Or had there been fine print he'd missed? Perhaps he should have had his lawyer look over the contract.

Or was there enough time to save the kids? Was the pick-up going slow enough?

He dropped the stop sign and ran for the kids. By pushing two of them, he was able to knock the others over to the sidewalk, where they were all safe. After that Clyde knew nothing but darkness.

—

When he woke up, he was no longer in a coma induced by an F-150. He was in Hell, standing in a street, dressed for duty.

Each time he tried to help a child cross, the poor kid was run down by an absurdly large SUV. Clyde Nebbins couldn't stop crying for the rest of eternity.

JESUS WAS DEAD FOR THREE DAYS!
CLICK HERE TO SEE HOW HE CAME BACK!

Dirk and I zap back in time, and he starts setting up his camera as soon as we arrive in the year 33 BC. I probably should say BCE, but fuck that sciency shit. I grew up with BC, and BC's the way it stays.

I've never been to this era before—and I've never been to Israel in *any* era—and the air stinks. Not like what we have at home. It's kind of a mixture between BO, shit and death. Jesus, don't these people fucking shower?

"These people." Heh. My boss would write me up for saying that. I play nicey-nice on camera, but I gotta be me on my own time.

Dirk mounts his camera on his shoulder. "Ready to kick ass, Brock?"

"I was born with my foot up that ass."

We struggle our way through the reeking, robed masses. Jesus Christ! Why doesn't someone go back in time and introduce modern cologne to these backward savages? Get them to used it, too. Stay until they get used to it. I know some Don Draper shithead could do that. Probably jerks himself off to sleep fantasizing about it.

There it is: Golgotha. The opening act is already finished; two guys have been nailed to crosses, silhouetted against the deep blue sky behind them.

"Get a shot of that!"

"Already rolling, boss."

The people part, and I can see Him arriving. He doesn't bear his own cross. His apostles do. He also looks nothing like in pictures. His hair is fro'd out, and he's got these flashy sunglasses. Literally. Bulbs of little lights blink at random. He smiles, and . . . come on. He's wearing a gold grill. Who the fuck got to him? Kanye West?

"Yo Jesus!" A black guy jumps out of the crowd and starts in with a ridiculously complicated handshake.

Jesus doesn't skip a beat. "Peace out, brah."

They reach the hill, and Jesus chestbumps every single one of his apostles. They hug and high five and fistbump and trash-talk each other. Shit. The viewers back home ain't gonna buy this. What is this, *Entourage*?

"Don't take Jesus! Take me instead!" It's a middle-aged tourist from the Bible Belt. She rends her hair and gnashes her teeth. People still do that shit? Fucking retards.

Jesus gets down to be nailed up. As Dirk and I get close, so does . . . holy shit. Kanye really *is* here. He's got a mic and backup singers. They start performing, and the crowd goes nuts. Jesus, is *everyone* here today a goddam tourist?!

The first nail goes in, and Jesus screams. "Motherfuck! Take it easy, brah!"

The Roman doesn't understand the words, but he sure feels the tone. Grinning, he puts the next nail in harder. Jesus screams harder, too.

When the Roman's done, other Centurions help him lift the cross and drop it in a post hole. This jerks the whole setup, bumping Jesus. He screams. "Damn, son! You just put these nails in me! You tryin' to rip 'em out again?"

The Centurions ignore him.

"That's some cold shit."

I gesture to Dirk, and he turns the camera on me. I hold the mic to my face. "Ladies and gentlemen, you have just seen the greatest moment in history, a moment so great we changed how we keep track of years because of it. Jesus of Nazareth, crucified at the age of thirty-three. As you can see this event has been changed by our invention of time travel. What you see may shock you. You may even consider it blasphemous. We're now going to get closer and see if Jesus wants to talk to TMZ superstar, Brock the Rocker Hardley. Stay tuned."

We push and shove, but only the guy in the KKK hood curses us out. The Romans don't want us to get any closer. They don't understand us, but we understand the swords they brandish at us.

"It's okay," Jesus says. "That's Brock Hardley. He's supposed to be here." No stupid accent or idiot half-words. Clear English for me. Nice.

Wait a minute. I'm *supposed* to be here? Can't be. I don't believe in this horseshit. But he *did* know my name. Maybe Kanye said something. Douchebag hates me, so it's possible.

The Romans let us through, and I look up to Jesus on the cross. He's shorter than I expected. Got a huge dong, though. Good for him.

"Anything to say to your future fans, Jesus?" I hold the mic up as far as I can: dick height.

He leans down. "I've said all I need to say to my followers. I *did* want to say something to *you*, though."

This can't be good. "What's that?"

"You're an asshole. All you spout is hate and disdain. Try being nice to people. You might like it, and it would sure brighten everyone else's day."

Dirk looks shocked around the camera. "Dude. Did the son of God just call you an asshole?"

"Did Kanye tell you to say that?"

"Kanye had no idea you'd be here," Jesus says.

Pfft. Right. Whatever. Fuck this guy.

"So long, fuckface," I say. "Hang in there, *brah*."

"See you in three days," Jesus says.

I stalk away, and Dirk rushes after me. "We going home, Brock?"

"No. We gotta stay and cover his ass. Besides, I want to make sure that cocksucker's dead when they put him in the cave. Let's find somewhere to stay."

Trump went back in time to do some business, so finding his hotel is not a problem. Dirk turns on the insanely large flatscreen and pulls up On Demand. "Brock, they have shows from the future. *Our* future, I mean."

I go to the bar and sink down an airplane bottle of swill. "Let's see how *The Walking Dead* ends."

For a while, that's what we do. But the more I drink, the angrier I get. "Jesus Christ had the fucking nerve to call *me* an asshole? He doesn't fucking know me."

"I *do*. And he's kind of right."

I pause, staring open-mouthed like a mongoloid.

"You talk too much shit, Brock. You're okay when you're on the show, but behind the scenes you push people around. You make fun of people. Your screed on Mexicans taking white jobs... I mean, shit. You're a handsome version of Donald Trump."

"Fuck you."

"My point exactly."

I get another drink while Dirk surfs through channels. I take that shit from the son of God, and I gotta take it from fucking *Dirk*? That muscle-bound pituitary freak? I'm almost certain he's a product of incest. He *did* call me handsome, though. Is he a fruit? Have I ever seen him with a woman?

"Oh shit," Dirk says. "Hey Brock! Take a look at this!"

It's a live feed from Golgotha. Wayne LaPierre has shown up with an AR-15 and is trying to save Jesus. He's gunning down Romans like he thinks he's Omar Mateen. And goddammit, it's Hunter Tucker getting the scoop! That son of a syphilitic cock!

"We gotta go back," I say.

"It's too late. Everyone will think we're riding Hunter's coattails."

"I'm not there for the story. I'm there to knock his capped teeth down his fucking throat."

It dawns on his face. Dirk has forgotten—until now—how Hunter fucked my wife—*ex-wife*—and my daughter at the same time. My dumb cunt of an ex? I expect that from her. But my daughter was a smart twenty-year-old, college and everything. *That* pissed me off. Still does, obviously.

I gulp down another airplane bottle and step into my shoes. Dirk now knows how important this is, so he packs up our gear, and we drive down to Golgotha. Trump built a parking lot there, but it's full. Fuck it. I park across two handi-crippled spaces, and we rush to the scene.

Fuck. It's over. Wayne LaPierre's been shot dead. I laugh at the irony. Anyway, Hunter's doing a new story about Pat Robertson, who had fainted dead during the crucifixion. His body is still here, so Hunter has his cameraman getting close-ups of the corpse.

"Hey dickhead!" I call out.

A lot of heads perk up, but his is the only one I'm interested in. It swivels in my direction, surprise on his face. "I didn't know you were here, Brock the Cocksucker."

I look to Dirk to make sure he's getting this, then I belt Hunter in his pretty fucking mouth. Not so pretty anymore. He falls back, spitting blood and teeth. Got the front ones, too. Good.

But he laughs. I don't get that, and it makes me madder. I'm rearing back to kick him in the balls when he stops.

"This is worth every second of my cock in your daughter's asshole. I never washed clean. You can still smell her ring piece on me. Wanna whiff?"

I lose time. I don't know what I did, but when Dirk pulls me off of him, I'm out of breath, and there's blood on my shoes. Hunter barely has a face, but somehow he's still laughing.

"You can't just kick a man to death," Dirk says.

"These are Old Testament times. He fucked my property. I can do whatever I want to that needle dick shit eater."

But he's right. I think Hunter and I are even now. I'm still going to hate his guts, but I think we're good.

Some Marines arrive to protect the crucifixion, so I do some broadcasting. A couple of interviews. You know, the ushe. In the middle of all this, one of the Marines rips off his uniform, showing a bomb vest underneath. He runs to Jesus, screaming some Muslim mumbo jumbo. Dirk covers it like a pro, and he gets every moment of that explosion.

I think maybe the bomber didn't get close enough, but he manages to knock over the crosses. We run up for a closer look, and *holy shit*! Jesus doesn't have legs anymore. Most of his dick's gone, too. He's in too much shock to scream, but his eyes look at his injury. Comprehension is clear.

Paramedics rush in. They're trying to save his life long enough to last through the rest of the crucifixion. How does that make sense? It's like sterilizing the inside of a murderer's elbow before giving him a lethal injection. What the fuck?

Jesus begins screaming. He screams so hard it breaks his vocal chords.

All right. Maybe I *am* an asshole. But I can't let this guy suffer just to be crucified again.

I sneak the gun off a Marine's belt. He's too busy staring at this madness to notice. I've seen the movies, so I know how to turn the safety off and jack a round into the chamber. Except it ejects a bullet. Guess this guy doesn't fuck around.

Before anyone can stop me, I fire at Jesus' face. For mercy. Instead I get him in the jaw. Blasts it off his face. His eyes roll in their sockets, and his body shakes. He's choking on his own blood. Yeah, he's going to die, for sure, but not fast enough for mercy. I shoot him again, this time in the forehead. His holy brains splat out the back of his shattered head.

Someone finally notices, and the Marines dog pile on top of me. I have never gotten a beating so bad in my entire life, not even from my father who regularly beat the mortal shit out of me. Luckily I pass out pretty early on. I only remember them breaking my ribs.

I wake up three days later. Dirk is sitting in the only chair in the room. I'm surprised to note there are no handcuffs on my wrist.

"What did I miss?"

Dirk tells me that every bone in my body was broken. Weird. I don't feel any pain, and I can't see bandages. Maybe I'm on some really good shit.

After I passed out, the Marines went as far into the future as they could to find the smartest doctors in history. None of them could put Jesus back together again. Also, a group of Nazis arrived to secure the body of Christ for Hitler. They'd stopped in the future for advanced weapons, but they didn't stand a chance against the Federation of Space/Time. They always have the best shit.

They finally decided that they'd just go ahead and put Jesus' body in the cave. The Federation put their best people on protecting the place. Kanye gave an amazing, emotional speech and signed autographs afterward. Scholars from Ancient Greece to the futuristic Scientists for the Preservation of Earth came by, eager to open the crypt after three days.

"Why am I not a prisoner?" I ask.

"Because—"

The door bursts open. "Because nothing can be proven without a body."

I look to see who it is and gasp. "Holy shit! I shot you."

"Twice. I remember." There is some irritation in Jesus' voice.

"But how?!"

"Resurrection, my brother. Now do you believe?"

I almost kind of do. Unless this is a dream. If I'm dreaming, why is my mind betraying me? Or am I dead, and this is Hell? Fuck that. Hell doesn't exist. I don't know what's happening.

He must see the confusion on my face. "You're the ultimate proof. Who do you think healed you?"

I flex my hands and arms. No pain. No bandages. He hands me a mirror. There is no damage to my face. I look as sexy as ever. Hell, I look *younger.*

"Take this gift I give to you," Jesus says. "Be nice to people. Change the world for the better. God bless you, Brock Nelson Hardley."

And he leaves, a peace sign held aloft.

Holy shi—er, poop. It's for real. All of it. I can't deny having my broken bones healed in a mere three days. Maybe I've been too much of an asshole. Maybe I should cool it. Start rethinking my viewpoints.

Why is my cameraman smirking at me?

"What is it?" I ask.

"You seriously believe that shit?"

"What do you mean?"

"He didn't magically heal you. He's a time traveler, too, so he picked up a younger version of you, brought him here, paradoxed you and boom. All better."

Funny. I don't feel paradoxed. Not that it's ever happened to me before.

"Wait. How? Did he use our equipment?"

"No, he's a natural."

"No. He'd have to be alive to do that. He lost his legs, and I shot him in the head. Twice. He was dead."

Dirk almost laughs. I can sense it. The prick. "He had a timer set. A flux in the continuum grabbed a younger version of *himself*. Brought him to the cave. He paradoxed himself. At least, that's my theory. I wasn't there for it, but that makes complete sense to me."

It dawns on me like a nuke going off in my brain. "That means he planned the crucifixion."

Dirk nods. "It was an inside job."

That phony son of a bitch. He almost got me.

"We have the scoop, right?"

"Eh." Dirk waves his hand sideways, back and forth. "No one else has said anything, but we don't have the proof. We can't do shit with it."

"No! Goddammit!" I cover my face with my hands. The biggest story in the history of the world, and I have to sit on it. Maybe I can run it past the ethics board, but I know what they'll say.

"There's always Alex Jones," Dirk says. "But you know how that'll go."

"Fuck," I mutter.

"It gets worse."

I grunt. "How? How could it possibly get worse?"

"He also paradoxed Hunter Tucker."

That motherfucking, cockbiting piece of human garbage.

"Pack up, Dirk. We're going to time travel across the entire continuum, and we're going to hunt down Jesus Christ. When we find him, we'll kill him. But first I have to rip out Hunter's still-beating heart. If he has one."

Dirk sighs. "Jesus. I should have kept my mouth shut."

"Jesus," I repeat. "Right. Let's get him."

CAPTAIN METH-MOUTH ON THE HIGH SEAS OF CHICAGO

1

How had a simple summer job turned into a way of life? Captain Dwight Fitzgerald looked at himself in the cracked mirror in his quarters and looked over his pirate outfit, now more rags than costume since he'd worn it every day from the time when the zombies killed civilization. The buttons on his coat, once shiny, now gave off a dull gleam through the tarnished, filmed-over spots, and what once was rich red material had thinned so much he could see his undershirt beneath. He'd long ago stopped wearing the fake beard, since he now had a real one, although he couldn't grow much on his upper lip. Even the tricorner hat he wore seemed ready to fall apart, and the skull-and-crossbones insignia had faded so much it was only a pale shadow at his brow.

The only part of his accouterments that remained fresh was the sword he kept strapped to his waist. It wasn't the phony one his boss had given him for the show. No, this came from his private collection, and he took good care of it every night, no matter what. He rarely used it, since he did his best to not let zombies get that close to him. He much preferred the .45 he'd found in Miami, and the assault rifle he'd picked up in Atlanta didn't hurt, either.

He tried to remember being a college student, but he couldn't conjure the memories. It seemed so long ago, like he'd been a different person back then. He'd only meant to be a pirate on the Treasure Island Adventure Show for a summer before going back to class. How had he come to this? He'd been so mild-mannered before, and now he helmed a boat full of survivors, and he'd had to kill a lot of people to keep his shipmates alive. How many? He couldn't even remember. How messed up was that?

Boots clomped down the wooden steps. Dwight turned and saw Lt. West, a musclebound man dressed completely in black, arms bulging under his tight shirt. A skull cap stretched over his bald head, and a light layer of thick whiskers kept his cheeks warm.

"Land ho, Cap. Looks like we're here."

Dwight stared at West, the only real warrior on this ship. West had been a Navy SEAL before the zombies. The crew had found him in New York on a suicide run, cornered by a herd of the undead. With a bit of luck and hard work they'd saved him, and when he joined the ranks, Dwight made him first mate. Since then West's expertise managed to not only keep them alive, but also kept them on track, even through the wilds of Canada. Even through the Niagara Falls nightmare. And as for Detroit? Dwight didn't want to think about it.

He nodded. "I'll be right up. Thanks."

As West made his way back up to the deck, Dwight took one last look at himself and straightened his sword. After all they'd been through, this was it.

They'd first heard the rumor from Benny, a teen they'd picked up in Miami. At the time they'd set anchor on the coast of the city, safe from the zombie horde. Whenever they ran out of supplies, they'd sneak to shore and forage what they could. Sometimes they rescued survivors, and sometimes they lost companions. They found Benny in a dumpster behind a McDonald's with two zombies trying to get to him. Later, on the ship, he said he'd heard that the government had a base in Chicago, that they'd restored a semblance of order there.

Supplies were running low, and each search party came back with less and less. Soon Miami would be stripped bare, and then what?

Dwight brought his advisors together. He could never get used to the pomposity of having advisors—they were just Julio, who used to sell him weed; Jocko, who played the first mate on the Treasure Island Adventure Show; and Tori, who worked at the concession stand—but being the captain, he was stuck with the idea. Everyone had agreed: they needed to get to Chicago.

None of them favored going over land, though. The ship had offered them safety, and they didn't want to give that up.

Over the course of the month they'd floated near Miami, they'd collected an entire treasure chest of batteries, just in case. They kept them in Ziploc bags to keep them dry, as they did with a GPS device Julio had scavenged from a grocery store. If they conserved enough energy by only turning it on once a day, they figured they could go up the coast to the St. Lawrence and take that through the maze of lakes and rivers to Lake Michigan and to Chicago. The only issue would be the cold, so they waited another month before setting sail.

Dwight smiled, thinking about old friends. Benny died in a freak accident in Atlanta. Tori bought it at Niagara. Julio and Jocko were gunned down in the Detroit massacre.

And only a half a year ago they'd all just been normal people eking out their mundane existences.

Sometimes Dwight lost faith in Benny's talk of rumors, but every once in a while they came upon a traveler or sailor who had heard the same thing. It wasn't always the government who saved the day, but every story agreed that Chicago was a safe zone, and that kept everyone going.

Dwight took the stairs two at a time, feeling the rough and splintered handrail scratch at his palms, and as he emerged onto the deck he saw West had gathered the troops. All of them lined up as if waiting for a speech.

He looked at their expectant faces and realized only one of them had been with him from the start: Hector St. Martin. They'd gone to school together but never really talked to each other, not even when they both got summer jobs on the Treasure Island Adventure Show. In fact, Hector had played the first mate of the invading pirates back then. Together with Julio, Jocko, Tori and a few others, they'd gotten the idea to hide out from the zombies on the ship they'd worked on, the S.S. Stevenson. They'd even decided together to start rescuing people, since they'd had plenty of room onboard.

Every single person who stared at Dwight now had been saved by him and his friends. His crew. Sure, it ran contrary to the pirates they pretended to be, but just because the rules of society had been canceled didn't mean everyone could act like a pack of uncivilized assholes.

Dwight cleared his throat. "It looks like we're finally at our destination. We've all been through a lot, and for all we know the rumors we heard are just that. We must maintain hope that order has been restored to the City of Chicago, but I want us to be prepared for the worst."

He turned to West. "How long do we have?"

The lieutenant cast his eyes up to the mast, where Dandy Jim kept watch with his telescope extended. "Probably a day. No more."

Dwight nodded and addressed the rest: "This is a cause for celebration, but by the time we have Chicago in our sights, I want us to be armed and ready, just in case—"

"Ship ahoy!"

Dwight glanced up and saw Dandy Jim pointing to the west, toward the city. Sure enough, another ship rode the waves. It looked like a fishing boat, and it was headed toward them.

It could be good news or bad. They'd come upon many ships in their journey. Most wanted to barter, but occasionally there were folks who wanted more. Folks who took their roles as pirates more seriously. Nobody onboard the S.S. Stevenson needed to be told to grab their weapons and ready themselves for battle. They scrambled about in a frenzy, but none of them panicked. They'd been through too much to panic.

Dwight stepped up to the helm and felt West's presence at his back. He knew the former SEAL held his M16 but did not point it anywhere, his finger resting on the trigger guard. None of Dwight's people aimed at anything yet. They didn't want to seem threatening, but they didn't want to look weak, either.

As the boat drew closer he could see their people doing the same. Their stony faces reflected the grim world they lived in, and the rags they wore indicated their squalor.

One man stood out from the rest, and as the ships started to line up parallel to one another, he stepped forward. To Dwight: "I take it you're the captain?"

"Dwight Fitzgerald. What gave it away?"

The guy looked puzzled for a moment, and then his face cracked in a smile. "Sorry. We saw the pirate ship and your clothes, and it got us kind of jumpy."

"Relax. We won't try to kill you if you won't try to kill us. Deal?"

This time the guy laughed. "I'm Nate Gables, and this is my crew. We're getting the hell out of Chicago, and when we saw you we thought you were, you know. Him."

Dwight exchanged a glance with West, but the lieutenant didn't acknowledge him; he was too busy looking hard at Gables.

Dwight turned his attention back to the other captain. "Uh . . . first of all, him who? And second of all, why leave Chicago? We heard it was a safe zone."

"You heard wrong. I take it you're not from around here?"

Dwight gave him the super-abridged version of their story and why they were headed for Chicago. When he was done, Gables nodded. "Well, you heard right about the zombies. There are none in the city. That's the good news. The bad news is, the guy who cleared them out is a lunatic. Some kind of street thug with delusions of grandeur. He's who we thought you were."

This confused Dwight, since in all his time at sea, theirs was the only pirate ship he'd seen. "Why?"

"He's got some kind of pirate fetish. Watched *Pirates of the Caribbean* one too many times, if you ask me. He has a boat just like yours, and he has an outfit like the one you're wearing, except yours looks store-bought. He had his tailored. I guess he'd have to, seeing as how big he is."

"Holy Christ," Dwight said. "Sounds off his rocker."

"I wish I could just dismiss him as crazy. He's a tough bastard, and he runs Chicago like a police state. It's a pretty violent place. He does the pirate thing for real, and he leads all the raids personally. His orders are shoot to kill, and any survivors . . . well, if they're men, he kills them. With his own hands. If they're women . . ."

"I get the picture."

Hector approached and whispered, "We're running low on food."

Dwight said to Gables, "Are you willing to barter? We don't have much food, but we have a lot of ammo. Some batteries."

Gables shook his head. "We're low on everything. Sorry. But I hope you change your mind about Chicago. You seem like a nice guy, and Captain Meth-Mouth will probably tear you limb from limb."

Captain Meth-Mouth? Dwight fought to keep from laughing.

How could anyone take someone like that seriously?

Instead of showing off his incredulity, he said, "I appreciate the advice. Where are you going?"

"I don't know," Gables said. "Anywhere but here."

"Stay away from Detroit. We barely got out of there alive."

Gables laughed. "That would've been good advice even before the zombies."

They wished each other well, and as Gables and his crew sailed away, Dwight turned to face his people. They'd gathered around him, waiting to hear what he had to say.

"You heard them," he said. "What do you all think?"

"This is bad," West said. "He must have an army, if he's able to keep the dead out of his entire city. We've got a ton of ammo, but we don't have enough soldiers. I say we cut our losses."

"We need to get supplies," Hector said. "We can't turn back. We need to stock up in the next day or so, or we'll be eating our own boots before long."

Ellis, a shaggy-headed, constantly grinning man stepped up. "Dude, he calls himself Captain Meth-Mouth. One, what kind of clown does that? And two, if he's a meth-head, we can take him. No sweat."

West regarded him with disgust, but he didn't say a word.

Dwight cleared his throat. "How about a compromise? We don't have to fight this Captain Meth-Mouth. We could always barter. Or maybe we can even join him. It sounds like Chicago is safe, just so long as you don't cross him."

"People like Captain Meth-Mouth don't barter," West said. "They take. And I don't live with any scumbags. I don't imagine anyone else here would, either."

"Good point. Do you think we could maybe sneak into the city and get some supplies? And then make off for our next destination?"

West grimaced, rubbing his stubbly chin. "It'd be tricky, but possible. It depends on how disciplined his men are."

"And they're probably street thugs, just like him. Right?"

"Maybe." West didn't sound convinced.

"Say we do that," a voice from the crowd said. "Say we succeed. Where would we go next?"

Dwight turned to see Kelly had joined the conversation. She'd been with him since the later Miami days. He and Jocko had saved her from a drug dealer who had kept her in his whorehouse, selling her for food and alcohol. The bastard kept four women as slaves. One had died in the confrontation, and the other two—twin sisters—decided to try their luck on their own. Only Kelly joined the crew of the S.S. Stevenson, and since then she'd been Jocko's girlfriend.

When Jocko died, Kelly withdrew from everyone else. She still did her tasks, but she didn't interact much with the others. This was the first time she'd said anything in months.

"We can't go back." This from Jo, a waitress they'd picked up in Norfolk. "We'd never survive Detroit again."

West nodded. "We're trapped in Lake Michigan."

Dwight tugged on his beard for a moment, rubbing at the rough strands of kinky hair. "What if we did here in Chicago what we did in Miami? Just sort of float out here and raid the city every once in a while?"

"No way," Hector said. "We didn't have Captain Meth-Mouth to deal with in Miami."

"He's right," West said. "In Miami, all you had to deal with were zombies and the occasional scumbag. It's too dangerous here. We might get away with it once, but I wouldn't dare try it more than that."

Dwight cursed and forced himself to stop playing with his beard. "I'm open to suggestions. Anyone?"

"Raid Chicago once," West said. "I'll take a team of three. We'll sneak in, forage what we can and get out. When we get back, set sail north for Milwaukee, check things out there."

"I actually heard Green Bay isn't too bad." From Jo again. Everyone sensed the blind hope in her voice, but no one tried to dispel it.

"Green Bay, then," West said.

Dwight nodded. "That sounds doable. Everyone else agree?"

A few yeahs and grunts of assent from those around him. None of them sounded very eager. He didn't blame them. They'd all hung their hopes on the stories of Chicago being true. Now things were starting to revert back to the early days of the zombie apocalypse, when everyone prepared themselves for the inevitable end of civilization and their own lives.

"That's it, then," he said. "Lieutenant, pick your team and prepare to embark on your mission. Ellis, ready the lifeboat for launch. Grafton, set anchor."

Everyone went their separate ways, and Dwight stepped up to the fore of the boat. Just beyond the head of the wood-carved naked lady at the bow, he could see the city of Chicago on the horizon. Gray and dirty, it looked like a layer of scum floating on the lake. He thought about what he'd hoped to find here, and he thought about what Gables had said. He prayed to any god who might be listening that this didn't turn into another Detroit.

2

Captain Meth-Mouth slit the woman's throat and backed away so he could admire her flailing body and the spraying blood and the way her friends all stared aghast at him. Yes, moments like this made his dick hard, and he instantly regretted not sentencing her to the brothel instead. Still, this bitch and her companions thought they could overthrow him as the King of Chicago.

Dumb. Real dumb.

Her man roared and tried to break free of the guards grasping his arms and shoulders. "You bastard I'll kill you! I'll fucking kill you!"

Captain Meth-Mouth nodded to Claudio, who then stabbed a fist into the prisoner's guts. The guy doubled over, gagging. A string of bile swung from his lower lip like a pendulum.

Captain Meth-Mouth grabbed the prisoner's chin and jerked up his face so they could see eye to eye. "You're him? The Turk?"

The Turk spat in Captain Meth-Mouth's face. A fat, bubbled glob struck his cheek and oozed down to his jaw line.

The captain moved like a mongoose. His bunched up fingers snaked around the Turk's nose and squeezed, forcing a choked groan from him. Captain Meth-Mouth twisted his wrist so hard he felt the Turk's nose creak like a rusty hinge. He held it on the very brink of breaking.

The Turk screamed and strained against the guards to no avail.

"Is it true you killed Murdock with your bare hands?" the captain asked. "Jerked his head back so far his neck broke, and his spine stuck out his throat?"

The Turk made a muffled sound, maybe a curse. Blood dripped from his pinched nostrils and colored the tip of his chin.

"I heard you call me Captain Faggot. Is that true?"

This time, all the Turk could do was groan.

"A real tough guy," Captain Meth-Mouth said. "Let's find out how tough. One hour. In the arena. You win, you and your friends live. You lose, your friends get butchered. It's been a while since I skinned a man alive." He turned to one of the other prisoners—this one had to be Quaid, since the others were women—and made a kissy face at him.

Quaid couldn't meet his gaze. Pale, he looked at the ground.

Captain Meth-Mouth released the Turk's nose and made a dismissive gesture. The guards took the prisoners away, leaving the captain alone in his throne room. He regarded the kingly seat, an ancient Egyptian masterpiece he'd taken from the Field Museum. He didn't know which pharaoh had sat in it all those centuries ago, but whoever it had been, he'd been pimp as all hell. The only thing it had needed were skulls on the arm rests, which Captain Meth-Mouth had added near the beginning of his reign as King of Chicago. One belonged to a former friend who had boned his favorite girl, and the other was a rival drug dealer who'd had the same idea to rule the city.

Whoops.

Behind Captain Meth-Mouth, someone entered and started cleaning up the Turk's woman. He slipped into his chambers to prepare himself for the coming battle.

He sloughed off his royal robes and shucked out of his boxers, and standing naked in front of the mirror, he flexed, smiling at the way his muscles bulged and danced under a thin layer of skin. Not bad for a former junkie. He could have been an MMA fighter, maybe even a Hollywood star. He wished he could grow out his hair and look even scarier, but he'd gone bald at an early age, before he'd even dropped out of high school. Not that it mattered; he shaved his head every day, and he still looked pretty scary.

The only thing that bothered him was his smile. Meth had done a number on him, reducing the remaining teeth in his mouth to blackened, monstrous fangs. Every time he saw them he wanted to have them pulled and maybe replaced with silver piranha teeth, but there were no dentists around these days. Even though it hurt, he could still chew, and he wanted to continue doing so for as long as he could.

He stepped into his workout pants and did a few stretches to make sure he had full mobility. Then he donned a wife-beater and slipped his feet into heavy duty boots. How often had he cleaned blood and bone off of them? He couldn't remember, but these boots had taken more lives than his sword.

He belted his rapier to his waist and gave the blade a quick examination. It looked kind of silly in his giant, scarred hands, but he knew how to use it and use it well.

Only one thing remained now. He went to his stash and pulled out a fifth of Myer's Rum. Not his favorite brand—rum was hard to come by these days, unlike corn whiskey—but it would do. He belted down three swallows and felt his gums burn and tingle.

More than ready, he made his way to the arena. He had another throne here, but it wasn't as majestic as the other. This one had been taken from an SUV and had been overhauled to his liking. It was made of velvet and bone with a cup holder made from the skeletal hand of an enemy. Above the headrest was a skull, mounted in such a fashion that it seemed like a crown when he sat in the throne, which he did now.

Below, in the arena, jesters pretended to do battle in kind of a pre-game to the main event. Already a crowd had gathered and was laughing at the antics in the pit. Even Captain Meth-Mouth cracked a smile at the jangle-headed fools.

Soon the hour drew to a close, and the jesters finished their show. Captain Meth-Mouth abandoned his throne and descended to the arena, ready to meet his rival.

Shortly the Turk made his appearance, struggling against the guards who practically dragged him to the pit. He'd been stripped to his waist and cleaned up a bit, but he certainly didn't look ready for this.

Captain Meth-Mouth removed his sword and handed it off to one of his go-fers. "Rules are simple. You die, or I die. You ready?"

The Turk tried to harden his face, but his eyes betrayed his fear. Too bad. Captain Meth-Mouth had been looking forward to a challenge, and he'd heard the Turk was a bad ass. He'd killed the Turk's girl, for Christ's sake! Didn't the anger overcome the fear?

"I'll give you the first shot," Captain Meth-Mouth said. Maybe that would make this more exciting. Probably not, though.

The Turk uttered a prayer in his own language, and it seemed to bolster his rage a bit. The fear left his eyes, and Captain Meth-Mouth felt hopeful for a moment.

The Turk bared his teeth and roared, rushing the captain with fists at the ready.

Not smart.

Captain Meth-Mouth sidestepped with ease, and he hooked an arm under the Turk's shoulder, flipping him like a burger into the chain-link fence that protected the audience from the violence. The Turk got up right away, and when he tried his next attack, he dropped his shoulder before trying to deliver the blow.

Pathetic.

Captain Meth-Mouth hammered on him for a while, just to wake him up a bit, and he backed away to see what his opponent would do next. The Turk, blood running freely from his nose and the sockets in his gums where teeth used to be, took his stance, like maybe he'd watched too many kung-fu movies when he was a kid.

Captain Meth-Mouth couldn't help but laugh. He played with his quarry for a while, trying to make things interesting for the audience, but after a few broken bones and a lot more blood, things got too slow.

The crowd was bored. They'd seen all of this before, so the captain got the Turk on the ground and straddled his torso. He leaned an arm on the Turk's throat and placed his reeking maw over an eye. Sucking with all his nicotine-addled lungs' ability, he felt the eye protrude from its socket as the Turk screamed. He screamed harder when Captain Meth-Mouth fit his charnel teeth around the orb and bit it from his head.

The Turk rolled on the ground, bleating out his pain with both hands clamped to his face. Captain Meth-Mouth turned to the crowd and held the eyeball in his teeth, proudly displaying it to his cheering fans.

Then, he saw Claudio by the fence. His second-in-command wore a grim expression on his face, so he clearly had bad news. Bad news took precedence over everything else, so Captain Meth-Mouth spat out the eyeball and chopped the edge of his hand down onto the Turk's throat as hard as he could. He felt his enemy's windpipe collapse like a drinking straw, and he walked to Claudio to find out what was wrong.

"Ship's been sited on the lake," Claudio said.

"So? Find someone to fuck their shit up and salvage what they can."

Claudio watched the Turk trying to breathe against all odds. He even went as far as trying to reach down his own throat, but he had no chance.

"What's up with you?" Captain Meth-Mouth asked.

Claudio turned back to his boss. "Sorry. This ship is different."

"Different? How?"

"It's a pirate ship, sir."

Captain Meth-Mouth froze, trying to process this piece of information. Finally, he said, "Don't you bullshit me. If you're lying, I'll fuck your ass 'til your momma feels it."

Claudio didn't pause. "It's real, all right. It should be here within the day."

Captain Meth-Mouth motioned, and his go-fer brought the sword. Distantly the captain strapped it to his waist.

Could it be? For as long as he'd been alive, he'd wanted to be a pirate. Now he had a rival? This opportunity could not go to waste.

"Prepare my ship. We leave within the hour."

"Aye-aye, Captain."

Captain Meth-Mouth strode off, eager for this new adventure. He was so distracted by this new development that he didn't bother to watch the Turk finally roll over and die. He didn't even wait to see his men tear the Turk's companions to pieces in an orgy of rape and blood.

All he could think of was a battle on the high seas of Chicago.

3

Dwight and West discussed some last-minute items while the men prepared the lifeboat to be launched on this desperate mission. They didn't get far into it. From the corner of his eye, Dwight saw Dandy Jim scuttling down the mast. He hit the deck running and rushed over to Dwight.

"You're not going to believe this, Cap."

Dwight recoiled at Dandy Jim's breath. He'd been homeless in Atlanta, and even though they had a supply of toothbrushes, he never used one. His missing lower teeth stood testament to the fact that he'd never been much for oral hygiene. The crew had voted him for look-out duty not because of his eyesight—which was exceptional—but because of his wretched halitosis.

"What's up?" West asked.

"I saw a pirate ship. It's coming right at us."

Dwight supposed a part of him had thought Gables's story of Captain Meth-Mouth had been bullshit, or at least blown out of proportion. Now he felt his stomach ice over a bit. He extended his telescope—another prop from the Treasure Island Adventure Show—and peered out toward the city. He braced himself against the rail and cast the telescope back and forth until he saw it.

And the cannons on the side.

The S.S. Stevenson had cannons, too, but they were merely decorative.

"Lt. West, your salvage mission has been scrapped. Get all hands to the armory and have them battle ready ASAP."

"Aye-aye, Cap."

As West moved to follow orders, Dwight took another look at the approaching vessel. This time he could see people, and one of them wore a tri-corner captain's hat much like his own. This man towered above everyone else, and his outfit strained against bulging muscles. The savage look on his craggy face really put him over, though; he was pirate-mean, no doubt. Blackbeard had nothing up on this guy.

In that moment Dwight felt the urge to retreat. Just run away. There was no way in hell they'd be able to take this guy. But no, Captain Meth-Mouth would probably chase them down. This would end in bloodshed one way or the other. Might as well make these bastards work for their victory and maybe even take a few of them down to boot.

Someone gently touched his shoulder, and it startled him enough to jerk away from the railing. Heart pounding, he turned to see Kelly standing at his side, holding a cloth-wrapped bundle. She handed it to him, and just by the weight alone, he knew what it was.

"You might need it," she said.

"I hope not."

"Just in case. I've lost too many of my loved ones. I don't want to lose you, too."

Before he could respond, she rushed swiftly away. He watched her go, puzzled. Did she sense the same doom he had? Hell, they *all* had to. One look at Captain Meth-Mouth was enough to turn his guts to worms.

West approached, holding out a rifle to Dwight, butt out. Dwight shook his head and patted his holster. "I'd rather have this one. I was never any good with the big guns, anyway."

"Suit yourself." West passed it on to Sully, a guitarist from Boston. His instrument had been destroyed in Detroit, blown to pieces by a shotgun, and a lot of his soul had gone with it. He took the rifle, but he did not seem to care much about it.

"Besides," Dwight added, "I hope I can talk our way out of this."

West cocked an eyebrow, testing the waters for Dwight's sense of humor. Finding nothing, he said, "That's crazy."

"It's worth trying. These guys can probably kick our asses. Let's try to avoid that, if we can. Hey Hector!"

Hector emerged from below deck, holding an assault rifle. "What's up, Cap?"

"Look at our stock. See what we can barter. I'll bet this guy has a taste for rum, so bring up a bottle. The good stuff."

Hector stared at him for a moment, his mouth twitching. Finally, he said, "What?!"

West shook his head. "Guys like him don't barter. They take. This is a bad idea."

"Maybe he won't," Dwight said. "If not, we go out in a blaze of glory. But maybe he will, in which case we set sail for Green Bay with our lives."

"You can't be serious!" Hector practically stuttered, he was so incredulous.

"We have to try," Dwight said. "Follow orders, all right?"

Hector looked to the lieutenant like a convict begging for a last minute reprieve.

West shrugged. "It could happen." Then he held up his own assault rifle and nodded toward it.

Hector understood. He opened his mouth as if to try one final time, but he knew it would be futile. He went back below.

Dwight and West stood at the bow of the ship, watching Captain Meth-Mouth's approach. The lieutenant said, "You're crazy, but I'll back you, even though we're probably going to die in a few minutes."

"Jesus, man. Try not to get my hopes up."

West cracked a smile, but his eyes remained flat and calm. "Might as well make 'em work for it."

Dwight remembered thinking that very thing not too long ago but coming from West it meant more. From Dwight, it felt like false bravado, but West meant it. Dwight shivered. It was always cooler by the lake, right?

"I don't know if his cannons really work," West said, "but he doesn't know that ours are just for show. It's worthy of a bluff if you really intend to talk this guy down. Regardless, don't take chances. Don't let him turn his side to us. He doesn't have artillery at the bow or aft, so let's keep on those sides, just in case."

Dwight could now hear the devilish war cries of Captain Meth-Mouth's crew, and he suddenly wished he was back in Miami smoking a bowl with Julio and watching some stupid movie on late night TV. The chill clawed at his bones again, and he pocketed Kelly's bundle, hoping he'd never have to use it.

4

Captain Meth-Mouth saw the pirate ship about a mile out from the city, and when he did, he felt his heart flutter for the first time since he'd named himself King of Chicago. He hadn't believed Claudio at first, but now that he saw it—a ragged Jolly Roger flapping against the wind at the top of the mast—he knew he was about to fulfill a childhood fantasy.

When he was five and staying with his grandma because his mom was too much of a junkie whore to take care of him, he'd seen a movie called *Captain Blood* on the broken down black and white Zenith the old lady kept in the basement, where felonious eyes would have to work really hard to notice it. The slow parts of the film didn't appeal to him, but the action scenes? He'd gotten his first hard-on that day while watching the swashbuckling adventure. He longed to be in sword fights, knife in his teeth, swinging from boat to boat amid gunpowder flashes and flying cannon balls.

He peered through his binoculars and saw his adversary had cannons on each side of his ship. While Captain Meth-Mouth had many cannons, all taken from historical markers from around the city, only one worked: the one he'd taken from the Field Museum. It was still enough to have a cannon battle, though. He shivered with anticipation.

A skinny fellow perched on the mast, and he shouted down to the others. People scrambled to and fro on the deck, probably getting ready for Captain Meth-Mouth's imminent arrival. He saw one guy—a giant who could have been a WWE wrestler— and hoped that he was the captain.

Then he saw the guy dressed in historical captain's clothes, just like himself. Captain Meth-Mouth had mixed feelings about this one. While he liked the style and recognized a kindred spirit, he knew he would have no trouble kicking his ass. The captain looked wiry, so there might be hidden toughness—and maybe he was even a sudden bastard—but Captain Meth-Mouth knew how a one-on-one fight would end.

"Sir."

Captain Meth-Mouth turned and saw Claudio standing by, armed with a shotgun. "What's up?"

"Should we shoot first and ask questions later?"

If anyone else had said this, Captain Meth-Mouth would have slapped the teeth from his mouth. His first mate, on the other hand, was too valuable. Tough in a fight. Merciless after.

"There's no fun in that," Captain Meth-Mouth said. "First we parlay. Then we kill them."

Claudio shrugged. "Sure thing, boss."

"Tell Markus to pull up beside them on the starboard side. We'll talk for a bit, and when I get bored I'll fire the cannon at them. Make sure it's loaded."

"Aye, aye."

Claudio retreated, and Captain Meth-Mouth felt his heart flutter again. On the other ship he saw they were pretty well armed. Assault rifles, shotguns, pistols. The guy on the mast had a sniper rifle, but he didn't look like he knew how to use it. It seemed like he scoped down on Captain Meth-Mouth, and it took him a while to find his mark through the eye piece.

Captain Meth-Mouth smiled and waved at him, knowing that he had better weapons and well-trained men. This wouldn't be like an old pirate battle, but it would be close enough. He thought their ship would look nice in his dock, so he promised himself not to hurt their vessel too much.

The people? They were fucked. He'd keep the women for his harem, and everyone else would either be put to the sword or thrown into the zombie gladiator pit he kept at Soldier Field.

The captain, though? He'd keep that guy alive. It had been a while since he made someone walk the plank over the shark tank at the Shedd Aquarium. It only seemed fitting that he'd do that to a real pirate captain.

5

Dwight stood at the bow—West at his right hand and Hector at his left—as he watched the other ship come closer. It tried to turn its side to the S.S. Stevenson several times, but Dwight had made it clear to Ellis, who had the wheel, to keep them face to face. Every time Captain Meth-Mouth tried to move to the side, Ellis countered perfectly.

The other boat finally gave up this maneuver, and the two ships floated bow to bow. Everyone remained silent until Captain Meth-Mouth made his way to the front and said, "Ahoy, cap'n!"

Dwight couldn't believe the size of this guy. He could probably fit two of West in there and still have room left for scrawny Dandy Jim. Even worse was the mouthful of jagged, blackened teeth. If he bit anyone, the victim would probably need a tetanus shot. As it was, he could smell the captain's rancid breath over the ten yards of lake between them.

"Hey," Dwight said. "How's it going?"

Captain Meth-Mouth thought even less of his opponent now that he could see him up close. He was just a wispy kid, the kind Captain Meth-Mouth used to mug for lunch money back in junior high. He also didn't approve of the cavalier way this guy conducted himself.

Fuck it. The shark tank, for sure.

"What's up, friend?"

Dwight cleared his throat. This Captain Meth-Mouth didn't sound too bad. He seemed laid back, in fact, not like the crazed warrior he'd been expecting. Still, he looked too dangerous to be trusted. "Wanna' trade?"

Captain Meth-Mouth touched his chin in the universal let's-see-here gesture. It struck Dwight as a pose, but he didn't want to jump at shadows yet. Why not give him the benefit of the doubt?

"We have some good shit," Dwight continued. "Are you in need of anything?"

"What have you got?"

It felt like a natural question, but the tone threw Dwight off. Captain Meth-Mouth had to be bullshitting him, but he wanted to pretend that it had been genuine curiosity. The alternative was too scary to consider.

"We have a lot of batteries," Dwight said. "More than we could use for quite some time."

"Cool. What else?"

"Well." He scratched his head. Then he remembered what he'd sent Hector to get. "You strike me as a rum guy. Do you like Captain Morgan's Special Reserve?"

He elbowed Hector gently, and his friend held up the bottle.

Captain Meth-Mouth's tongue felt saturated with saliva, and he had to swallow repeatedly to stop himself from drooling. The Reserve was his favorite, and he'd run out of it a long time ago. He never thought he'd see another bottle in his life.

Dwight saw the look on his adversary's face and smiled. "Tell you what. This bottle's free. As a gesture of good faith."

Captain Meth-Mouth ran the back of his hand across his lips and then wiped it on his shirt. "Toss it here."

Hector glanced at Dwight, eyebrows raised. Dwight nodded. "Go ahead."

"What if I miss?" Hector asked.

"Don't you worry," Captain Meth-Mouth said. "I'll catch it."

Hector stepped back and slowly underhanded the bottle. It sailed across to the other vessel, where Captain Meth-Mouth caught it one-handed. He admired the bottle for a while, running his thumb across the label. "Got more of these?"

"Hector?" Dwight asked.

"A few," Hector said. "We also have some Sailor Jerry. Some Bacardi, if you're desperate. We have more whiskey, though."

"I'll take the lot," Captain Meth-Mouth said.

"That's great!" Dwight said. "Listen, I was hoping we could trade the booze for some food. We're running low on . . ." He trailed off when he saw Captain Meth-Mouth shaking his head.

"Come on," Dwight continued. "You're on land. You've got to have food to trade. We're so desperate we'll take Ramen, if you've got it."

"I'm not in the barter business," Captain Meth-Mouth said. "In case you can't tell, I'm in the taking business."

Dwight felt that familiar fear creep back into his belly. West tensed next to him, his finger slipping inside the trigger guard of his assault rifle. Hector shrank back, trying to hide behind his captain.

"I take it, then, that there's no peaceful way out of this?" Dwight asked.

Captain Meth-Mouth stepped up to the very brink of the bow. "Son, I've waited my whole life to get in a pirate battle at sea. There's no way out for you at all."

West whipped up his gun and took aim at Captain Meth-Mouth, ready to send a short burst through his torso. Claudio expected this and fired his shotgun at the lieutenant. West saw the shotgun barrel turn toward him just in time and ducked down, dragging Dwight with him. Buckshot turned the helm into a cheese grater. West caught a light peppering high on his shoulder, and two bits had furrowed into his jaw and neck. Nothing serious, but it burned fiercely. He gritted his teeth against the pain, neglecting himself to make sure that Dwight was fine.

The captain hadn't even been winged. Hector, on the other hand, hadn't been so lucky. He stood in silent shock, his blackened face more bone than skin, his windpipe and upper ribs open for the world to see. One eye stared out in horror while the other slipped down into his sinuses in a yellowish, viscous form.

"Cap! You okay?"

Dwight barely heard West's question. All of his attention fixated on Hector's body as it folded in on itself and slumped onto the deck. The death-blind eye met Dwight's gaze, and he couldn't look away. Firearms exploded all around him, bullets strafing the world, and he didn't even flinch.

"Dammit, Cap! Don't do this to me!" West jerked his hand up and down in front of Dwight's face. Dwight turned and watched as Ellis crouched behind the wheel, trying to keep the boats head to head and still not get shot. Kelly used the mast as cover while she took pot shots with her pistol. Grafton ducked down behind the edge of the rail, and he fired his shotgun without looking.

West briskly slapped Dwight's cheek, and the captain blinked, coming back to himself. The gunfire and screams suddenly seemed louder.

"We need you, Cap. You ready to kick some ass?"

Dumbly, Dwight nodded. He glanced down at Hector—his oldest friend on the ship—and realized he didn't even have time to mourn. He remembered pretending to do battle with Hector every day in Miami for the amusement of hundreds of kids. The script dictated that Hector die each and every time. Now he was dead for real.

Suddenly he hated Captain Meth-Mouth, and anger boiled in his guts, simmering in his head. Why had he refused the assault rifle earlier? He wanted to murder every single one of his enemies.

Something on his face must have changed, because West smiled and clapped him on the shoulder. "Good to have you back."

"How fucked are we?" Dwight asked.

A chunk of the bow splintered away and flew by West's face. He jerked his head back and tried to hunch lower. "We have a chance."

"But not much of one, right?"

West shrugged. "We need better cover. I'm going to pop up and strafe as many of those bastards as I can. When I do, take Grafton and make for the anchor crank. If you get there, give me some cover fire so I can get behind the lifeboat. Got it?"

Dwight nodded, even though he didn't like the sound of "if." Still, he motioned to Grafton, who seemed to understand the pantomimed plan. Then West stood, blasting away at full auto. Dwight watched from the corner of his eye as men on Captain Meth-Mouth's ship dropped dead in their boots.

Dwight pushed Grafton down behind the thick metal crank and started firing back the way they'd come. West retreated from the bow, shuffling back and to the side, keeping his eye on his adversaries.

He almost made it. About a yard away from the lifeboat he roared, dropping to his knees. Blood sprouted from his calf and pooled quickly on the deck. Growling like a beast, he muscled his way to cover, but when he did, his foot flopped back and forth like a dying fish.

Grafton cursed and held up his empty shotgun. "I'm out, Cap."

Someone from above screamed, and Dwight looked up just in

time to see Dandy Jim riddled with bullets, flailing as he fell to the deck, his thin body snapping like popped bubble wrap.

Bullets pinged and whizzed off the crank, but Dwight barely noticed. All he could see were his shipmates—his friends—crying and yelling, sending as many bullets as they could into Captain Meth-Mouth's ship and men. A surprising amount of Captain Meth-Mouth's pirates poured their hot blood onto the deck, but he still had so many more standing and pouring hot lead into the S.S. Stevenson.

Captain Meth-Mouth saw something different. He saw scared people, and some of them were even women, as they tried to pitifully strike back against certain death. So much for the epic pirate battle he'd hoped for. These wannabes were ready for the end. Time to oblige them.

He ordered his men to break out their grappling hooks.

Dwight saw Dandy Jim's sniper rifle nearby. He tried to kick out and snag the strap, but it was just out of reach. He had plenty of ammo for himself, but he needed Grafton to be armed with something. Dwight tried with his foot again, but this time a bullet nearly found him. Instead it tinged against the scope, obliterating it.

Well. Grafton didn't need the scope. He needed a loaded gun. Dwight took a deep breath and charged out from behind cover, gun at the ready, reaching for the sniper rifle.

Captain Meth-Mouth and a half-dozen of his men swung across the gap and thumped down on the deck of the S.S. Stevenson. Two of them shot down Gillian and Riggs right away. Both of them, lovers Dwight had found in Atlantic City, the former a school teacher and the latter a cab driver, jerked and heaved and died before they even hit the boards.

Dwight felt his balls shrivel as he saw the pirates split up. Two of them tried to get to Kelly behind the mast. Two of them went for Ellis. Just as Dwight scooped up the rifle, Captain Meth-Mouth found him and smiled.

An assault rifle chattered, and Dwight saw muzzle fire from behind the life boat. Two of Captain Meth-Mouth's men went down, but he just looked annoyed.

"Corner that weasel!" he yelled. "Smoke 'im out!"

Dwight scurried back as all of Captain Meth-Mouth's men focused on the life boat. Grafton grabbed the sniper rifle and moved to jack a round into the chamber.

Captain Meth-Mouth drew down on him and fired, blasting Grafton's brains out the back of his head just as casually as if he'd used a remote control to change the channel.

"You son of a bitch," Dwight said.

"Fuck 'im. He wasn't invited to this little dance. Now I see you got yourself a sword, too. That real, or is it as phony as the rest of this outfit?"

Dwight saw in his mind—just as clearly as he'd just seen some of his closest friends die—a vision of Captain Meth-Mouth cutting him to pieces with his rapier. Again his belly chilled, and he felt worms crawling beneath the skin at the back of his neck.

But then he remembered the look on Hector's face. The scream Dandy Jim had made. Even West's pained grimace as he struggled for cover.

Dwight would be damned if he was going to let this motherfucker win so easily. He drew his sword and held it out, ready to meet his maker standing up.

Captain Meth-Mouth whistled. "You got some steel there, son." And then he unsheathed his own sword, aiming the point at the spot between Dwight's eyes.

Ohshitohshitohshit! Over and over the thought raced through Dwight's mind. He felt something moving in his guts, and his legs quavered, a cold tickling sensation at the backs of his knees. He looked at Captain Meth-Mouth's dancing gray eyes, then down to his grin. His teeth could have been broken shards of a black vase.

Dwight saw himself running. He wanted to do this so badly. But he knew the instant he turned to flee, Captain Meth-Mouth would lop his head off.

No. If he had to die, he wouldn't go out like a bitch. Time to be the pirate he'd always pretended to be.

He sneered. "You gonna' fight? Or are you gonna' to twiddle your sword around all day?"

Captain Meth-Mouth's smile vanished. "It's on now, boy."

His sword flashed, and Dwight put his own up. The blades clashed with a spark, and Dwight felt the force of it go up his arm, kind of like hitting a line drive in baseball. He almost felt pushed back, but his strength managed to hold Captain Meth-Mouth at bay.

"Is that the best you—"

Captain Meth-Mouth roared and turned into a dervish of slashes and thrusts. Before Dwight could think about it, his training took over. What he couldn't dodge, he parried, and he did so with the élan of an acrobat. All of those years spent fighting in the Treasure Island Adventure Show came back at once, and he felt like a true swashbuckler again. He could almost hear the crowd's applause.

Captain Meth-Mouth stopped. "Damn, boy. You're living up to expectations. Too bad I'm going to kill you."

Dwight didn't want his opponent to see he was almost out of breath, so he slashed at Captain Meth-Mouth, catching him on the side of the head. If Captain Meth-Mouth hadn't recoiled, he would have had his eyes cut from his face. Blood slipped down from a gash showing more than just a little bone.

Captain Meth-Mouth didn't hesitate with banter. He came at Dwight in a fury, and when their swords crossed down to the hilt, he kicked, nailing Dwight in the chest. The air was crushed from his lungs, and he fell back. Luckily he remembered to tuck and roll, pistoning his legs out at the right moment so he'd come back up on his feet in a flash. Gasping for air, he tensed up, ready for the next salvo of blows.

They came hard, but Dwight managed to weather them. In a distant part of his mind, he couldn't believe this was happening. As Captain Meth-Mouth and he beat their blades together, gunfire and screams filled the air around them. Dwight barely noticed it when a bullet blew back his hair a little. Captain Meth-Mouth didn't flinch when the cannon went off, taking out the mast of the S.S. Stevenson, showering him with wooden shrapnel. Blood and metallic flashes filled their world, and Dwight felt separated from it all. He didn't even feel like he was in charge of his own body as instinct and training gave back everything Captain Meth-Mouth could throw at him.

But as his muscles flared up, and it became harder for him to lift his arms, he knew he couldn't win. Captain Meth-Mouth was stronger, and he had more stamina. No amount of training would keep Dwight alive for much longer.

Captain Meth-Mouth couldn't believe his luck. As blood roared through his body, driving him harder and harder against Dwight, he knew this was the battle he'd always wanted. This guy didn't look like much, especially considering how he'd started this while wearing a hopelessly scared face, but Captain Meth-Mouth would put him up against any of the scum he'd killed in the pit. The pain just above his ear proved that. The threat of danger filled him with a rush of adrenaline, even though he knew he'd win this eventually.

Dwight's arm couldn't get up in time, and one of Captain Meth-Mouth's slashes finally got through, opening Dwight's face up from temple to chin. His flesh hung in a flap, and Captain Meth-Mouth could see Dwight's teeth through the laceration.

The searing pain brought Dwight back to himself as he touched his cheek. Thick blood filled his palm, and when he touched the wound, pain flared up, blinding him for a moment.

A moment was all it took. Captain Meth-Mouth used the flat side of his sword to hit the hilt of Dwight's. It sailed from his hand, and Captain Meth-Mouth jammed his palm against Dwight's throat, driving him back against the wheelhouse. Captain Meth-Mouth heaved and lifted Dwight up by the neck, pointing his sword against Dwight's belly.

Panic flooded his brain, and he lashed and flailed against Captain Meth-Mouth's grip, trying to breathe. He felt the sword cut through his tunic and sink ever so slightly into his skin.

"It's been fun, chuckles," Captain Meth-Mouth said. "You've enhanced my life. Just so you know."

Kelly's surprise. Dwight felt it heavy in his pocket. If ever there was a time for it, it was now. His right hand, feeble from loss of oxygen, managed to get into his pocket and pull out the pineapple grenade they'd found in Atlanta among the possessions of a drug dealer who fancied himself to be Scarface. No one knew if the thing still worked. He hoped it would as he somehow found the strength to pull the pin and lift it up.

Captain Meth-Mouth felt pressure at his neck and laughed, surprised at this kid's tenacity. Even though he knew he was doomed, the kid still fought with everything he had left. But then Dwight's hand went higher and pressed against Captain Meth-Mouth's chin. Only then did he see the object Dwight held.

Grinning, Dwight pushed the grenade against his enemy's mouth, and just as Captain Meth-Mouth tried to pull back an explosion rocked the decks of the S.S. Stevenson. Dwight felt a surge of pain, followed by a bright flash, and then darkness.

6

The first thing he saw when he opened his eyes was Kelly. She sat by his side, reading a book. He couldn't focus on the title, but he didn't think he'd seen it on the ship before. He tried to sit up.

"Oh! You're awake!" Kelly gently touched his chest. "Don't. Just stay down. Do you remember . . . ?"

Yes. He held up his right arm, not very surprised to see that it ended in a bandage. No hand. Part of him wanted to freak out, but he just couldn't muster the energy.

"How am I still alive?"

"Your hand absorbed most of the explosion." Lt. West. He stood on crutches at the foot of the bed, grinning at his captain. "You have no idea how lucky you are. That was the ballsiest thing I've ever seen."

Dwight tried to look at the rest of himself. "How bad is the damage?"

"You got off light," West said. "Aside from the hand, that is. You got a nasty cut on your cheek, but you'll probably wind up with a kick-ass scar. There are some burns on your face. You caught some shrapnel in your belly. But all things considered, you should be dead."

"Then . . . we won?"

"Kind of," Kelly said.

"We agreed to disagree," West said. "As soon as you blew Captain Meth-Mouth's head off, his men lost the will to fight. His first mate Claudio almost seemed relieved. I think he's wanted the top spot for a while but was too scared to go for it. Anyway, he's in charge now. He let us set anchor up north— safely away from him—so we could repair the ship. We bartered for some supplies. We even got a doctor for you."

"How about you?" Dwight asked. "I saw your foot was pretty bad."

West glanced down at his plaster-encased foot. "Separated at the bone. The doc fixed me up, though. I'll probably have a limp, and I'll be able to predict rainstorms, but I'll still have my foot."

"Where are we now?"

"Claudio wanted us gone, so we're headed for Green Bay, like we talked about before."

"Good." Dwight eased himself up, ignoring Kelly's look of

disapproval. He staggered over to his mirror and looked upon his ruined face. He'd been moderately attractive before, but now he looked tough and raw. He reached up to touch the puckered stitches on his face, forgetting that he no longer had a right hand. How the hell was he going to survive the zombie apocalypse minus one hand? He'd always favored that one. Why couldn't it have been his left?

"By the way, I have a present for you, Cap." West approached, holding up a hook with a long leather rig attached to it. "It's something Ellis has been working on."

"For what?" Dwight asked.

"For your hand. Ellis says a pirate with only one hand should have a hook for his stump."

Dwight nodded, but he couldn't find the words to tell West that he didn't want to be a pirate anymore. It had been fun in Miami, and even when he'd been fighting zombies it was still kind of fun. But then he started fighting the living. His friends started dying. And now, this.

Still he took the offered gift and cupped it to his stump, strapping it up to his elbow and shoulder. It did look cool, and he had chosen this path, after all.

Might as well see it to its end.

THE LAST OF HIS KIND

"And this, I'm sure, is the display you've all been waiting to see. Preserved for the last hundred years, he's the last intact specimen we have of *homo vampiricus*. I present to you, the last of his kind, Richard Wheeler!"

Dean Johns stood on tiptoes so he could see the glass case that contained the vampire's body. The room was dimly lit in order to keep the corpse from breaking up into dust. The display was roped off to prevent people from getting too close, and for those who got beyond the velvet barrier and the silent robot sentry, there were wires leading to an alarm.

How many times had Dean gazed upon Wheeler? He'd lost track, but each time he admired the sharp anorexic cheekbones, the long peacocked dark hair, and the ghostly alabaster flesh, it felt like the first time. How odd that society thought such a frail shape to be so dangerous. The authorities said Wheeler was still alive, even though he didn't breathe, move or, according to medical technology, think. Yet they guarded the staked vampire with alarms, shatter-proof glass, cameras, and a robot guard. Ever paranoid that someone would pluck the stake from his chest like one would a flower from the ground, they kept constant watch over the shell of the last vampire.

Dean remembered the first time he'd seen Wheeler at the American Museum of Natural History. He'd taken the tour because he had no friends, and he had nothing better to do with his Saturday afternoon. Yet when he'd seen Wheeler, it felt like he knew the vampire, maybe from childhood? But no, Wheeler had been locked in his glass case like a mummy for the past 103 years, so he couldn't have been a childhood friend. Dean, at twenty-three, knew that would be impossible.

Maybe from a past life? Dean didn't think so, as he didn't believe in such things, but the *déjà vu* filled his mind so much, he could think of nothing else.

When the tour guide mentioned why they needed so much security around Wheeler, Dean asked, "If he's so dangerous, why keep him around?"

The guide didn't seem to understand, so Dean rephrased his question: "If you're so scared of someone bringing him back to life, why not destroy him?"

"Why do we keep smallpox around?" the guide said. "Mr. Wheeler is a scientific document, a testament to a bygone era. Granted, the vampires were not good people, but it's something we must remember since it's a part of our history."

Dean was too young to remember the vampires, so when he got home, he went online to the library and read up on the subject. Due to a glut of books and movies about sympathetic vampires, real vampires decided to come out of hiding. Since the Draculas, Varneys, and Barlows were a thing of the past, society welcomed these genuine bloodsuckers with open arms. None of them sparkled, as was the hope of many teenaged girls, but their adult counterparts thrilled to the idea that they could finally live the *True Blood* fantasy.

Too bad their intentions weren't quite as pure as the fictional versions of them.

When the killings began, they seemed pretty random. People turned up every once in a while dead, empty of blood, and the cops thought they were isolated incidents. So the vampires had killers among them, just like humans. It happens. Soon people started uncovering vampire clubs, where mortals were tortured and murdered. When it became clear that all vampires were out to kill, the living declared war on the undead.

That didn't seem right to Dean. It sounded a bit too much like "all black people are criminals and welfare cheats," or "all gay men are pederasts." Vampires clearly had minds of their own, regardless of their tastes, so clearly they had choices. Some of them could have been whatever their version of vegan is, right?

Dean continued to slog through the politics of the war. He didn't understand all of it, but he grasped the gist. Long story short, the world's nations joined forces and killed all the vampires. They kept a few for research purposes by staking them. According to trial and error, it would render them immobile. Not dead, just sleeping.

Most countries destroyed their specimens at the conclusion of their experiments. America kept theirs on display for the public. As of 2125, there were four in the nation.

Now, in 2213, there was one.

Dean visited Wheeler on a regular basis, wondering what the vampire thought of his predicament. Or did he think? Could he possibly be aware of his surroundings? Did it hurt? Did it drive him crazy?

According to the placard on the case, Wheeler had been in the museum for 103 years. He'd been experimented on for 10 years before that. No one knew much about Wheeler before he became an artifact, but they estimated his age at nineteen before he'd been turned into a vampire. It was impossible to tell how long he'd been in existence for sure, but at the very least he was 132 years old. Most of that had been spent paralyzed.

Dean tried to imagine what that would be like, and he shuddered, hoping that Wheeler really wasn't conscious.

At least once a week Dean would visit Wheeler, sometimes with the tour, sometimes on his own. Whenever he could, he'd get as close to the velvet ropes as he could and try to determine if there was any sign of life. Any sign of consciousness. Any sign of recognition. According to the history, vampires had hyper-awareness. Could Wheeler smell him? If so, did he know who Dean was? Maybe even read his mind?

If he could manage it, when no one else was in the room, Dean would talk to Wheeler. Ask him questions. Try and notice some kind of movement, even if it was just REM.

He never saw anything.

Not surprising. More than a century ago, scientists had hooked Wheeler up to a brainwave scanner, and he'd emitted nothing.

Dean didn't know when he'd started making up conversations with the staked vampire. At first it struck him as laughable, just a private joke, but before long he started looking forward to these little chats. He started taking them seriously. He would say something aloud to Wheeler—if they were alone—and he would make up Wheeler's reply in his head. Dean recognized there was something odd about this practice, but he couldn't help it. He had no one else to talk to, not even at his job. He worked as a data entry clerk, making just enough money to squeak by, and everyone there thought he was too introverted to hang out and have a good time. Truthfully, he was too shy to attempt to change their minds.

A month ago he asked Wheeler how he felt about being stuck in the glass case, on display like ancient pottery. Wheeler's response came quickly in Dean's head: "It's driving me crazy. Please. Help me. Set me free. I'm not a bad guy. I've never killed anyone who didn't deserve it. Murderers. Rapists. Child molesters. Never regular people. Please. I need to walk free again."

Dean had never before gotten a response like that. Usually Wheeler kept it short and impersonal. It jarred Dean so much that he wondered if it really had come from himself. Up until now it had just been a silly game. What if Wheeler really could communicate with him?

Dean looked it up online: vampires could communicate telepathically. But Wheeler had no brainwaves. Surely a staked vampire could do no such thing, right?

Even if he could, what if he'd lied? What if he'd lied so he could resume a killing spree and maybe make a vampire army to get revenge? They were certainly capable of grand manipulation.

Dean felt a little dirty, thinking like that, like he'd just discovered a racist part of himself.

When he went back the next weekend he tried to ask Wheeler if it was really him talking back. He got no response. Every time his frontal lobe burned to say "yes" in his mind, but nothing legitimately came from Wheeler.

Last week Dean thought he might have seen Wheeler twitch. It couldn't be a trick of the light, because there was only a black bulb over by his display. Could it have been his imagination?

It was then that he decided it didn't matter. Wheeler was a victim of society's mistreatment and prejudice. Killing animals for any purpose—even food—had been outlawed about fifty years ago because it was cruel. The same for circumcision seventy-five years back. Cruelty to babies. Why should this atrocity be allowed to continue?

Dean thought about petitioning the museum and the city to pull the stake, but he knew it would never happen. Too many people feared Wheeler, remembering how his kind had ruthlessly killed people back in the day.

No, he'd have to do it himself.

He could do nothing about the alarm, but he figured by the time it went off, he would have already saved Wheeler. The problem would be getting through the shatter proof glass without a guard seeing him. They were robots, so eluding them wouldn't be difficult. The only thing he knew that could break the glass was a laser, but that might injure Wheeler.

On the other hand . . . the exhibit next to Wheeler was a dinosaur display, the bones of a tyrannosaurus rex held together by a metal frame. After doing a little research he determined it would be possible to use the weight of the fossils to shatter the case. All he had to do was use a laser to cut the right part of the frame in just the right way. Since Wheeler was a vampire, being beaten down by the exhibit wouldn't hurt him. Considering how sturdy the bones were, they shouldn't be damaged, either.

Earlier today Dean slipped his utility laser, no bigger or longer than his thumb, into his pocket and headed out to the museum. For some reason he felt a bit paranoid, as if he thought the museum officials knew what he planned for Wheeler, so he put on a wig of long hair and stuck a beard to his face. He wanted to wear sunglasses—just in case—but Wheeler's display was too dark. Dean needed to see to pull this off, and the light of the laser wouldn't be good enough.

Now, standing with his fellow tour-attendees, he tried not to pay much attention to the staked vampire out of fear that someone might be watching him. However, he directed one thought to Wheeler: *Don't worry. You'll be free soon.*

Thank you. The words in his mind startled him. He supposed they could have come from the deepest folds of his subconscious, but he preferred to think that Wheeler had actually thanked him.

The tour moved on, and Dean stayed in the room, alone except for the silent robot that guarded Wheeler. Dean moved over to the t-rex, pretending to admire it. It wasn't dangerous, so there were no guards and no velvet ropes, just an alarm. Kids liked to get up close and touch the ancient creature's remains. This is what Dean did now, caressing the bones of something that lived 65 million years ago, wondering what it would be like to be the most fearsome hunter in a forgotten world.

He'd run simulation after simulation, and after so much research he'd determined that he needed to make four cuts in order to topple the giant predator. The first two would be easy since they were close together. The last two? They would be easy if a utility laser could legally have a reach longer than six inches. The alarm would certainly go off, and the robot guarding Wheeler would be on Dean in seconds.

The only thing he could do is spray paint on the robot's sensors. Ever afraid of lawsuits, the museum couldn't let robots resort to extreme action. As a result, it would always give the human a chance to stop what they were doing. Dean felt confident enough in such a plan.

He took the cap off his utility laser, and as he held the canister of black spray paint in his free hand, he made the first two incisions with ease, releasing a steel bar, which clanked to the floor.

The alarms exploded like a battery of cannons, and Dean felt pain hammering at his ears. Instinctively he wanted to cover them, but he knew there was a lot more at stake here than his comfort.

The robot approached, and it said something, but Dean couldn't hear the words clearly. The machine leveled a rifle at him, and although he knew it was loaded with rubber bullets, he hoped it wouldn't go off.

He sprayed the paint at the robot's head, nailing its sensors perfectly. It emitted an electronic yowl somehow louder than the alarm. The pain crescendoed, and Dean could feel it swelling in his eyes as he rushed to make the last two incisions. He sliced through the steel frame, and just as another section fell away, a heavy dose of foam came gushing down from the ceiling.

Fire retardant. Dean hadn't thought of that. Hands slick, the laser squirted out of his grip and vanished in a snowbank of the stuff. He gasped against it as it tried to fill his mouth, and he frantically rubbed his eyes trying to keep from going blind.

A tremendous crash overcame the alarm for a moment, and when Dean finally managed to look, he saw that not only had the t-rex busted open Wheeler's case, it had also taken out the robot.

More had to be on the way, so Dean waded through the foam, now up to his waist, until he stood next to Wheeler. Surprisingly, the bones hadn't messed him up too badly. He still rested in place with his hair a bit mussed. A large bone rested across his middle. Had he been human, it would have pinched him in half.

Brushing nuggets of glass away from Wheeler's cold, rocklike face, he gripped the stake and hoped it wouldn't be too hard to yank out, as he now heard robot reinforcements approaching.

The stake came out quickly, as if it had been greased. Dean marveled at it in his own hand, and he wondered if Wheeler would need blood. Being incapacitated for so long, he probably needed some right away.

Dean was okay with that. He just hoped Wheeler wouldn't go overboard and kill his only friend.

Wheeler's eyes slipped open, showing filmed-over pupils, and he blinked a few times until the slight caul cleared up. Dazed, he sat up, swaying as he gained his balance.

Dean tried to think of something cooler to say than "hi," or "how's it going?" or "welcome back to the real world." Was that how friends talked? It seemed that way on iTV.

He watched as Wheeler took in the chaos around him and realized that if the alarm practically killed himself, the vampire must be suffering more. In fact everything probably shocked him, even though he seemed to take it calmly.

Finally Dean found the courage to say something. "Hello, Mr. Wheeler. I woke you up."

Wheeler turned his gaze on Dean. Confused, he said in Dean's mind, "*Qui êtes-vous? Je ne parle pas l'anglais.*"

Now Dean felt out of place. What kind of ancient vampire language could that be? It sounded like French. Wouldn't it make more sense for Wheeler to speak English?

Wheeler opened his mouth, perhaps to further elaborate, when the air sizzled around him, and his head rolled away from his freshly cauterized neck. The body remained still for a moment before it exploded into ash. It mixed with the foam, turning it gray.

It took a moment for Dean to realize what had happened. Then he couldn't help but scream. Somehow he didn't even hear himself over the sound of the alarm. He barely noticed as the guard robot, which had decapitated Wheeler with a laser pointer, now prepared a taser to subdue Dean.

He felt the hooks catch in his skin, and his world ignited with blue fire before it extinguished with a muffled whimper.

—

Dean dreamed of a perfect world in which Wheeler had a chance to tell everyone he meant no harm. In which he told everyone he just wanted to live in peace. In which everyone celebrated the cultural differences between vampire and human, and everyone benefited from this.

Dean envisioned hanging out with Wheeler, talking about art, about philosophy, about the state of the world. He envisioned getting married and having Wheeler as his best man. He envisioned Wheeler acting as uncle to his kids as they grew up.

No one could ever decipher these things from Dean's brainwaves as they studied him in his coma. The government wanted to understand what such a terrorist thought about, but since he never woke up, all they had to go on were his wildly active charts.

Years later, after careful consideration, they concluded Dean's trial, finding him guilty. It had been decades since someone had committed a terrorist act, so they preserved his life and hooked him up to machines so that anyone who wanted to study him could do so.

Not that it mattered to Dean. He had his own life to live.

GOING DOWN

Tonight is the night. I know because yesterday I could kiss the tip without even trying. Everyone on Fuckbook will know my name.

The camera is in place. The floor mat is ready. At first I wanted to just use my bed, but the springs make the situation unpredictable. Too many things can go wrong without a stable surface. I might dip out of frame, and what's the point of doing this if I don't record it for everyone on Pornhub to see?

Will people think it's in bad taste, so to speak? Yes. So will the authorities. They'll want to pull the video as soon as possible, but by the time they do it will be too late. I'll be viral, like herpes. I'll be the footage slightly blurred on your nightly news. I'll be the subject of conversation in your office lunchroom as you make your morning coffee. I'll be the bookmark you don't want your mom to find out about.

I will be Porntube.

I will also be a monologue joke on Conan. A dated joke on Saturday Night Live for you to laugh at five years from now. But humor is always the extension of shock. It's logical, and it doesn't matter. My mark is on you already. You will be forever changed by what you see on Newbie Nudes.

I limber up. No sense in straining anything. I go through my yoga moves, and my muscles lengthen and stretch. They become rubber. I know I am ready when I can touch my thighs to my forehead. Snizzshare is ready for me.

It is time to change the world. I switch on the camera recorder and settle into the frame so everyone can see my skinny, supple body. I am hairless by choice. I want the world to see everything. My natural hirsuteness must not shadow any detail you might want to see on Redtube.

Off screen, porn plays. A compilation of my favorites. Not too old that I'm bored, but not new enough to be unfamiliar. I am hard as a rock in moments.

Don't you feel weird watching a guy stroke it on Porn 2.0?

My dick is huge, I know. That's what draws your attention. I'm using two hands and there is room for a third. The old saw about women wanting me and men wanting to be me? It's okay, I'm used to it. Playfully, I thump my cock against my breastbone.

But you knew that, viewer of Xshare.

According to my first plan I started out with the moment of glory. But people like a little foreplay. They like to spend a little time with their subjects before blowing their load. Gives them a sense of intimacy. And people worry that YouPorn and the internet are tearing society asunder.

Here's the moment you're waiting for. I scooch down the mat, mindful of where the frame limits are, and I throw my ass into the air. Theatrically my feet protrude out and my hard-on hangs halfway down to my face.

Are you getting this, Xvideos?

My knees thump down on either side of my head, and my dick plunges toward my wet, open mouth. I grab the shaft and squeeze and pull. Pre-cum glistens on my helmet as I coax it closer to my lips. Closer.

Are you ready to blow your wad, VHO?

Gently I kiss my own penis. I can taste the spice of my seed as I flick the tip with my tongue back and forth. I know I don't look like much. How many of you on Sex Tube Guide think you can train yourselves to do this because of my example?

I take myself into my mouth and electricity shoots down the length of my member. Orgasm boils at the base of my cock, but I can't let go. Not now. I can't let down my viewers on the Best Porn.

I pull my dick back and look directly into the camera. My glans is held gently, firmly, in place with my teeth. And I bite down. I bite with all the force my jaws can muster, and the pain makes me want to shrink away. My teeth don't let me.

I gnaw at my dickhead until it pops like steak-fat in my mouth. Blood gushes down my throat and around my lips and I continue to chew on it as if it were gristle. My mouth is full of bitterness, and I swallow it away again and again, but my heart pumps fast and my glans snaps off and my head is full of heat from being doubled over like this and I gag as my throat works at getting my cockhead down and I want more YOU want more and I slurp at my dick as it convulses in my mouth OH GOD I'VE NEVER CUM LIKE THIS and I'm chewing at a beef stick, sucking down hunks of meat and my blood and cum tastes charged like Gatorade and I choke and gnaw and slurp and suck and my chin is wet my balls are in my eyes can I get them too and pop them like grapes between my molars jerky it feels like jerky on my tongue and blood creeps in my nostrils I can't breathe but HOLY FUCK I'M STILL CUMMING I can't keep swallowing it overwhelms me and I keep chewing at the ragged stump just barely in my mouth and one of my balls rolls through the torn stub and I suck at it like an egg and THERE!

Between my teeth. For all of you to see on Shufuni, I bite the testicle, and lights go off in my head. Shock sets in. I can smell electricity. My vision sears.

The ecstasy ebbs, and the weight of my legs holds me down. Did the camera get it all? I try to draw breath, but there's too much of me clogging my throat. There is me everywhere, even on me.

Even on the red light of the recorder, winking at me as if to say good job. You're the best. Never shot anyone better.

I unfold and reach for the camera, ready to upload the footage to Hard Sex Tube. To Boyztube. To the world.

But this doesn't happen. My numb tingly legs prevent me from straightening out. I can't breathe because I'm choking on me. I'm suffocating on me. My guts and throat and nostrils and eyes are stuffed and caked over with me.

I am everywhere. I must be everywhere. I absolutely NEED to be—

RUMBLE IN THE RETIREMENT HOME

Everyone felt bad when they sent Ken "the Bruiser" Butler, addled from a lifetime of concussions, to the Sunny Hill Retirement Home. He'd been such an integral part of so many kids' lives that they—now adults—lamented the passing of a piece of their childhood. Even though he was sixty-five, they all secretly dreamed of a comeback, but now he would never body slam another opponent. No more clothesline strikes for the Bruiser. His days of jumping off the turnbuckle to double hammer his enemy on the chest were over.

But everyone fucking loved it when his career-long arch-nemesis, Carl "Stark Raving" Madsen moved into the very same home ten years later. The Madman, as his fans called him, had turned seventy-six and started suffering from dementia. When he no longer remembered who he was, his family brought him to Sunny Hills for the care they couldn't provide themselves.

The media exploded. The Jimmys—Fallon and Kimmel—had barrels of jokes written about the situation. Fans liked to speculate what it would be like for the bitter enemies to be stuck together in the same home in their respective wheelchairs. The fans would giggle maniacally about it.

The attention died down when everyone realized that they were just a couple of old men, and maybe no one should be making fun of their very real mental problems. Their families did not appreciate the attention, to say the least. Eventually even the paparazzi gave up trying to get a picture of the two of them together. The crowds thinned, and everyone forgot about the geriatric wrestlers.

That was the way Mickey Butler liked it. He no longer had to fight through crowds of busybodies in order to see his father. The

Bruiser had good days when he seemed like himself, and he had bad days when he didn't acknowledge his son, but dammit, those days were now private.

At least there was one person in the world who understood: Laurie Madsen, the Madman's daughter. She suffered by Mickey's side through thick and thin, and now that the circus died down, he liked to spend the afternoon after his weekly visit hanging out with her at the onsite coffee shop, which was creatively called the Li'l Coffee Shoppe.

After, he didn't have much of a life. He didn't have friends because everyone he ever knew always wanted something from him. Sometimes it was money, because they assumed that the son of a celebrity was rich. Most times, though, they wanted to meet his father. Or they wanted his memories. What was it like growing up the son of the Bruiser? No one liked him for *him*, so he led a private lifestyle. Read a lot of books. Saw a lot of movies. Even took up painting, even though he never liked his work. It seemed too childish.

Laurie never wanted anything from him, and he liked that. She'd grown up the exact same way, except she had more friends. Friends who liked her for *her*. She even had boyfriends. Plural. Mickey tried to remember the last time he had a girlfriend, and he realized it was back in college. He'd broken up with her when he learned she'd only dated him so she could meet his father. So she could call TMZ and report their location. So she could maybe be in the shot when they took pictures. So she might possibly end up on TV.

At the age of thirty-five, he missed the feeling of being with someone. He hadn't inherited his father's frame or good looks, so he found it hard to meet someone in that capacity.

Laurie didn't have that problem. She looked like a clone of her mother, a supermodel who still knocked 'em dead at the age of fifty-seven. Mickey wished he could be more like Laurie, but he settled for their weekly cup of coffee.

"You should really get out more," she said.

They never discussed their fathers. Their topics of conversation usually began and ended with their activities, or how they dealt with the press. Once he'd made the mistake of confessing to her that he hadn't dated in more than a decade.

"That's unhealthy," she said. "People need someone to love, or they start to wither. I don't want you to wither. I like you too much."

She offered to set him up with friends, but it sounded too scary for him. He'd been out of practice for so long, and he didn't want to fuck up and have Laurie's friend talk shit about him. The very thought devastated him.

"Why don't you hang out with your work friends?" she asked.

Well, he didn't have any. Just work acquaintances. Sometimes they'd invite him out for five o'clock drinks at Pally's Pub, but he always turned them down. Booze might loosen him up too much, and he didn't want them to find out who his father was.

"Did you see the Iron Sheik on Conan last night?" she asked.

A man pushing a cart rattled by the Li'l Coffee Shoppe. Startled by the loud clatter, Mickey looked at him. The man looked back, and then he shifted his glance to Laurie. At first it seemed like he recognized them, like maybe he wanted to say something to them, but then he pushed on. A little faster than before.

"I never knew that about him," she said.

Mickey hadn't heard what she'd said before. Instead he thought of a time when the tabloids thought he and Laurie were dating. They'd even gotten pictures of them at this very table. TMZ made fun of his balding hairline, and they wondered what a beautiful woman like Laurie was doing with a schlub like him. He would have liked it if they were together. He didn't trust anyone else to be that close to. But he didn't want to risk screwing up their friendship. If he lost this beautiful, tiny part of his week, he didn't think he could stand it.

"Are you even listening to me?" she asked.

He snapped out of it. "Sorry. I was thinking about that guy."

"What guy?"

"The guy with the cart. I think he recognized us, but for some reason he didn't say anything. Just kept moving."

"Are you complaining?"

Mickey chuckled. "Not really. Just thought it was odd."

Laurie waved a dismissive hand. "Forget about him. He probably just got scared."

Neither of them knew that they'd spend the rest of their lives thinking about a man they would later learn was named Justin Burt. Justin, like a lot of men his age, had loved the

Butler/Madsen rivalry as a child. Unlike his peers, he didn't have any friends, only his grandma's cat, Moses. While everyone else practiced wrestling moves on each other, pretending to be their heroes, Justin could only play make believe with Moses. He had the scars on his arms and neck.

Justin still had no friends except for an invisible cat he called Moses II, but he had an undying affection for the two wrestlers. He'd sat with them numerous times, even though neither knew it. He tried asking questions, hoping for a fanboy moment he could tell Moses II all about, but nothing ever happened. Though he was no psychologist, he felt certain that these two old men had merely forgotten what their glory days had been like.

Justin knew the grand duty fell upon him to remind them. He just had to jog their memory, and they'd finally be the icons he needed them to be.

Fortune smiled upon him! Both Butler and Madsen sat in their wheelchairs next to each other in the Sun Room, which was kind of built like a greenhouse. Glassy enough to promote a healthy feeling of solar warmth, but metal enough so it didn't become a sweltering pit of sweaty geriatrics dying of heat stroke.

It couldn't be better if he'd planned it this way. Gleefully he pushed the cart to the empty space between them.

"Hey guys. It's me. Justin. You're looking good today."

Butler squinted at him from under a pair of eyebrows so bushy they looked fake, which was a horrible contrast to his shiny pate, bare except for a fringe around the back and sides. "Do I know you, kid?"

Justin beamed at being called a kid. At fifty, his head was as bald as the Bruiser's. Had been since Justin's teenage years. "I see you almost every day, Mr. Butler. You and Mr. Madsen."

"Huh?" Butler cupped a hand behind his ear and leaned forward. "Speak up, kid. Hearing ain't what it was."

Justin hooked a thumb toward the Madman. "You and Mr. Madsen, sir. You remember him, right?"

"Are you a friend of Mickey's?"

Justin looked to Madsen for help, but empty eyes looked back, his mouth drooling slightly. Not bad enough to be wiped, just bad enough to be noticed.

"No sir. I'm *your* friend, and I'm about to give you the greatest gift ever. You ready?"

"What?"

Justin uncovered the old bell on his cart. It had taken him a long time of combing eBay, searching to find it, and it had cost him a lot, but it was an official World Wrestling Group ring-used bell. Worth every penny. With a rushing sense of wonder and awe, he struck the bell.

Though Butler didn't hear much anymore, the stark clang cut through the fog, and his heart rate went up. It brought him back to the old days, back to before even Mickey had been born. Back when he lived up to his knees in pussy and cocaine. Back when he got arrested for a DUI and his agent managed to cover it up.

The crowd roared around him, and he saw the Madman sitting next to him, blinking and old but still one of the best in the business.

"Fight!" the ref shouted.

The Madman shuffled out of his corner, bewildered, trying to remember where he was. He could have sworn he'd been in a nice, sunny room in a comfortable wheelchair, but the ring around him couldn't possibly be an illusion, could it?

The Bruiser certainly wasn't, and he shambled forward, ready for battle.

Hell with it, the Madman thought. He chalked it up to being blackout drunk. Again. It wasn't the first time he came back to himself in the ring.

The two old men locked arms and clumsily circled each other. Delighted, Justin found himself traveling back in time to when he was a kid. To when Daddy used to put cigarettes out on poor Justin's five-year-old arms. To when Grandma made him eat peas. The only thing that kept him locked in the moment was the fact that his grandmother was dead, so he'd never have to eat that bitch's peas ever again.

"Get 'im, Bruiser!" he said.

The other old folks stirred, mumbling among themselves, confused and afraid. Finally one of them hobbled off on a walker to get help.

She passed the Li'l Coffee Shoppe, where Laurie smiled at Mickey. He was such an adorable goof. Meek Mickey, her friends called him, usually derisively, but they never saw him like she did. His shyness never allowed him to open up to anyone, so no one knew his endearing personality. His quirky humor. His delight in odd things. No one except for her. He trusted her. She wished he'd let more of the world in. Sometimes she wanted to pick him up like a baby and rock him to sleep.

Did she feel attracted to him? A little bit. There were a couple of times when she felt like kissing him in more than a sisterly way. But ultimately she didn't think she could be with him like that. She pitied him too much, and that didn't mix well with being in love.

She wished she could find someone for him, though.

A roar from the Sun Room startled the both of them. Each jumped in their skin, but only Mickey rose. He walked to the entrance to the Li'l Coffee Shoppe and peered around the corner. A crowd had gathered, blocking much of his view, but he thought he saw two people fighting.

Wait. They looked kind of old. Were they residents?

"What's going on?" Laurie, from her seat.

"A fight, I think. It's hard to tell."

She got up and joined him. "Holy shit, you're right. Huh."

The sudden, chilling thought occurred to both of them at the same time, and they stared wide-eyed at each other. They didn't have to speak, and they didn't want to believe the horror such a thought meant. Both rushed down the hallway, forgetting Laurie's purse at their table.

Mickey didn't have to push through the gaggle of onlookers like he thought he'd have to; they scattered when one of the old men pushed the other, like he'd been setting up a clothesline strike against ropes that didn't exist. Sure enough, the pusher extended his arm, waiting.

Dear Lord, Mickey thought. *Pops.*

Madsen stumbled against retreating gawkers, and he tripped over a table, falling back on top of it. The glass surface shattered, and he fell into the mess, lacerating his hands. His robe protected the rest of him.

"Dad!" Laurie cried.

The Madman shook his head and ignored the pain in his hands. The Bruiser had tossed him too hard into the turnbuckle. Whatever. That asshole was supposed to win this one. Might as well put him over . . . but not too much. Just to make things hard on the champ, the Madman got up on the turnbuckle, ready to drive himself like a missile into the Bruiser's midsection.

"No! Dad! You'll hurt yourself!"

The Madman turned and saw his little girl in the audience, tears in her baby blues. She never liked to see him fight, but he'd explained the show to her before. She had to understand.

He winked at her and took the plunge.

The Bruiser knew that look in his opponent's eyes—just before he jumped—and knew what was happening. The Madman didn't want to make this show easy. He wanted to make this victory hurt a little. Fuck that. Just as the Madman hurled himself into the air, the Bruiser turned just a little, enough to sidestep the brunt of the attack, but not so far that he couldn't hook an arm under one of the Madman's, twisting so he could drive his opponent to the mat, face first.

Mickey watched, his insides rioting, trying to push his heart out his throat. When he was a kid, he'd watched his father on TV in the ring, and he felt the same thing back then that he felt now. He remembered hugging his father fiercely when he came home. Then Mickey said, "Why did that bad man—" Meaning the Madman, that night. "—want to hurt you so badly?"

Butler rustled Mickey's hair a bit. "Forget it, kid. It's all make-believe. We don't hurt nobody." Grinning. Showing off the dentures he'd earned in his prime when a folding chair nailed him in the teeth instead of the crown of his head.

Little Mickey didn't care. He never watched his father fight again . . . until now.

Madsen leaped from the chair he stood on, but he didn't go as far as he would have in the good ol' days. Instead of nailing his opponent, he fell short, but his grasping hands managed to latch onto Butler's robe. The two of them tumbled to the floor in a pile of wrinkled, sagging limbs.

The room gasped, and most of the people had to look away. Not Justin, though. He leaped up, pumping his fist, cheering. He hadn't been this happy since his father got killed in a car accident.

"Isn't someone going to stop them?" an elderly man asked.

"Fuck you!" Justin said. "No one's stopping this! This is totally rad!"

This snapped Laurie out of shock. She rushed in to help her father, but Justin blocked her path.

"Back in the crowd, honey." To emphasize his point, he

grabbed her shoulders to force her back.

Mickey snarled, surprised at how much rage flowed through him in that moment. "Hey asshole! Get your hands off of her!"

Did he really say that? Damn. That sounded kind of cool.

The Madman noticed the ref's back was turned, so he went for good old-fashioned eye gouge. The Bruiser saw it, though, and grabbed the Madman's pinky finger, putting him into an arm lock. Then, with some deft maneuvering the Bruiser managed to get his opponent into a strong headlock. Fingers scrabbled at his arm, trying to find purchase, finding none.

Time to end this one. With a quick hop in the air, the Bruiser went to the mat ass first, his arm still around the Madman's neck.

On the way down, the Madman knew this would be the final act. He saw his daughter in slow motion, being held back by the ref. She looked so adorable. He couldn't wait to get home and cover her chubby little face with kisses.

Mickey had never struck anyone in his entire life. In fact, he told everyone he was a pacifist. No one was more shocked than he when he shoved his fist into Justin's face, causing the stranger to release Laurie and hold his nose.

Mickey stared at his fist, and he fancied he could see the pain throbbing, making it puff in and out like on a cartoon. He couldn't believe what he'd just done.

Neither could Laurie. She'd never seen Mickey so passionate! So alive! Meek Mickey was all but in this moment. She wanted to kiss him so badly. He'd stuck up for her! And with such emotion!

And then Justin, who determined that he didn't feel much of anything, only a slight numbness reminiscent of being out in the cold for five minutes, pushed past Laurie. He planted his fist into Mickey's jaw, breaking it and sending him reeling, his teeth dribbling out his mouth, covered in blood.

Rage exploded out of Laurie, and she fired her foot into Justin's crotch. Later she found out it was hard enough to rupture one of his testicles. All the air rushed out of him, and he couldn't take any in.

Laurie eased the misery by cold-cocking him on the ear. Justin's eardrum popped, and he fell to the floor, bleeding and unconscious.

Later, as Justin rested in his hospital room, handcuffed to the bed railing, he cursed himself for passing out too soon. If only he'd stayed awake for three more seconds. Because of that bitch daughter of the Madman, he'd missed the end of the match.

Laurie had three seconds to admire her handiwork, and then two cracks rang out in the Sun Room, loud and nauseating.

Both old men were on the floor, one sitting and the other seemingly under the first, face down. Immediately Laurie knew what one of those cracks was. Screaming, she ran to her father's side and tried to get him out from under Butler's lock. Madsen's head lolled too loosely, and his neck sounded like a sack of marbles being rattled.

She looked into his empty blue eyes—once sparkling and full of life—and she broke.

Butler, shocked back to reality by the incredible pain from a broken coccyx, finally released his opponent and slumped to the floor, slipping into a coma. His arm fell away from Madsen's neck, and Laurie took her shattered father into her arms, cradling his head, rocking and sobbing and screaming and shouting and cursing.

By then Mickey came to and saw his father. Scared out of his mind, he went to Butler's side. Desperate, he moved his hands all over Butler's neck until he found a pulse. Strong, too.

Relieved, he fell back on his haunches and watched as doctors and nurses finally showed up. They went to work immediately, and before long they'd moved Butler into surgery.

"We should look at *you*, sir," one said to him.

Only then did Mickey feel pain in his jaw. It throbbed sharply, and he became aware that his lower front teeth were all missing.

But then he saw Laurie, and he ignored the doctor and the pain and the broken teeth. He went to her side and put his arm around her shoulders. She turned her red slick eyes to him, and her cries fell silent.

They watched each other for a while, and it took Mickey a moment to realize he had tears in his eyes, too. They spilled down his cheeks and dripped down his throat.

After a while Laurie gently placed her father's head on the floor, and she pivoted toward Mickey. They wrapped their arms around each other and held on as tightly as they could. Balanced on their knees, they held each other for a very, very long time.

-

For weeks, Laurie never left home. She cried constantly, and when she didn't—when she was too tired for tears—she wanted to die, if only to take the pain away. Her friends wanted to help, but she drove them all from her.

All except Mickey. He came over every day, and they wept together. He held her for hours on end. He did everything for her, from cooking meals to cleaning up around the place.

But one day she felt she had to push him away, as well. He looked a little too much like his father sometimes, from the right angle, and it hurt too much.

"I think I need to be alone for a while," she said.

Mickey, who had a nice set of dentures for his lower jaw, understood. "You have my number if you need me."

He was okay. He wanted to help, but he also knew it would give him more time to see his father, who remained in a coma and likely would for the rest of his life.

Unfortunately the Rumble in the Retirement Home, as the media called it, reignited interest in the Bruiser. Reporters and fans alike swarmed Sunny Hills, and they constantly tried to get information out of him. He didn't even acknowledge the fucking cannibals.

Mickey spent a lot of time with his father, and when the circus died down again, he liked to take up his old perch in the Li'l Coffee Shoppe. Alone. He missed Laurie, but he didn't mind the comfortable environment and the lustrous scent of coffee.

The doctors said surgery would be necessary to fix the broken tailbone, but considering his age and condition, they didn't think they should do it. They'd needed his permission to not treat the injury, and on the day he finally relented and gave it, he retired to his coffee. He stared into the black depths of his cup, feeling like he'd given the doctors permission to pull the plug instead. Not that there was an actual plug, but still.

"Mickey."

He glanced up, surprised—and pleased—to see Laurie. She'd lost some weight, and she had more lines around her eyes, but she was beautiful as ever.

"How's your father?" she asked.

He told her about it, and she sat down opposite of him, leaning in. As he told the story, she reached across the table and took his hands in hers. She squeezed, and he squeezed back.

"How are *you* doing?" he asked.

"Better. Not good, but better. I'm glad I found you here."

"I'm glad you're here," he said. "I missed you."

"I wanted to tell you something. I love you, Mickey. Without you, I would have . . . I would have done something bad. Thank you for being there for me."

He blushed. "You'd do the same for me."

"I want to do something for you in return. I want to introduce you to the world. I want you to be a part of it."

His heart pounded. "But I—"

"No more cutting yourself off from people. I want you to bloom like a rose and live your life. For real."

"I—" He looked down and tried to swallow. Something seemed stuck in his throat. "I'm scared."

"I know. I'm going to help you."

He looked back into her eyes, and he found himself on the brink of weeping. "I love you, too."

"I know. Come on. Let's get out of here."

They stood together, and they walked out of the Li'l Coffee Shoppe holding hands. Outside the building they paused, and Laurie kissed Mickey softly on the cheek. "Welcome to the rest of the world."

Mickey felt the weight of his solitary existence lift from around his neck, and the two of them watched the sunset before they stepped into their new lives.

LATE START

My eye cracks open. It's unusual for me to wake up before my alarm clock goes off. I check my phone and—*holy shit!* It's 8:29 am! I have to be at work in one minute!

I don't have time to eat or brush my teeth. The commute from Elmhurst to Schaumburg can take between twenty to forty minutes. I can't afford to be so late.

I dress and rush out the door to my car. I drive as fast as I can to the expressway. Thank Christ it looks like traffic is moving swiftly. I get over to the left lane and get up to eighty-five miles per hour. No one's ahead of me, so I gun it to ninety-five.

I check the dashboard. Still 8:29. Good.

Oh shit. I just passed a cop. Please don't see me. Please don't see me. Please—

Fuck. He saw me. Lights flash, and he zooms up to my ass. He's gotta be pissed, but I can't be late. I press my foot down as far as it can go. I check the time. Still 8:29.

I look up just in time to see that traffic has stopped, and I'm about to crash into the car that has magically appeared in front of me. I scream, twisting the wheel to the left. I veer away from the jam and hit the ditch so hard that my car flips. The roof caves in, and I hang from my seatbelt. The airbag goes off and punches me in the face.

Son of a bitch. I'm not going to make it to work on time. The dashboard is crumpled, so I can't check the clock.

Someone knocks on the driver's side window, and I remember the cop car. I'm in serious shit. I see the cop's legs, and they seem too white for this world.

He opens the door and cuts me free of my seatbelt. He helps me out of the car, and when I straighten out, I see it's Andy

Griffith. Or Andy Taylor, rather.

"You're in a spot of trouble, son," he says.

"You're darned tootin'!"

I look around Andy to see Barney Fife rushing up to me, wagging his finger in my face. Both he and Andy are in glorious black and white.

"Am I going to jail?" I ask. "I need to call my boss if I am."

"You know what we oughta do, Andy? I think we oughta *rape* him!"

What. The. Fuck.

"Now, now, Barn. We can't just go around rapin' folks. He *is* going to jail, though. Turn around, son."

Shit. I comply. He fits the handcuffs on. They're tight and cold against my skin. He pushes me forward until we reach the cruiser. Barney opens the back, and Andy gently eases me in.

But I'm not in the back of a car. I'm in a castle. I turn around to see a door-shaped hole, but when Andy closes it, reality fills in.

"Good evening."

I turn back around to see Dracula standing at the top of a staircase. Not Lugosi or Lee or even Langella. It's Gary Oldman.

"Um," I say, "do you have the time? I'm going to be late for work."

"You shall be much later, then. Girls?" He gestures at me.

There are three women suddenly around me. All are incredibly hot, and they wear gauzy see-through gowns. They grin, showing off their fangs.

"Take good care of my guest. Don't hurt him . . . too much."

They lead me into the next room, a bedroom. They tie me up to a chair and drag me over to a computer on a table in the corner. They start to bicker over who gets to show me their blog first. They settle on Cauldron of Goth. It's so bad I kind of wish they'd drain me of blood and be done with it.

Just when I consider chewing my own tongue off to choke myself, the door explodes. I whip my head around to see Alex Jones bearing a cross and holy water. He charges the brides of Dracula, driving them back hissing and glaring.

"That's right, you undead concubines!" he says. "Stay back! I'll toast your ass!"

"When did you become a vampire slayer?" I ask.

"Just after I was Bill Hicks. I created Alex Jones as a cover. I've been killin' vamps ever since."

He makes short work of my bonds—even the handcuffs—so I thank him as I stand.

"I'll hold 'em off," Alex Jones says.

The door he came through is gone, just a brick wall, so the only way out is the window. But we must be a hundred feet up. There's no way I can do this.

"You have to climb down the wall!" Alex Jones shouts. "Hurry! I can't hold 'em off much longer!"

Here goes nothing. I grab a hold of the wall, and I'm shocked by how easy this is. It's like I'm Spider-Man. I crawl down face-first until I reach the ground.

There! About a block away! I see my office building! I rush across the grassy field and feverishly work at opening the door with my badge. I dart in and slam my ID card against the machine that punches me in.

It beeps.

The time switches from 8:29 to 8:30.

Whew!

PIETY

Judah Crenshaw used to be the most pious man he knew. He went to church every day, sometimes more than once. He gave more to the collection plate than any other parishioner, and he sang hymns louder even than the preacher. Not a day passed without his fervent prayers.

All of this changed when he saw Reverend Jordan torn to pieces by a savage beast unlike any he'd ever seen before.

It happened late one cool and crisp night as autumn crept up on the world. Judah's wife busied herself with cleaning dishes while his two sons knelt before their bed in the other room, whispering their prayers. The farm fell silent as it usually did at this hour. Only the crickets sang from the fields under the velvet, star-bedazzled blanket of night.

Judah sat by the fireplace, packing his pipe. It was the only vice he allowed himself, and anyway he felt certain the Bible said nothing about smoking. Still, it bothered him, so instead of striking a match, he decided to visit the reverend and find out the good Lord's take on tobacco.

He made his excuses to Rachael—who graciously understood her husband's ways—and went out to the barn to saddle his horse.

The stirrups creaked as he stepped into them, hauling himself up into position. A tiny little throb of pain spoke up in his back, barely noticeable but there. At the age of forty he figured this to be the beginning of his descent into decrepitude. Soon his sons would bear the brunt of the work around here, and that suited him fine.

The horse clopped its way down the dirt path, and Judah felt swallowed by the night. The illumination from his house faded behind him, and now he saw only with the aid of stark moonlight. The whirring sound of the crickets grew louder, punctuated by an occasional owl hoot.

It reminded him of home. He hailed originally from the backwoods of Pennsylvania, where he'd misspent his youth helping his pa brew moonshine, and though he never firmly believed in it, he took part in his ma's bastardized powwow ways.

Out west, in the rich fields of Nebraska, very little reminded him of the peaceful, almost lazy ways of home. Only the night made him feel like a child again, when darkness shrouded the fields, and he could close his eyes and pretend to be in his native woods.

Before long he reached town, where the sounds of drunken debauchery dispelled his reverie. Civilization tended to do that to a man. Had he never gone to Philadelphia, he would never have become enchanted with the ways of the Christian church. He'd still be an ignorant yokel, sinning with his old man and practicing empty and meaningless magic with his mother.

He never would have met Rachael, either. He never would have found true happiness.

He rode past the rows of saloons, ignoring the raucous, tinkling music from within. Harder to ignore were the sounds of revelry. Laughs, cries, shouts, declarations. The rhythmic stomping of dancing boots.

All of the stores were closed. The only other building that showed a sign of life was the sheriff's office. A candle burned in the window, and someone made a loud, metallic rattling sound. A disgruntled prisoner, perhaps?

Judah turned a blind eye to it all, and as he reached the end of town, where only the church resided, its white steeple in sharp contrast against the sackcloth sky, the noise of late-night city living passed away. In fact, he could hear nothing but the deafening ring of absolute silence. Though the church had a huge yard out back, no crickets could be heard.

The horse slowed. Judah hadn't given any commands, so he nudged the animal forward. It stopped, a small whine in the back of its throat.

"Come on, Sue," he whispered. "Get going." He dug his heels in a bit, and the horse continued. Its head shook back and forth in a skittering way. Though it was night, Judah figured Sue had wind of a snake.

He tethered his horse to the hitching rail and made his way up the steps into the church. Inside a few candles burned, but he found no one around, not even the reverend. Thinking Jordan was in the rectory, Judah walked down the aisle, pausing to take a quick knee before a statue of the crucified Christ, and made his way around back.

Before he reached the rectory, he felt kind of funny. His arm hairs stood up uncomfortably, and the back of his neck tingled. He hadn't felt this way since childhood, when his pa's still was about to be raided by the local deputies.

And then he sensed an odd animal smell, almost like a bear's yet muskier.

He heard a loud thunk as something fell over in the rectory. Someone wearing heavy boots clopped along the hardwood floor. He wanted to call out the reverend's name, but his throat seemed suddenly small. He couldn't even squeak as he moved toward Jordan's private chambers.

The smell in here was worse. It mixed with the deep, gassy smell of shit and something else. Something . . . coppery, like when Rachael was on her menses.

A light breeze pushed his hair back as he realized that the window had been broken. No, that wasn't quite right. The window had been torn clean out of the wall. The sill stuck out in all directions, a splintered mess.

And then Judah saw the reverend—what remained of him— and the hulking beast hovering over him.

At first his eyes refused to process this unholy thing before him, but after a moment he started categorizing it in terms his mind could comprehend. A diadem of horns—akin to a buck deer's antlers—topped its bear's head. The rest of its seven-foot-tall frame was a shaggy pelt not unlike a buffalo's. It had no feet but hooves, exactly like a goat's.

But its face and hands were pure human, and evil shone from its almond eyes and razor-toothed grin. Its taloned claws— opposable thumbs and all—rooted around in the reverend's body, or so it seemed at first. Judah peered past the mess of blood and sundered flesh to see that Jordan's legs had been broken and twisted away, giving the beast easy access to the reverend's most private of parts.

The beast had dug its hands into Jordan's groin—deep—and now it uprooted his genitals in one awful scoop. It brought the handful of obscene flesh to its mouth and bit into it, yanking its head back like a dog working a bone, and chewing its prize with the sloppy, slobbery chaos of a hungry animal.

In that moment, as Judah watched this horror, he knew that there was no God. No all-powerful being would ever consent to the existence of such a monster.

It lowered the final piece of Jordan's genitals into its mouth like a delectable morsel and chewed, blood slipping down its hairy chin. Its eyes closed in ecstasy as it smacked and slurped until it swallowed. Then it looked directly at Judah and grinned, showing off teeth that belonged to a mountain lion.

Fear flushed through Judah's system, and his consciousness fled him. The next thing he knew he woke in his own bed, body slicked and sticking to the sheets. Relief flooded his thoughts as he realized that the horrors of last night couldn't have been real. The beast had been a fevered nightmare, perhaps brought on by a bad piece of food at supper.

But then he found Rachael in the kitchen, preparing breakfast. As he sat down to a plate full of eggs, toast and bacon, she asked how he felt.

"A bit shaky," he said. He thought he might mention the nightmare, but perhaps the subject matter would be too strong for the fairer sex.

"You came home an absolute mess," she said. "I don't know what you got into, but you were terrified out of your mind. All you wanted to do was hide in bed. You trembled so much I thought you'd break the bed. What happened last night?"

Judah didn't tell her anything. He had to have dreamed the whole thing. Monsters didn't exist, and if they did, God would protect him from them. So not wishing to seem like a fool to his own wife, he remained reticent on the matter.

Yet when he went outside to begin the usual chores, he found his horse outside the barn, breathing heavily with its flanks practically whipped away. Had he done this to the poor animal in an attempt to flee . . . something?

Then he heard the news. A neighbor stopping by for some water and a quick jaw told him that something had gotten to the reverend. "Must've been an animal. Tore him to pieces, it did. Ugly sight. Even the undertaker puked."

Judah felt something move uncomfortably in his guts, and breathing became difficult, as if he wore an ever-tightening girdle. He flashed back to last night, to the beast reveling in the reverend's severed works. He felt that horrible fear again and fought the urge to look around just to make sure the beast hadn't snuck up on him.

That night his fear became more real. As he closed up the barn, ready for dinner, he smelled the unmistakable musk of the monster, and he felt like he was back in Jordan's rectory. His heart flailed against the inside of his chest as he whipped around, deathly afraid that he would see the monster a split second before it did to him what it had done to the reverend.

Nothing. No movements. No sound. The musk faded, but he took his pitchfork with him back to the house. Once more he barricaded the door, and when he went to bed, he kept the pitchfork close at hand.

When he did this a third night in a row, Rachael said, "What's gotten into you?"

Judah fumbled with words, trying to express confusion at her question. It was a futile attempt, and she made sure to let him know with her next breath. Finally, he said, "I can't explain it. Something . . . happened. I—"

"You don't say your prayers anymore," she said. "Whatever happened's been eating you pretty bad."

He blanched at her choice of words. An image of the beast eating Reverend Jordan came to mind, and he shook his head, trying to banish the gristly scene.

"You've got to tell me what's wrong," she said. "I'm your wife, Judah."

She looked so concerned, but he knew she'd never believe the truth. As for himself, he didn't *want* to believe, but it stuck in his thoughts like a piece of corn between his teeth.

But the truth had to come out of him. It was all he could think about, even as he toiled at work on the farm. It poisoned him, and if he didn't talk about it, it would wither him into a man old beyond his years.

"I saw what happened to Reverend Jordan," he said.

"How—?"

"I went to see him that night, remember? And . . . and I saw the thing that et him. It was . . ." He trailed off because something didn't seem right. Though it was a calm night, he could hear nothing. No crickets, no birds, not even the grunting sound of pigs in the pen out back. His neck tingled, and he sniffed the air for any kind of musk.

"Judah," Rachael said. "What—?"

His eyes darted to the window, and for a split second he saw the face of the beast leering at him through the glass. It grinned, eyes twinkling, and then vanished from the pane.

Judah grabbed up the pitchfork and rushed to the window. The whole thing had happened so quickly he wondered if he'd imagined it. He didn't know what he feared more, catching a retreating glimpse of the monster, thereby confirming his fears, or nothing at all.

"What's wrong?" Rachael asked.

Swallowing, he forced his hands to stop trembling. "They're saying a bear mauled him. Well, it weren't no animal that done it." He then described the monster as he stared out the window, looking for any sign of it.

Rachael couldn't look at him when she asked, "Did you stop by the Lady Gaye that night?"

This remark hurt him, and then he realized it shouldn't have. Sin couldn't exist if God didn't. "You know I've never had a drop to drink."

"You came home in a state that night. You don't even remember it. Maybe—"

"It wasn't drink, Rachael."

Silence. Then: "Why do you keep looking out that window?"

"I'm afraid that creature might've followed me home."

She didn't look at him quite the same since then. His demeanor thereafter didn't help, either. As soon as the sky started to darken in the east every day, he barricaded the house and refused to let their kids outside. He stood vigil at the windows with a newly purchased rifle. Before, he wanted nothing to do with guns. Now he stayed up late in his chair, his rifle across his lap, a finger in the trigger guard.

All of this had a bad effect on Jeb and Jubal Crenshaw. The former, older by three years, hated his old man for this new tyranny. He wanted to see his friends after supper and maybe do a little hell-catting. At fourteen he'd just begun developing an interest in things in which his parents would disapprove. The nightly lockdown inspired anger and sulking in him. However, the latter bought into Judah's paranoia. It got so bad he spent his evenings hiding in the bed he shared with his brother.

Rachael couldn't tell which of the two had it off worse. As for herself, she couldn't bear to sleep next to her own husband. He screamed a lot while dreaming and shivered so hard the bed shook. At times he would flail out and accidentally strike her.

She wanted to give him the benefit of the doubt, but in this present state he was dangerous, not just physically but emotionally. Who knew how badly he'd already stunted Jubal's growth?

One morning, while the boys were already at their chores, Rachael sat at the table next to Judah and said, "I want to leave, and I want to take our kids with me."

He gazed at her through heavy-lidded, sleep-deprived eyes. More veins than iris looked out of their puffy cocoons at her, the whites covered in a red, cobwebby film. He said nothing.

"Darn it, I don't want to go, but you're making this impossible. Have you even seen that . . . whatever it is since that night?"

He ignored her and turned his attention to the window. Even though the sun shone down on every inch of the farm, he still felt concerned whenever the kids were outside.

"You're not going to fight me on this?" When he said nothing a third time, she uncharacteristically cursed. "I want to protect them. From you. But if you just talk to me, maybe we can figure this out."

He jerked, as if someone had startled him from behind. "From me? Why? I'm trying to keep them alive."

"From a figment of your imagination. I've never seen that thing, Judah. And I think you see it, but only in your nightmares. Sometimes you scare me."

He stared dumbly at her. It hurt that she thought for a second that he would do anything to hurt his family, and he wanted to burst out at her. But then he thought that this might work out for the best. By taking the kids away from here, she'd be saving them from the thing that killed Reverend Jordan. He swallowed hard, forcing his indignation back into his guts, where it festered like an infected boil.

"To hell with you, Judah. I don't know why you're doing all of this, but I'm not going anywhere. From your silence, I have no choice but to think you want us to go. Maybe now that you don't live up to your religious beliefs, you want to play around a bit. Maybe go to a few saloons. Maybe even find a new woman. But I refuse to let you do this. You won't get out of this easy."

No. She couldn't stay. She and the kids had to leave, even if he had to make them. Yet he didn't know if he could. He'd never raised a hand to her in all their years together. What if she called his bluff? Would he really have to hit her?

"Get over yourself." His voice was hoarse and dirty, and it hurt his heart to utter these words. But he knew her very life depended on it. "Don't you get it? You're not wanted here. You want the kids? Take 'em. Get out of here, you no good cunt."

The last sentence came out awkwardly, as he was not used to cursing. But as he watched her face wilt at the words, he knew he'd gotten the job done.

He let his eyes glaze over, and he did not acknowledge her for the rest of the morning, not as she packed her bags, not as she wept in the kitchen, not even when she tried to say goodbye. It took all of his power to not break down in that moment. His heart yearned to break through his chest, to take back his awful words, but he refused to let himself give in.

Finally, the door closed. He stood and rushed to the window, where he watched her and the boys on the wagon, headed for town and the stage that would take them to her folks in Kansas. The sun still hung in the middle of the sky, so he knew they would be safe.

As he watched the backs of the heads of his children, he wished he could have said goodbye to them. He wished they would at least turn around to give him one last glimpse of their faces, something to hold with his memory as he tried to go to sleep at the conclusion of each day.

They did not comply with his wish.

That night, just before the sun slipped from the sky, Judah went to the barn to lock up. He stepped inside to make sure all of his animals were present when he nearly keeled over from the powerful odor of beast. It normally smelled bad in here, but now it overwhelmed him, causing his eyes to water and his chest to hitch. Then, just as the stench became the most unbearable, he remembered what it signified. His blood juddered to a halt in his veins, and he gasped, desperately trying to breathe. He didn't have his rifle because such monsters could not walk in daylight. Now he had no means of defending himself.

He turned to run, but his feet tangled up against each other, and he fell to the straw-covered floor. He did not hesitate to push back up to his feet and sprint for the safety of his house, to his rifle. As he went he could have sworn he saw a pair of eyes glittering out at him from the darkness of a stall.

Judah spent the entire night going from window to window, clutching his gun at the ready. He routinely sniffed the air for the telltale musk of the monster. At every sound, even those as quiet as the house settling, he jumped like a frightened child, but he kept up his vigil until dawn. Even then he waited for sunlight to bathe his entire property before he ventured out to the barn.

Outside he could smell the musk, but it was so faint the beast couldn't still be around. Inside he discovered all of his animals slaughtered, their bodies split and torn, their blood painting the walls and straw, now drying to a rusty shade. Had it been this way last night, and he'd been too scared to see it? He didn't remember hearing the animals, and wouldn't the presence of the beast have driven them mad with fear?

Then he realized it had eaten none of them. At least, not entirely. While all the females had just been torn asunder, all the males had lost what made them male. All that remained were ragged holes surrounded by teeth marks.

There was no way he could clean up this unholy mess, so he got some kerosene and razed the barn. He watched from his porch as the fire billowed up, licking at the light blue sky like fingers reaching for Heaven.

He thought back to his youth, to the powwow he'd practiced with his mother. Had she ever heard of an animal like this? Was there something in her books that could explain this monstrosity? He wished he'd kept his copy of *The Long Lost Friend*. Maybe then he could do a little research of his own.

His sister Ruth had taken over for his mother after she passed away. Judah considered telegraphing Ruth, but he knew he'd never get an answer soon enough. Even so, any telegraph agent entering those woods would be shot for a federal officer by Old

Man Crenshaw, who still moonshined in those parts.

No, Judah was on his own. If only he could gain mastery over his fear. Then, perhaps, he could shoot the beast and find out if bullets could vanquish it.

He considered going to town for help, but he dismissed the idea. Who would believe him? Besides, he thought about all that open land with no shelter and shuddered, even if he would be making the trek in daylight. Home it would have to be.

Instead of doing chores, he did necessary tasks. He made sure he had enough water in the house. Since he didn't have any more animals, he stopped by the smokehouse to load up on jerky beef. Lastly, he tore down his fence and used the wood to cover up all the windows of his house and to reinforce the door. He made an extra crossbeam to use as a barricade.

At the end of his labors he sealed himself off in his house, even though the sun still lingered at six o'clock, and sat down to eat. When he'd staved off his hunger, he cleaned the rifle.

Later, as Judah tried to relax by the fire, he heard someone knock on his door. Annoyed—after all, it had taken him a long time to bar the entryway—he went over to the front of his house and said, "Who goes?"

No one answered him.

He regretted not adding a peephole so he could see who was out there. Then again, it would only have weakened the door to the creature. Besides, would the monster politely knock like a neighbor? He decided to open up and see who it was.

Just before he touched the knob, the knock came again. It sounded kind of forcible, so he drew back. "Who goes?" he asked again. Once more he received no answer.

"God damn you! Speak up!"

The knock came a third time, harder than before, and this time it didn't stop. With each hammering blow, the door juddered wildly in its frame. Judah backed away, holding the rifle close to his chest, shocked that the wood didn't splinter.

Bracing himself, he aimed the gun at the door and waited, resisting the desperate urge to run. But he knew he couldn't run. By barricading himself in, he'd given himself no way out.

The door stopped convulsing, and everything became quiet again. Only the monotonous tick of Rachel's grandfather clock filled Judah's ears as he continued to stare at the barred entryway. "Hello?"

Laughter. Deep, rich laughter came through the door, reverberating in his chest like a loud song, but there was nothing delightful about the sound. Judah's mouth dried up, and the back of his neck flushed and tingled. Now he felt the urge to put the gun in his mouth and pull the trigger, ending this madness in the most merciful way he knew.

"Little pig, little pig, let me in."

God! It could talk! He felt like screaming, but he knew he'd never find the breath for it; he couldn't even find any with which to *breathe*.

Finally the fear built up so much he couldn't hold it in any longer. "Go away!" he howled. "Please! Go away!" He dropped the gun and cowered in a ball on the floor. He no longer cared about survival. He just wanted this to be over.

He barely noticed that the monster no longer tried to gain entrance, nor did it speak again.

It was dawn before he gained the courage to open the door. Only a lingering whiff of the beast's stench remained, as well as scuffed hoof marks on the porch.

His hands couldn't stop shaking, so he hunted down a bottle of grain alcohol Rachael used for disinfectant. After a few belts he felt calmer, and he wondered why such a wonderful feeling should be railed against by men of God.

Judah spent the next couple of days locked up, eating poorly, sipping at that bottle. Nothing happened, but he kept up his seclusion, not even going outside to defecate. On the third day, however, the stink got to him. He was also out of alcohol, and he wanted to eat something—anything—other than jerky beef.

At noon he took up his rifle and headed outside with the intent of shooting some veal. He cautiously wandered outside, even though the world shone with brightness. There were few shadows, but he watched them regardless, just in case.

After an hour, though, he let his guard down and started feeling human for the first time since he'd went down to visit Reverend Jordan, which seemed like a lifetime ago. He took in the fresh air and could practically taste the rich, fecund scent of corn. His belly rumbled, but he restrained himself from raiding the crop too soon.

Motes of dandelion fluff dotted the air around him, and he

playfully blew a cirrus scrim of them away. As he did he saw movement from the corner of his eye.

There. From the line of corn stalks. A woman stepped out, throwing her gorgeous head of dark hair back from her face.

Rachael? It was either her or a heretofore unknown twin sister. What was she doing here? Did she come back for him? He felt a longing twinge in his heart. Oh, how he'd missed her. He missed her presence at the dinner table, her thoughtful discourse at prayer time, the way she felt next to him at night.

Her eyes met with his, and the twinge migrated lower in his body. Soon the front of his pants felt pinched and tight, and he moved forward, eager for his wife's embrace.

"Oh Rachael," he said. "I've missed you so. I'm glad you came back to me."

She stepped forward, a smile spreading across her face like the buttery light of the rising sun. "Judah. I had to see you. I missed you, too." She held out both hands to him.

Even as she folded her arms around him, he felt like something was off. Rachael didn't quite sound herself, but he didn't think too much about it. The building heat of his loins took precedence, and he shuddered when their bodies pressed together, and his rigidness prodded her just below the waist.

"My. You *have* missed me." Her hand wandered down to the bulge under his belt and caressed him, rubbing gently.

Heat exuded from Judah's body, and it practically evaporated off the top of his skull. He moaned as she unbuttoned his trousers and unlimbered his manhood.

Rachael primed his pump, gently squeezing, and Judah could feel his climax burning within him. Too soon. He leaned forward and kissed her, touching her face with his field-scarred hands.

Odd. Her cheek felt like his after a couple of days without shaving. His impending orgasm threatened to distract him from this quandary, but there was something too strange about her.

Something shifted in her face just as she dipped her head down toward his sex, mouth open and ready. Excited as he was about Rachael's intentions—she'd never done anything like *this* before—he almost dismissed it as a trick of shadow. Then, he noticed for a split second that it looked like she had deer's horns on her head.

Just like the beast.

The image of Rachel melted and flickered away, and Judah watched as the beast raised up his penis toward its razor sharp teeth. He screamed, going soft immediately, tearing himself from the monster's grip. He stumbled away and rolled backwards, almost striking his head on the base of a tree.

The smell of nature vanished as if someone turned off a switch, and his nostrils filled up with the beast's musk. He flailed around in the dirt, seeking his rifle and finding nothing. Now the beast loomed over him, grinning down at him, licking the palm it had used to stroke Judah's sex.

Where could the rifle be? He cast his eyes wildly, hoping it was close enough to reach, and then he saw it at the monster's feet. Casually, the abomination stooped and picked up the gun. It examined the weapon briefly before snapping the barrel in two like it was a twig.

Just like he had at the church, Judah fled, and when he came back to himself later—locked away in his house—he had no memory of it. All he knew was the beast had nearly killed him, just as it had killed the reverend.

And it had done so in broad daylight.

Now he had no refuge in the sun. He had no weapon. And considering its strength, the beast could easily get inside to him. He had no hope. He felt certain that he would die within the hour.

Why hadn't it killed him before? Was it toying with him? What did it want from him? Could it be just the taste of his flesh?

Something thumped on the porch. Again. A third and fourth time, each sound growing louder. He imagined those heavy hooves clopping closer, and his heart picked up its pace. The dark reek of the monster permeated even through the thick reinforced door. A loud rending noise battered at his ears, and the door—along with a goodly portion of the frame and wall—disappeared.

The beast's monstrous bulk stood in the threshold, a silhouette against the blazing sun behind it, and it took its first step into Judah's house. The creature opened its mouth, showing off its slavering chops, and reached a hoary hand toward its victim.

And in that moment, as fear practically tore Judah's heart out, searing every nerve in his body, epiphany struck, and he knew the only thing that could save him. Mustering all of his strength, he shouted one word: "*Wait!*"

The beast paused, and its thickly furred eyelids fluttered.

Laughing, no longer master of his own body, Judah rushed to his mantle, where he kept his Bible, and threw the book into the fireplace. As it had not been lit, the tome thumped down in the ash and sent up a cloud around it.

"I renounce Jesus Christ!" Judah shouted. He spat onto the dusty cover. "I was deceived, and I regret every moment of my worship of a false god. I feel like a fool!"

The beast smiled. Instead of finishing off its prey, it leaned back, its stout arms crossed, and waited.

"I should have seen the sign," Judah whispered. "As soon as I saw you, as soon as your existence disproved God's, I should have known. I should have started worshipping you right away."

The beast chuckled. "Go on."

"You are clearly a powerful being, the most powerful I've ever seen. You have abilities. You must be a god. And now, if you'll spare my life, I'll spend the rest of my days dedicated to worshipping you."

The beast's arms came untangled and swung at its sides as it straightened its body. "You know what I require of you, Judah Crenshaw."

Judah thought back to Reverend Jordan and to his slaughtered animals. A part of him thought he was mad for even considering this, but when he reflected on the matter, it would be a small sacrifice, especially since it had almost gotten him killed earlier.

He rushed to the kitchen and retrieved a butcher knife. When he returned, he undid his trousers and let them slide down his legs. He took hold of the head of his penis, stretching out the entire organ, and placed the blade against the shaft.

"No. It must be erect."

When Judah looked up, he saw Rachael again. Completely naked. Before the kids had been born, which meant no loose skin. No stretch marks. Just young, taut womanflesh.

Judah grew bigger in his hand as he watched this specter of his wife fondle herself, and just as he came closer to climax, he knew what the beast wanted.

Just before he cut himself, the beast said, in Rachel's sweet voice, "Don't forget the balls."

Judah pressed down with all his might and sliced. Fiery pain burned along his flesh as the blade bit into him halfway through the shaft. Blood exploded from the wound, and he felt his final orgasm rocket through his body, shooting thick crimson spurts onto the floor.

And even though it hurt him like nothing else on earth ever had, he forced himself to pull back and slice again, desperately hoping he could get the whole thing this time. He got the rest of the shaft and hit no resistance as he reached the sac. His testicles unraveled, and his manhood held on only by a strip of scrotum.

Judah couldn't bear to use the knife again, so he gripped a handful of his genitals and tore it away from his body. Blood audibly pattered down on the hardwood floor as he stumbled forward, holding his gristly prize aloft.

The beast had banished the image of Rachael, and now it reached out to Judah's gore-slicked hand. Daintily, it plucked the jumble of meat like picking a piece of lint off a shirt and lifted it up to its mouth, where it popped it in like a piece of candy. It chewed, absorbing all the sexual energy he could from this charged piece of flesh, and its own member stood up, tumescent and large like a man's forearm.

Judah collapsed, still feeling the dying pulse of his orgasm as blood pumped from the ragged hole between his legs. "May I . . . live?" He barely managed to get this gasp out.

"You may, my servant. There's just one more thing."

Gently, the beast turned Judah's trembling body onto his back and knelt down between his legs. Throbbing pain, combined with the animalistic stench from the beast, smashed whatever remained of his sanity as he howled with laughter. Part of him knew the beast's intention, and that part had made peace with it.

He spread his legs wider to accommodate the monster's girth. The hole, where once his genitals had been, stretched—not unpleasantly—as the beast thrust into him. Judah could feel his guts compress to make room, and he clutched the beast's hairy back, screaming its praises, worshipping it as loudly as his cracked and ruined voice would allow.

And that was the last thing he remembered for a quite some time.

Days later, he awoke in his own bed, but not once did he wonder if it had all been a nightmare. He felt the closed, knotted flesh between his legs and knew this wonderful dream had been true.

How would he tell Rachael and the boys? *Could* he? No matter. They were gone, abandoned him what seemed like years ago. All that remained of his life was the slight bulge in his belly.

He smiled warmly down at it and thought he felt something move inside of him.

BLACK FRIDAY

It's 11:59 pm, and Rick Denning is ready. He's worked in retail for thirty years, and he's watched Black Friday get worse and worse. He knows this one will be bad. The crowd pushes against the doors, eyes rabid and rolling.

The clock hits midnight. It's official. He nods to Erik Vasquez and Dina Trevor. They're young and quick, so he has every confidence in them.

They approach the doors, and in unison unlock them. Dina is fleet of foot; she jumps back and takes cover against the wall. Erik is not so lucky. The door swings open and breaks against his face. He screams, shards of broken glass leaking blood down his cheeks. He falls and is promptly trampled. He might make it, but . . . never mind. Someone steps on his throat.

The rush is over. The screams and fighting have begun in the store. Rick and Dina approach Erik's ruined body. He twitches, trying to breathe through a crushed trachea.

"Sorry, son," Rick says. He unholsters his weapon and aims it at Erik's head. "You did good."

Erik closes his eyes, and Rick puts him out of his misery.

Dina sniffs and wipes away a tear. "He was one of the few cool guys around here."

"I'll miss him. Now let's make sure everyone behaves."

Rick sees an altercation brewing in the toy department. Two grown men wrestle with a giant Millennium Falcon set between them. A little boy clutches at the leg of one of them.

"You're an adult!" the father yells. "This is for my kid!"

"Fuck your kid! I love *Star Wars*, and he can't have it!"

The father stomps his enemy's foot. The other guy screams and lets go of the toy. "Ha! You lose, asshole!"

The other guy doesn't hesitate. He kicks the five-year-old in the face, crushing his skull. The father howls and drops the Falcon. He cradles his dead son as the asshole picks up his prize.

Rick shoots him in the face. Can't suffer a guy like that to live. The asshole doesn't even hit the ground before someone else grabs the Falcon and runs.

Gunfire erupts from sporting goods. Shit. Time to upgrade. Rick goes to the office for his M16. He has always hoped it would never come to this, but he'd been a military man going back to the Boy Scouts. Damned straight he is always prepared.

Two groups of gun nuts stand off against each other by the hunting supplies. They only have handguns, but this has to stop. Rick knows talking will get him nowhere, so he switches to auto and mows them all down. Blood and guts splash all over the floor, but now there are no more gunshots.

He reloads. Just in case.

In lingerie Rick finds a young woman trampled to death. A middle-aged fat man drags her toward the dressing rooms while he rubs the lump at the front of his pants. Rick draws down on him.

"Wait! Don't shoot!"

"You gonna tell me you weren't going to rape her corpse?" Rick asks.

"Rape? No! She's dead. You gotta be alive to be raped. This won't bother her none."

Rick fires, turning the rapist's head to mush. Then he looks at the clock. Only one hour has passed? He thinks he's getting too old for this shit.

—

"Mr. Denning! We have a serious problem!"

Rick stops trying to put a customer in a headlock and buffaloes him with the gun barrel. The guy, who had been trying to shoplift a mannequin dressed in a bikini, goes down with a dent in his skull.

"What's going on, Jenny?"

"There's a guy in lawn and garden crucifying himself!"

"Well, so long as he's not hurting anyone else . . ."

"He's denouncing Black Friday! He's trying to talk our

customers out of buying stuff!"

"We can't have that, I guess. Is he using our nails?"

"Yes! And our hammer, too!"

"Tell him he's got to buy them first. If he doesn't, stab him in the ribs. I'm sure he'll appreciate that."

"Yes sir!" Jenny, a cute little college girl who has never worked retail on Black Friday before, looks excited as she runs away. Probably never stabbed a customer before. Adorable.

"No! Mine!"

Rick turns and sees two young boys playing tug of war with the new Playstation set. Both snarl at each other. One of them suddenly pushes. The other, taken off guard, stumbles back and falls.

"Mine," the winner says.

The loser draws a 9 mm pistol and shoots the winner in the face.

It's been a while since Rick has had to shoot a child. It never feels good. As he reaches for his sidearm a teenage girl rushes in to grab the Playstation. The boy turns his 9 mm on her. Just before he fires Rick shoots him in the head.

The girl grins. "Thanks!"

"No problem. Be careful on your way to checkout."

Rick patrols the aisles, and he sees an old man and an old lady dueling with their canes over a toilet seat lift. He hopes this one doesn't require him to shoot one of them.

"Stop. Do you realize how ridiculous you two look?"

The old man growls. "Go fuck yourself, junior. She's not winning this one."

"I divorced you thirty years ago, George! I'm never going to let you win!"

George nails her in the face, and her cracked dentures fall out. He laughs and cries with victory.

Rick shoots him in the leg. George screams and falls. "Just be lucky I like old people, George."

The woman happily claims her toilet seat lift.

Now it is noon. Time for a break. Rick hands off command to Laura Deen. He trusts her. She'd been a Marine for years before coming to the store. She can handle these mad bastards.

Rick takes a nap.

-

When Rick wakes up at five the store is on fire. Some customer lost the new iPhone to someone else and was so pissed that he covered the guy in lighter fluid and flicked a lit match at him. The entire Apple department burned to a crisp along with three customers and a sales associate. It was only Ed Barnes, a slacker who was probably going to be terminated anyway, but Rick takes the death of anyone working for him as an insult. Luckily Laura kneecapped the firebug and nearly has the fire under control.

"What do you want to do with this shit splat?" she asks.

"Send him to apologize to Ed," Rick says.

Laura doesn't hesitate; she blows away the customer executioner-style.

Back into the fray. A family of four is brawling with a young couple over the last 3D TV. Rick only has to shoot the father from the former group to stop the fight.

Later he finds Dina with a broken arm. She'd tried to stop a customer from killing another customer's Seeing Eye dog with a baseball bat. She succeeded but got hurt when the customer swung it at her. She shot him dead in return. Rick escorts her to the triage team in the warehouse. There are three sales associates and two managers with various injuries being tended to. Dina is the least wounded, so the nurses sit her down and give her an oxy for the pain.

Rick's walkie-talkie goes off. It's Tim in shoes. "I had to kill some guy's wife to resolve an issue, but her husband took it real personal. He's got me pinned down, and I need back up."

"On my way."

Rick takes the escalator up to the second floor. He sees Tim crouched between two shelves and the gunman trying to shoot him.

"Why do we do this every year?!" the gunman screams. "We risk our lives for *what*?"

Rick shoots, aiming for the head. The gunman moves at the last second and gets it in the chest instead. Puking blood, he manages to get one last sentence out: "Viva la revolution." He dies.

"Thanks, Rick. I owe you a beer after this."

"No problem."

Rick looks at the clock. It's six. Only six hours to go.

-

Rick stops by lawn and garden to see how Jenny is handling herself. She is covered with blood, but she's smiling because none of it is her own.

"I got to stop a fight with a lawnmower," she says. "It's interesting to be on this side of Black Friday for a change."

In hardware Rick checks in on Chin Xiang, the manager. Everything's fine. No one's been killed in four hours. "But I keep hearing something about some kind of revolution."

Rick thinks back to the gunman in shoes. "Keep your ears open. Let me know if you learn anything else."

—

The tide turns at nine. Most of the good stuff in the store has been sold. Many of the shelves are empty, and the fighting has petered off. Rick feels he no longer needs his M16, so he locks it up and carries only his sidearm.

This is a decision he now regrets.

An army marches down the escalator. The man in charge, a giant sinewy guy with an eye patch and a beret, holds aloft a spear with a head on it.

Poor Tim from shoes.

"Who's in charge here?" One Eye asks.

Rick steps forward. "I'm Rick Denning. Who are you?"

"You may call me White Friday. We in the resistance have grown sick of this ghastly holiday dedicated to unrelenting commerce and the wanton violence it causes. Other groups are attacking other megastores as we speak. You will concede this place to us. We will give you an hour to discuss the matter with your lieutenants. If you do not concede, or you wish to fight . . ."

His army all raised their weapons. Many are assault rifles. Some even have bayonets fixed.

"One hour, Denning. We meet back here. Don't make me come and look for you."

Shit. Rick gets on his walkie-talkie and calls all of his managers to the back office.

—

Rick is now strapped with his M16, two gun belts criss-crossed at his waist and a few hand grenades. He paces in front of his fully armed troops.

"In all my years at this job I've never seen anything like this. I'll be honest, I don't think our chances are good. We're well armed, but so are they. They have the numbers, too. But goddammit I refuse to give our store over to those anti-American heathens! We will stomp them into the dirt or die trying! Who's with me?!"

They shout and cheer. Rick's got a good feeling about this.

"They're expecting us at ten. We've got to hit them before that. Reports from the sales associates are telling us that they've broken up into groups so they can take over individual departments. That's good. They've divided themselves which will make them easier to conquer. Talk to your teams. Make sure they're armed and in position. When I give the word, attack."

More war cries. They filter out of the room, eager to rile their teams up. Now it's just Rick and Laura.

"Do you think we'll make it?" she asks.

"We got something those terrorists don't have." Rick looks her in the eye. "We've got grit."

—

Rick gives the signal at nine-forty, and the battle begins. Constant gunshots ring throughout the store, mixed with screams and victorious roars. He and Laura enter the fray side by side and begin to shoot the rebels to pieces.

The war lasts an hour, and it all seems like a blur to Rick. His muscle memory kicks in from when he was a SEAL, and he lets this murderous instinct take over. At one point he sees Jenny with a lawnmower strapped to her chest. She roars like a beast as the blade spins, bloody meat still stuck to it.

Not everyone on Rick's side is doing well, though. Lingerie falls early on to the enemy. So does electronics. Then juniors. Each report breaks Rick's heart a little more. Still they must fight. They must fight for the American way.

As ten-fifty approaches Rick finds himself face to face with White Friday. They draw down on each other, faces sweaty, but they don't fire. The rest of the world ceases to exist. They are the only two people alive.

White Friday grins. "We don't need guns for this, do we, old man?"

"You think you can whip me? I've taken shits tougher than you."

Both slowly lower their guns until they let them go on the floor. They circle each other, fists at the ready. White Friday fires a quick jab, just to test the waters, and Rick slaps it away with little force.

"Where'd you fight? Grenada?"

"Classified," Rick says.

White Friday lunges, catching Rick at the belly. They stumble back into an empty shelf. Rick brings both fists down in a double hammer on White Friday's back. The thump echoes, but White Friday hangs on, throwing awkward and weak punches into Rick's lower ribs. Rick grabs White Friday's belt and kicks with all his might, pulling back. White Friday loses his grip and flips over, freeing Rick. He jumps to his feet, but before he can stomp White Friday's head White Friday crawls back and pulls himself up.

"You've got some stone in you," White Friday says. He then draws his knife and starts weaving.

"Pussy," Rick says.

White Friday slashes, and Rick brings both fists up, hitting White Friday's knife hand from beneath. The blade flies up and behind White Friday. He looks to try to catch it.

Instead he catches Rick's fist with his mouth. White Friday reels back with a few broken teeth rattling around in his head. He spits them out in a bloody wad, but that's all he has time for. Rick batters him with a flurry of solid punches until White Friday's legs fold. Dazed, White Friday can't move.

Rick plucks a grenade from his vest and puts the tip into White Friday's empty eye socket. He stomps down on it until most of it is inside White Friday's head. Rick pulls the pin and walks away.

White Friday screams until his head blows up. Rick doesn't look back.

After this the fight goes out of the rebels. Some even jump ship and disappear into America. By midnight the last of them is swept up, and Rick gratefully locks the doors.

Laura's report is good. Very few store employees were killed in the battle. There is extensive damage to the building itself, but it's nothing that can't be repaired in-house. All told they sold an estimated $30.8 million worth of goods.

"We did a good job, sir."

"We did," Rick says. "Tell everyone they can go home. We'll clean up tomorrow."

"Goodnight, sir."

On the way out Rick runs into Jenny. She's covered in blood and is wearing a headband Rambo-style. A necklace of ears covers her cleavage. "That was a lot of fun, Mr. Denning! I can't wait for next year!"

He watches her walk out to her car, and he worries about the next generation. The things he's done . . . but he never *liked* it.

Black Friday, much like war, is Hell.

THE WORM

The stairs creaked, and Pete Jervis ground his teeth. A soft thump, followed by another, reverberated in his skull, and while the gentle sound shouldn't have been intrusive, to Pete it was almost as bad as a rusty chainsaw.

He forced his eyes to the papers in his hand. There were copies of several contracts on and around his desk, but most of them weren't worth the paper they were printed on. Only one showed promise, but he would have to go to great monetary risk before convincing a financer to invest. It was *step* a tough decision *step* and he really couldn't *step* have his thoughts *step* interrupted at such a vital—

"Petey?" The low tone of his mother's voice stabbed into his ears like a baby's cry in a theater, an unanswered phone ringing and a dentist's drill all combined into one. It took all his willpower not to yell, "What?!"

Instead he turned his gaze to her, eyebrows raised. From the look of things she was at least five sheets to the wind, and from the way she gripped the handrail, she was ready for seven to ten more.

"I know you're busy," she said, her face scrunched up. She wasn't even looking at him. "I was wondering . . . ."

"Yes?" His voice was sharp, and he didn't feel bad about it.

"Do you have anything? I'll pay for it."

He thought about the bottle of Ten High he'd hidden in a trashcan between his bookcase and a bunch of filing cabinets, where he knew she couldn't reach. He used to keep his whiskey under the bed, but he noticed some of it would occasionally go missing, and it didn't take a rocket scientist—or even a math teacher—to figure out what was happening.

"I don't have anything." Pete turned back to the contract.

"I'll give you ten bucks, just please give me something."

Pete could feel his jaw groan, and he tried to unclench his teeth. "I told you, I have nothing." He read the same sentence for a third time and hoped desperately that he could make it through the rest of the paragraph.

He did, but he didn't need ESP to sense his mother's unmoving presence at the foot of the stairs. *Maybe she's so drunk it's taking a moment for my words to sink in,* he thought.

New paragraph. Halfway through the first sentence, she said, "Could you go out and get me something. Please?"

Pete sighed through his nose. "Look, I have a lot of work in front of me. If I'm ever going to move out of this place again, I need to work, okay?"

Her nose started turning red, and she was squinting, sure signs that she was about to cry. When she inhaled, it sounded like she was snorting the dregs of a milkshake up through her nose. "I'd go myself, but I'm not well right now. I need something! Please! I'll give you money. You can keep the change. I just . . . I'm not okay right now."

There once was a time when he would have refused her request. Back then he'd been a much more optimistic man, but recent events had crushed his faith in the world. Back then he'd thought he could cure his mother, but now he knew better.

Now he knew that all he could do was get her off his back.

Pete held out his hand. "Fine. What do you want?"

She gave him a twenty. "Tequila. I need something that will put me down quick. And get the kind with the worm in it. I like the worm."

Pete grimaced. It was actually a butterfly larva, and the beverage was technically called mescal, but he couldn't understand how anyone could drink anything with an insect in it. A turd by any other name . . .

He pocketed the money. "I'll be back in a few."

———

As it turned out his gas tank was nearly empty, and he only had five bucks, which was only good for about one gallon in these godforsaken times. So his mother's change would probably help out, at least until the next unemployment check showed up.

It rankled him to live with his mom at the age of thirty-seven, especially since he'd been worth several million dollars only a few years ago. Like many businessmen, Pete had been swept up in the dot-com craze, but like many less-than-shrewd businessmen, he was too busy flashing green and getting laid to notice that the bottom was about to drop out. He'd lost everything, and now he spent his days writing business proposals and sending them out to any venture financer who would talk to him. It was a shame most of the contracts turned out to be stupid. The few he'd managed to get signed either went bust or he barely managed to break even.

The one that held promise was practical, but he needed to kick in fifty thousand dollars, of which he only had half. He could probably hunt and scavenge for the rest of it, pull in every favor he was owed, but if the venture failed he'd be back to square one, and probably working at a McDonald's to make ends meet.

He pulled into the lot and parked near the door. The sign above said WILLIAMS LIQUORS, but only the latter part was lit up. The rest was dirty, gray and cracked. A bullet hole in the window was taped over, and a dark stain by the door reeked of puke and piss. At least it was fall; the stink was worse in the summer.

Pete walked in and was greeted by the clerk. They didn't know each others' names, but they were familiar enough for the usual how's-it-going-nice-day-isn't-it-getting-lucky?-etc. He went to the tequila section. Most was of the usual non-worm variety, but on the bottom shelf he found a bottle of mescal. The worm looked different, however. Usually it was red or on occasion white (much to the purists' dismay), but this one was flesh colored. If not for the segments, he would have thought it was a pinkie finger.

It twitched.

If he hadn't been holding the bottle with both hands he would have dropped it, and his mom would never let him hear the end of it. When he peered in the bottle again the worm was still, and he decided the movement had been a hallucination. Too many hours writing too many contracts.

He considered getting a different bottle, but then he realized it didn't matter. His mother was only going to swill it down; she probably wouldn't even taste the booze, much less the worm. He rubbed the bags under his eyes and went to the counter.

After dumping eight-fifty-six into his gas tank, he went home and surrendered the bottle to his mother. She didn't thank him, she just shuffled off to her room like an old native wandering into the wilderness to die.

Pete retreated to his basement bedroom, to the contracts. He considered taking a snort of his Ten High, but he knew it would lead to nothing good at this late hour.

—

While her son went back to work below her, Mindy Jervis settled into her couch and began flipping through TV stations. Absently her fingers wrapped around the cap and tugged until the neck ring broke away. She placed the cold circle of glass to her lips and drank from the bottle. When she was younger she used to pour it into a cup, but she was a much different person now.

Now she realized the futility of extra receptacles. Besides, she'd only have to wash a cup later. With a bottle, all you had to do was throw it away.

She didn't grimace as the gasoline-like fluid went down her throat; she barely felt the burn. Though many images flew past her blank eyes, she stared *through* the TV screen as if it was a Mind's Eye puzzle.

The secrets of the universe were not divulged to her.

All she had were her thoughts and memories, no matter how hard she tried to smother them with drink.

It was on this very couch that Petey had been conceived. In those days it had been in her parents' house, but when she married Phil she took it with her. When her mom and dad were out at a party, Mindy had invited Phil over. One thing had led to another, which had in turn led to Petey.

She was really grateful for her son's existence. After him there had been two pregnancies, and both had been stillborn. They had also ruined her body inside and out. There would be no more children for her, and even if she weren't barren, her saggy frame would repel any suitors. If they could get past her flabby breasts and floppy folds of loose flesh, they would probably not get by the ring of stretch marks around her torso. If all else failed, she was certain *no one* would get past the c-section scar. Hell, *she* couldn't get past it. She couldn't stand the sight of her own body.

Neither could Phil. He cheated on her for a while, and then he divorced her. The alimony was nice, but Mindy would trade it all in an instant for the loving touch of a man, which she had not felt for about twenty years.

The bottle was already three-quarters empty. How long had it been since Petey had given it to her? Just a couple of hours?

She tried to slow down, but her need wouldn't let her. A half an hour later—not that she was aware of the passage of time—she was down to the last inch . . . and the worm.

Mindy had drunk her share of tequila in life, and she'd never seen a worm like this one. They were usually red or white, but this one looked flesh-colored.

In fact, it looked kind of like a withered penis.

She laughed, but it sounded like a gagging noise to her own ears. *Wishful thinking,* she thought, and she sucked down the rest of the bottle's contents.

The agave worm seemed thicker in her mouth than it had appeared in the bottle. It felt as stout as her tongue when she swallowed it. For a moment she thought it had lodged itself in her throat, and she would start choking at any moment, but then it eased down into her. All was good.

You did it the wrong way.

She started. Had Petey entered her room? She looked around to find that she was alone.

Besides, she thought, *it sounded more like Phil.* And he'd had a heart attack last year, which he hadn't survived. She shivered.

Get me out. You put me in wrong.

She felt the urge to stick a finger down her throat. There was no reason, she just wanted to do it.

No, she couldn't. The tequila would come up, and that would be a shameful waste.

As it turned out she needn't have concerned herself with this inner struggle; her head went down, and her throat closed, clogged with rushing vomit. Though she hadn't felt sick, it came spewing out of her like water from a faucet. It stank of pure alcohol, and there were no chunks.

Except one: the worm.

And it was spasming.

Pick me up and put me in right.

Her hand moved toward it, and there was nothing she could do to stop, even if she wanted to. Once it was in her grasp it calmed down, and when she lifted the bottom of her nightgown, it went rigid and began to hum.

—

She stepped so softly he didn't hear her until her hands were on his shoulders.

Pete had been pouring over the specifics of the most promising contract, trying to write in loopholes where he might escape financial culpability. His lawyer could probably come up with something, but Pete was an old hand at this, so he hoped to work a bit of fine print in on his own.

His eyelids were starting to droop. The hour was late, and he figured it was time for bed. He was naked to his boxers and very comfortable, so he knew that if he didn't get under the covers now, he'd pass out at his desk.

When her pale hands slipped over the bronze mountains of his shoulders, he thought he'd fallen off the fence between reality and dream. When she squeezed and began to massage, he looked up to see his mother's face hovering over him, her long hair nearly tickling the top of his head.

"What's up?" he asked.

"It's two in the morning," she said. "You work too hard. You should get in bed."

"Yeah, that's what I was thinking."

He stood, letting her hands fall away, and went to his bed, where he sat on the edge. Only then did he notice how red her eyes were, as if she'd been crying for hours. "You okay?"

His mom bit her lower lip. "Not really. I've been thinking about your . . . your brothers, but mostly about your dad. And how empty I feel without him."

Pete sighed. This was the last thing he needed right now. Drama before bed was never good. Still, his mother allowed him to live here, so . . . "Aw, Mom. You should go out and date, like I always tell you. You wouldn't be so lonely."

"I can't." Her voice cracked on the second word, making it

almost unintelligible, but she didn't bother to try again. "I'm ugly. No one would want me."

"Oh, come on. You're fine, Mom. You'll do okay."

She looked down at herself. "Do you think I'm ugly?"

Pete didn't think she was pretty. Good-looking, maybe, but definitely not ugly. "Trust me, Mom, you'd do fine."

Tears sprouted from the corners of her eyes, and she sat next to him on his bed, pressing her hot wet face into his shoulder. Pete put his arm around her and whispered, "Shh. It's okay. You'll be all right. Do you want me to carry you upstairs?"

She sniffed. "You couldn't lift me. I'm too fat."

"Don't be ridiculous. I can pick you up."

She laughed through a throat full of snot. "Just sit here for a moment. I just want to spend a minute with my son."

He rubbed her shoulder and clasped her tighter. "Take your time." *It's not like I'm going to miss work tomorrow, or anything.*

She kissed his cheek. "You're a good son."

He closed his eyes, hoping she wouldn't take much longer. His pillow cried out to him.

Suddenly there was a soft pressure on his lips, and his mouth was filled with tequila fumes. His eyes popped open, and he was looking at his mother's face, which was too close to his own.

"Whoa," he said, pulling away. "I think we need to get you upstairs."

Her face scrunched up, and she began sobbing. "Oh God, I'm sorry Petey! It's just that you look so much like your father, and I wish he was here. Please forgive me!" She placed both hands on his thigh and squeezed. By pure happenstance, one of her hands clasped down on the tip of his penis, pressing it against the inside of his leg. She didn't notice, but Pete did.

Though the horror of the situation had filled his belly with roiling, ulcerous fire, his traitorous body reacted.

He pried her hands away and crossed his legs. "It's okay. We'll just get you upstairs, right?"

Both of her hands enveloped one of his, holding it so tightly she trembled. "I'm really sorry. Please forgive me, Petey. Please!"

His captive hand was suddenly warm and sticky, as if he'd put it in a freshly baked cake. Looking down, he noticed his mom had shoved it under her nightgown. His knuckles were sinking into her flesh, and he gagged.

"Mom! Stop! You need to go to bed!"

"I want you inside me," she whispered. Her head leaned forward for another kiss.

Pete backed away. "Look, I've got to get to bed, and so do you. I'll—"

"No!"

If she started struggling, and from the way her body tensed, it looked like she was getting ready to, there was no way he was going to be able to carry her up to her room. *Maybe I should just leave her down here, and then go upstairs to sleep.*

"Here, lean back," he said.

She didn't object as he pushed on her shoulder until she was on her back on the mattress. Then, just as he grabbed a handful of his blankets to throw over her, she opened her legs wide, showing off a pad of pale flesh with a thin scrim of dark pubic hair. A river of scar tissue, not unlike the white worm found in most tequila bottles, cut through the scant foliage between her legs. She was open and sopping wet.

He threw the blanket over her. "Goodnight."

Much to his surprise, her eyes were already closed, and her even breath indicated that she was finally asleep. He was about to sigh, but he had to restrain himself out of fear that she'd hear and wake up.

Sickness crawled up his guts and tickled the back of his tongue. Something burned inside of him as he looked down at her slumbering form. Could this be the same mother who had raised him? The same mother who volunteered to be a den mother for his Cub Scout pack when he was a kid? The same mother who had put Band-Aids on his skinned knees when he was trying to learn how to ride a bike?

I want you inside me.

The voice in his head was his mother's, and he knew nothing would ever be the same again.

You want me as much as I want you.

Again, it was his mother, but when had she said that?

You're poking out of your shorts, Petey.

He was. It was like the air was tugging on it, aiming it at his mother, as a dowsing rod would pull toward water. Revulsion ate its way through his stomach as he pushed himself back in and to the side. Without another glance at his mother, he headed for the stairs.

Don't go! Think of the things we could do!

He ignored the voice until he threw himself down on the living room couch. Then it grew stronger.

Think of all the women you could have brought home, it said. *You couldn't because you didn't want them to know you lived with your mother. No less than seven women this year alone! Isn't that pathetic?*

It was. His erection throbbed between his thighs.

Forget about them. They may be beautiful, but I will never stab you in the back. I will never embarrass you. I will always satisfy you.

He thought about what was under her nightgown. She'd told him she'd needed a c-section to get him out, but he'd always envisioned a Frankensteinian nightmare whenever she mentioned it. It hadn't looked that bad, actually.

Come downstairs. I'm waiting.

When was the last time he'd been laid? Back when he was rich, of course. He couldn't bear to bring women home to his mother. He was thirty-seven, for Christ's sake! He should have been out on his own again! What was wrong with him?

His erection throbbed so hard it felt like the glans was going to pop off, and he was no longer thinking with his big head.

Pete stood and allowed himself to pop out of his boxers again as he went downstairs and lifted his mother's blanket.

———

The next day, neither mother nor son could meet each other's eyes. They pretended nothing had happened, and while both suffered from stomach flops and burning throats, neither said a word. They avoided each other, and only said hi. Their tones were terse and clipped.

Months later, Mindy Jervis—who was once barren—was pregnant, and no matter how badly she wanted an abortion, all three million of her children did not let her get one.

DREAM QUEST FOR DOPE

"Dude! Why didn't you kill yourself tonight? I paid, like, ten bucks for this ticket. What the fuck?"

GG Allin didn't even break stride. Barely aware of the beer bottle in his hand, he brought it up and smashed it upside the guy's head. Long hair flung up in a sweaty tangle, and the guy fell on his back, rolling like a turtle. Not that GG noticed. He strode with purpose away from the ugly scene, rage boiling in his head. The cocksuckers didn't even let him finish his show. Fuckers.

The guy, still on the ground, started giggling. "Dude! GG Allin just broke a fucking bottle over my head! That rules!"

Dressed only in a skirt and combat boots, body soiled with his own feces, GG somehow managed to hail another cab, and this time the driver didn't freak out. GG slumped into the back seat and closed his eyes, trying to banish the clusterfuck of a show from his mind. He thought about the dope the promoter had scored for him. Ten lovely bags. That should be enough to do the trick.

When he got back to St. Mark's, he went up to his room and went for his works. Cooked. Shot. And let chemical bliss take him down from a day's worth of deli coke and booze. He let the comforting cloud fill his head and lungs like cotton candy, and it felt so wonderful he had to remind himself to breathe. He rested with a soiled arm over his equally soiled face and rode the wave of dopamine.

But it wore off too fast. Cheap shit. Did GG really expect something more from the asshole at the Gas Station? You couldn't trust people anymore, could you?

He could only trust in one thing, and he stumbled around the

140

room, seeking out his private stash. There, taped under the bottom of one of the dresser's drawers, he found a rolled-up baggie, much bigger than any one of the ones the promoter had given him. Unfortunately the contents left much to be desired. There was so little he might as well not even bother.

But . . . well, maybe on top of the cheap shit, it would do the job. It would be just enough to get him into that headspace to get more.

Just as he prepared to cook again, Johnny Puke and the girls showed up. From there, it was a whirlwind of shit. Just a few more bumps and some whiskey to even it all out, and the next thing he knew they were at Johnny's place, snorting more cheap-shit dope. GG hated putting heroin up his nose, but Johnny hated needles. Distantly he hoped he'd thought to pack up his works before leaving St. Mark's.

Quickly, he checked the pockets of his jean jacket. Thank fuck. It was there. He barely heard himself telling the others he had to take a shit, and soon he perched on the toilet in the bathroom, preparing the last batch. It took him a moment to find a good vein. So many had collapsed of late he started looking at the ones in his feet. Not yet, though. This shot deserved a special place.

A spaghetti noodle of a blue vein rose ever so slightly from the back of his hand, and he made quick work of it. As he depressed the plunger, he whispered the words he'd learned from so long ago, words that would make no sense to anyone else save for the select few who pursued forbidden knowledge. Not even he knew what they meant, but he knew that they would get him the most potent dope he'd ever had and lots of it.

This shit got him in a place the garbage couldn't reach. It went deep, scratching an itch in his bones. The world became hazy, and he stashed his works, knowing it would be his last chance to do so before the super dope hit him full force.

In a haze, he staggered out of the bathroom and donned his ragged jean jacket. Johnny jabbered about some kind of European tour, but with no music. Just words. Fuck that. GG wanted to scare the shit out of people, and a lecture just wouldn't cut it.

Numbness burned slightly throughout his limbs, and he thought he'd close his eyes for a minute. He got down on the floor and stared at the ceiling, waiting for the rush, the rush that no other dope ever had for him.

His eyelids fell, and while his companions thought he had just passed out, GG found himself hurtling through the cosmos. He didn't know how many stars he'd passed, and he never questioned why he didn't need an astronaut suit while in space, but before long he flew through mist and into the Dreamlands.

When he opened his eyes, he didn't see the desert. Nor did he see the mountains and the sun. Instead he found himself in a dank cemetery full of broken stones and rotting trees. Tombs yawned open and hoary graves all sported deep holes, their contents long since raided.

"What the fuck?" GG said. "This ain't Leng."

"You're off by several thousand miles."

GG whirled on the strange voice, and he found himself confronted with a grungy, dog-faced man with long, yellowed fingernails and jagged teeth. He stank of the grave, and when he breathed, the odor of rotten meat wafted over. GG barely noticed through the screen of his own filthy stink, and that alone impressed him.

"Who the fuck are you?" he asked.

"In days of old, I was a painter by the name of Pickman," the creature said. "Now I'm but a lowly ghoul. The worm flails, you know."

GG didn't know, and he didn't care. "Painter? What kind of shit did you do?"

"Ghastly stuff, old boy. Things that turned the stomachs of the high and mighty."

"I can dig that. I do some pretty fucked up art. You should see 'Blood, Shit & Cum.'"

Pickman sneered. "Sounds . . . wonderful."

GG grabbed a handful of the ghoul's ratty shirt and yanked him close. Then, without ceremony, he head-butted Pickman, opening a gash up on the painter's forehead. Pickman yelped and staggered back, holding his face.

"Why?"

"You talk shit, you get hit. Now tell me how to get to Leng."

Pickman's lower lip quivered. "No. You struck me. You can find help elsewhere."

GG stepped forward, reaching out, and Pickman backed away,

lightning fast. He jumped and landed on top of a gravestone. Perched like a raven, he didn't even sway. This didn't deter GG, who rushed the ghoul, face screwed up in a snarl. Again, Pickman leaped away, this time into the cradle of a creaky tree bough above.

"Stop," he said. "You can't catch me."

GG kicked the tree, his combat boots hitting solidly. The tree gave out a shriek, and the deadwood snapped in two, sending Pickman sprawled out on the loam. Before the ghoul could scrabble to his feet, GG grabbed a handful of his hair and yanked his head back.

"No! Stop! I'll help you! Just don't hit me!"

GG released Pickman's hair but gave him a solid kick to the ass, sending the ghoul rolling away. Moaning, Pickman managed to stand up, rubbing at his backside. "Why do you want to go to Leng? There is nothing for mortals there."

"My dealer lives there," GG said. "He's got the best shit I've ever had, and I need my fix."

"Ah." Understanding washed over Pickman's face, and he smiled. "*That* I can understand. It's very powerful and dangerous, but it is also very good. You are a long way from Leng. It would take you weeks, and while you're in the Dreamlands, it would still be too arduous a journey. There are so many things that can go wrong. Gods, monsters, death in all shapes and sizes."

"I don't give a fuck."

"By the time you got there, you wouldn't need Leng's opiates. You will have kicked the habit."

"Then think of a way to get me there quicker." GG's hands balled up into fists without him realizing it.

Pickman noticed right away. Message received. "I could help you, but I would want something in return. I've been seeking out a friend, Randolph Carter, from days gone by. The last I heard, he was in an alien's body. I would like—"

"No." GG didn't need to say another word.

"But . . ." Pickman saw the resolve in GG's face and knew he wouldn't be able to barter with this man. The need for Leng's pleasures was too strong in his soul. "Fine. You'll need a Nightgaunt. That will make the journey much shorter. You'd be in Leng within the hour."

"Good. Go get me one."

It had been a while since Pickman had summoned and bound a creature, and he didn't know if he could do it. Still, he understood the Dreamlands very well, and he knew he had a lot of power here. He had to try it. Besides, he wanted to get rid of GG. The sooner this lunatic was gone, the sooner Pickman could get back to his life of seclusion.

GG sat on a grave and watched Pickman go to work. He created a circle of stones and lit some candles. He said some mumbo jumbo bullshit, like the kind of thing that brought GG here in the first place. He still couldn't figure out how that had gone wrong. It never had before. How fucked up had he been when he tried?

Not fucked up enough. He got bored and started throwing rocks at tree trunks. More often than not, his arm was strong enough to knock the fuckers over. It gave him an idea for a song, but he didn't have anything to write on. He thought about writing in his own shit on a gravestone, but he wouldn't be able to take it with him.

The sky darkened, and GG looked up to see a gangly monster with giant talons and wings gliding down from the heavens. It looked cool as all shit. The fact that it didn't have a face thrilled him even more. He wondered what those assholes back in the real world would think if he confronted them with one of these. He wished he could bring it back with him.

The Nightgaunt softly landed in front of Pickman and knelt before him, offering its back. Pickman spoke to it, pointing at GG. It turned its faceless head toward him and waited.

"It's all yours," Pickman said. "It knows exactly where to bring you. Just climb on its back, and you're ready to go."

GG hopped up on the creature's back, gripping its leathery flesh with his balled-up fists. He thought he could probably stab this fucker, and the blade would break.

"Good luck," Pickman said.

"Hold it," GG said. "Where do you think you're going?"

"I summoned the Nightgaunt for you. My job here is done."

"Climb up behind me. You're coming with me."

Pickman grimaced. "Why?"

"Because you're a useful fucker. I want you with me if I need something."

Pickman sighed, resigned to his fate. Just to avoid another altercation—his head still stung from being butted earlier—he climbed up on the Nightgaunt and held on tight to GG's waist.

"Get your hands off me," GG said.

He did not have to ask twice. Pickman clutched at the Nightgaunt's back, tightening his legs around it, hoping that would be enough.

"How do you get this thing to go?"

Pickman uttered one word in ancient Plutonian, hoping that the velocity of take-off would be enough to send GG off into the ether, never to return. The Nightgaunt soared into the sky at a frightening speed, but GG held on so tightly the beast's back creaked.

Cold wind cut through to GG's bones, and tears welled up in his eyes. He kept blinking, trying to keep them warm, but it only produced more moisture, forcing it out into streams that cut through some of the shit still smeared on his face. His teeth ground together as he bunched his muscles up to tighten his grip. Behind him, Pickman whined. It was hard to hear with the rush of air all around them, but it disgusted GG. He wondered how Pickman would cope with one of his concerts. Pussy.

Land flashed below them, changing from dank forest to farmland to village and back again. GG marveled at how fast the Nightgaunt could go. Fuck cars and trains and shit. If he could travel by Nightgaunt in the real world, he'd do it every time. He lifted a fist defiantly into the air and loosed a primal howl, most of it lost to the wind. *This* was rock and roll. Perfect for the one true king.

Woods gave away to mountains, and they soon gave away to desert. Almost there.

"I hope you know where you're going," Pickman said.

GG didn't, but he knew he'd figure it out when he saw something familiar. They soared over the endless sand, dotted with the occasional sun-bleached skeleton. When he saw the plains ahead, he knew he'd reached Leng in record time. It had felt only like a half an hour. Not bad.

The Nightgaunt lowered until it skimmed over the surface of the world. Domiciles were holes in the ground, and they were everywhere. People loitered and roamed, going about their daily business, but they weren't really people. Those in Leng looked like the satyrs of ancient Greece: naked to the waist and covered with fur from there on down. Hooves instead of feet. Horns crowning their heads. Giant cocks swaying between their legs. And the most frightening grins known to humanity, full of a carnivore's sharp, pointy teeth.

GG recognized this village, and he steered the Nightgaunt until they reached his dealer's place, at which point the beast slowed to a hover and flapped its way to the ground.

Pickman fell off, his hands bunched into tight fists. Grimacing, he tried to open his fingers, but they were too stiff, and his muscles ached from holding onto the Nightgaunt like he had. He didn't think he could stand.

GG stepped down with a bit more dignity. He flexed his hands to get some of the creakiness out of them and glanced at Pickman's pathetic form. GG shook his head and approached his dealer's home. He positioned himself over the hole and put both hands around his mouth in a funnel shape. "Yo! You home?"

"I'm coming!"

GG stepped back and waited, listening to the scrabbling sound of someone ascending the ladder. Soon, a Leng man poked his horned head out of the hole and smiled. "GG! I've been expecting you."

"Then you know what I need, Yith Wagge," GG said.

"You liked the batch I gave you, then?"

"Fucking loved it. I need more. How much?"

Yith climbed the rest of the way out, showing himself to be shorter than average. He squinted up into GG's eyes with an odd expression on his face. GG thought it might be regret. That son of a bitch better not hold out on him. GG was in a head-butting mood.

"About that," Yith said.

"You better have my shit."

Yith's grin turned into a pained smile. "You know how I've been expecting you?" He didn't wait for GG to respond: "It's because you've, um, been summoned here."

"What the fuck does that mean?"

Pickman felt an odd sensation in his stomach, kind of like whenever he thought about Carter's dream quest so long ago. While GG was distracted, Pickman inched toward the Nightgaunt.

"It means that someone wanted you here," Yith said. "We have a visitor, and he'd like to talk with you."

A gust of wind blew out of the hole, and a figured levitated stiffly out, setting himself down gently next to GG. The stranger had dark skin, and he wore robes and gold as a pharaoh of Egypt would, topped off with a regal turban. A long goatee grew out from his chin like a handle, and his dark eyes gazed majestically out from thick eyeliner.

"Who the fuck is this?" GG asked. "You a cop?"

"You're late," the stranger said, "but that's fine. I caused your trajectory to vary slightly, just to give us enough time."

GG turned back to Yith. "What the fuck's going on? Where's my dope?"

Yith shrugged. "It's not my show. Sorry, man. I really am."

GG turned back to the stranger, about a hair's length away from trashing him from foot to turban. Yet when he looked into the stranger's eyes, he felt odd. Not necessarily high, but distant. The rushing blood in his veins slowed, and he felt himself falling under the stranger's sway.

"We've been waiting for a remarkable man like you for centuries," the stranger said. "Your dedication to danger is second to none. You live your life without lies, suffering no one. There haven't been many like you throughout history. I'd wager you're a one of a kind."

"You gonna' suck my dick now?" GG asked. His words slurred, as if some force wanted him sedated, but nothing could stop these words from escaping him.

"You are seen by your fellow man as utterly disgusting," the stranger continued. "A pariah on nearly all fronts, except for your loyal followers, the ones who love it when you strike them and fling feces at them. In short, you're a disgrace to society, which makes you the perfect gate."

"For what?" GG asked. This surprised him. He didn't give a fuck, but something inside him wanted to find out more about the stranger's plans for him. He tried to draw back his fist for a punch, but his arm remained limp at his side.

The stranger produced a crystal ball from his robes and held it aloft. "Look, GG Allin. Back to the waking world."

An image materialized in the crystal, and it was Johnny and the girls. And there was GG himself on the floor in the background, passed out. A Polaroid camera came out, and Johnny posed with GG, grinning drunkenly.

"Your friends don't know it yet," the stranger said, "but you're dying. Soon, they will retire for the evening, and when they wake, they'll find your corpse."

"I'm not dying," GG said. "I'm right here."

"Your dream self is right here, but I assure you, your physical body is dying. Too much heroin, as I'm sure you can surmise. Right now, you're suffering from respiratory failure."

Right away GG knew the stranger was telling the truth. It made sense after a life of insanity, and he didn't even feel bad about it. He only regretted not being able to kill himself on stage. That would have been awesome.

"You're not in your body," the stranger said. "When you die, you'll be stuck here. Your reanimated corpse will be our gateway to the waking world. My kind will pour through and completely destroy humanity. They don't deserve their planet, anyway. We're clearing the way for a new race."

"You mean, I'm going to cause the end of the world?"

"The end of the human race," the stranger said.

GG smiled. That was even better than onstage suicide. "Cool."

The stranger glanced sidelong at him. "This doesn't bother you?"

"No." GG shook his head faintly, almost sadly. "Those assholes have become complacent. In the tooth and claw world, they wouldn't survive. It's time to remind them of that, don't you think?"

This time the stranger laughed so hard he almost dropped his crystal ball. Out of breath, he put it back into his robe. "You truly are a remarkable man, GG Allin."

"Nah. Hank Williams, that dude was remarkable."

"I'm familiar with him. He made the journey to the Dreamlands, as well. I'm sure if you wander long enough you'll find him. Do you want to watch the end of your kind?"

"I don't give a fuck. I just want my dope."

Yith cleared his throat and kneaded his hands together. "There's, um, no dope. That other batch was made specifically to lure you here. It would take years to make more."

GG stared at him. "There's. No. Dope."

Yith grinned sheepishly, producing a tiny baggie with some of the super dope in it. "This is all I have left. It's not even worth using. Might as well just get some black tar."

The stranger said, "We can always get you something else. We have dreamers bringing new drugs in every day. It's only a matter of time bef—"

GG shot forward like a dart and brought his forehead down on the bridge of the stranger's nose. A sharp crack resonated down the plain, and the stranger gargled as blood filled his throat. His nose looked cracked in half, and the bottom of his face shone red in the sun.

"You dare?!" the stranger said through crimson slobber. "You dare head-butt Nyarlathotep, messenger of the Outer Gods?!"

GG jabbed his foot out and connected with Nyarlathotep's kneecap, snapping it and bending the leg backward. The Outer God fell to his hind, snarling. Then, just as GG stepped forward to deal another blow, Nyarlathotep's face split down the center, and a gigantic tentacle emerged. His shape grew, and his skin split. His shoes exploded, showing not feet but hooves.

Pickman almost made it. When GG started beating the stranger, Pickman had managed to reach the Nightgaunt and was about to jump on its back and make his escape. Then he saw Nyarlathotep bursting through the skin of the man, showing off one of his other forms.

Panic rushed through Pickman's body, and he felt like he'd been touched by lightning. He wanted nothing more than to get away from this horrible mess. But he couldn't let Nyarlathotep be loosed in Leng. Somehow, he had to be dismissed.

Once upon a time, Randolph Carter had given him a stone with an odd design on it. He'd told Pickman that it would ward off even the toughest of gods, should he ever need it. Now, he fished through his ratty pockets, seeking it out. He weeded through a few spare bones and some lint before he finally found it at the very bottom.

GG watched as Nyarlathotep shed the final vestige of his human form. It didn't have much effect on him, though. He'd seen a lot of crazy shit in the Dreamlands, and this was just one more thing. He wondered if he could jump up high enough to head-butt Nyarlathotep now.

In that moment, Pickman lunged between the two of them, holding aloft the elder sign. "Back, Nyarlathotep! Get you gone!"

Nyarlathotep shrank back from Pickman like a vampire from a cross. Then Pickman started babbling in another language. GG thought it sounded like nonsense, but it had too much cadence to be anything else but actual speech.

Nyarlathotep turned his red, blazing three-lobed eyes to GG. "It's too late. As soon as you die, the human race will end, and we'll have our way with your miserable planet."

GG didn't care about humanity. How could anyone take the fat bodies seriously? He did care that this piece of shit, who didn't even have the super dope from Leng, was going to get his way. Fuck that. He stepped toward the Nightgaunt, but he then saw Yith, cowering away from them. He still clutched the baggie.

Yith noticed GG staring at him and gauged the distance between himself and the hole in the ground where he lived. It did not look good to him.

He didn't have to think about it much longer. GG threw a haymaker into Yith's jaw, knocking the Leng man back and into unconsciousness long before his head hit the ground. Then GG swiped the baggie and jammed it into his pocket. Only then did he turn back to the Nightgaunt. He stepped around Pickman.

"What are you doing?" the ghoul asked.

GG ignored him as he got on the beast's back and thought about how Pickman had gotten this thing going before. He thought he remembered, but he would probably butcher it. He sighed and leaned toward its ear. Gently, he whispered the Plutonian word, and the Nightgaunt took off immediately.

Land shrank away from him as they soared into the sky. Clouds swirled as if they were going down a drain, and GG felt his stomach drop down to his feet. They flew higher and higher, and he could hear his ears popping. He hazarded a look down and saw that even Nyarlathotep from this height seemed like a doll on a play set.

GG let go of the Nightgaunt and felt himself fall away from the beast. He dropped like a stone, but he didn't like that he was falling back first. He managed to turn himself around so he could watch the ground rush up at him. He never understood those pussies who wanted to be knocked out for surgery. He always wanted to be awake so he could watch what they were doing to him.

The figures below became larger and larger as he came closer and closer to the ground. Nyarlathotep tried to get around Pickman and his elder sign, but the ghoul remained steadfast, keeping the Outer God at bay.

"No!" Nyarlathotep roared.

GG grinned, and his lips flapped about his face in the wind. Then, just before he struck the ground, he gave the god the middle finger.

He hit the sand so hard he could see every grain of it in stark clarity, and then he passed through it into the cosmos. Stars and planets whirled around him as he blasted through galaxies like a rocket. He pinwheeled through existence, leaving a vapor trail behind him as he came closer to the Milky Way. Closer to the Oort Cloud. Through the Kuiper Belt and past the gas giants. Plowing through the asteroid belt and Mars. And there!

Earth.

His trajectory slowed until he floated through the atmosphere and down. Through the roof of Johnny's apartment. Into the living room. Hovering above his physical body. He eased into the cradle of his flesh, and he felt almost grateful to be home, even though he could sense his impending death.

GG struggled for consciousness, desperate to see if he'd managed to bring the super dope back with him, but his body was too far gone. Fuck.

Too bad the human race didn't die, though. That would have been a hell of a thing to have to explain at the pearly gates. Not that GG believed any of that shit, not after everything his father had put him through. But still.

It could have been a kick ass song.

—

The next day, after they'd found GG's body, his friends tried to hide all their drugs before calling the cops. Johnny Puke patted down GG's jacket, just to make sure, and he found a small bag. There was hardly anything in it, but it looked different. Sparkly. Potent, almost like magic.

He stashed it away. For later. He couldn't wait to try out the shit that killed GG Allin.

I AM THE END

Cthulhu lives in my ass. I can feel him moving there. Every slither. Whisper. Grunt. He roils and schemes in my guts.

I found him when I had to take a momentous shit after an evening recovering from booze and Taco Bell. I sprayed that porcelain bowl for nearly an hour, and when I wiped with a mummy's hand of toilet paper, I felt *it*.

A skinny strand dangled from my balloon knot. It could have been a tape worm, but I knew better.

Tentacle.

What else could it be?

I pulled on it, trying to free it from the tyranny of my bowels, but it shot back inside me like a spaghetti noodle. I stuck my fingers into my anus, hoping to feel the bugger out, but all I got for my troubles was a shit-greased hand and blood.

Fucking hemorrhoids. They get in the way of everything.

I called my parents for advice, but they've never liked me, not since they found me fucking raccoon road kill in the backyard by the clapboard shed where the spiders lived. Hey, I was a kid, only twenty-three. Anyway, my father refused to talk to me, and Mom thought I was joking even when I offered to show her. I told her I'd come over, and she said not to because the restraining order said I couldn't. I said I was her son, and she couldn't turn me away. My father talked then. Mostly yelled. Said he'd call the cops.

Parents. They say they're there for you but never are.

I don't have any friends, so I asked my prostitute to come over and have a look up my ass. Hey, I don't pay for sex. Sex is free everywhere. I pay her to leave when I'm done with her. I learned that on TV.

I gave her a flashlight and spread my cheeks and asked her to see if she noticed anything different. She thought it was a game, so she stuck her hand inside me to the wrist and wiggled her fingers around.

Just the way I usually liked it, but I wasn't in the mood for jokes, and I was about to yell at her to be serious when something moved through my colon and grabbed her. At least I think it did, because I couldn't see that far behind me, and anyway she yelped about how something had her wrist, and she yelled something about Jesus Christ.

"No!" I shouted. "Not him! Cthulhu! You're looking for Cthulhu!"

But she didn't say anything because a giant tentacle shot out of my ass and wrapped around her head so hard her brain burst out the top of her head like pus from a popped pimple. She farted pretty badly and pissed herself and flailed around for a bit before Cthulhu dragged her into me, which sounds very painful, but it wasn't because I'd been shoving things in there since I was three, which is why I was flexible enough to hide a god in my poo-gun in the first place.

Too bad. I wanted to fuck that prostitute, but this way I saved money, I guess.

Well, I still had a part of her, so I stuck my dick in her medulla oblongata for a while, but it just didn't feel the same, so I yelled and threw it against the wall where it made a loud splatter sound. I ranted and raved at Cthulhu for a while because now I had blue balls and my collection of leper porn couldn't get me off anymore. Harry—he's my neighbor and an alien and a spy—hammered on the wall and told me to shut the fuck up. Normally he scares me because he listens to my thoughts by putting his head in his microwave, and he writes them down in code and sends them off to his home world because they need me as a stud to repopulate their planet, but I won't do it because they don't have vaginas and they talk too much about *Seinfeld* which is the worst show ever, but they love it so much and the last episode hasn't reached them yet, so I want to spoil it for them, but I can't bring myself to watch it just for a satisfying fuck-you.

But now I have a Great Old One in my digestive tract, so I'm going to go over to his place someday and ask to borrow butter or sugar or whatever the fuck neighbors borrow from each other, and I'm going to suck Harry into my asshole. "Cthulhu saves, in case he gets hungry later."

I learned that from a bumper sticker.

The day after my butt ate a whore, I called in to the factory where I shoveled shit for a living and told them I didn't feel well, so I wouldn't be in for a while. They told me to see a doctor, but I kind of liked having Cthulhu inside me and besides, I don't have insurance. You can't trust the system. They take pictures of your little penis and send them around to their colleagues and laugh at your tiny manhood. You think that stethoscope listens to your heartbeat? Wake up! That's how they get you.

Anyway, I hung up on my boss and drank a fifth of tequila because I thought Cthulhu might want to get fucked the fuck up, and instead I got hammered and puked up a lot of gas station hot dogs and blood. I was hungry, so I ate the hot dogs again and tried to put my blood back where it belonged, but blood never listens, not like the dog at the Victrola, the god in my guts.

I told Cthulhu everything, like the time I jerked off in a confessional, or the time I lost a finger in a lawnmower when I shoved a baby bunny into the blades, and he laughed because he likes my stories, especially the one when I dick slapped my sister so hard her eye popped out.

But not even that one cheered him up after the tequila incident, so I thought he had to be upset with me. How do you make a god happy? Human sacrifice, of course.

At first I wanted to sacrifice Harry, but that didn't make sense because if you're going to sacrifice someone, it needs to be someone you love. If it's someone you hate, you're not giving up anything.

I don't have friends.

But I do like Cliff on *Cheers*, and I would miss him a lot of I had to feed him to the god in my anus, so I tried to get a hold of John Ratzenberger by pretending to be a producer, but his manager saw through my ruse and told me to fuck off.

Who else did I like? The guy at the liquor store, but I didn't want to shit where I ate, as the saying goes, so that left the girl at 7-Eleven with the braces, the guy who always smiles at me and works the late night window at Wendy's, and the guy with the bad dentures at the Shell station on my way to work.

I picked the Shell guy because it would be funny to see a

toothless man be eaten, so the next graveyard shift he worked, I went in for some Slim Jims and a hot dog, just like always. He never suspected a thing—he even made small talk as I made my selections—and then I hit him with a sock full of quarters right on the head. Floored him with ease.

I saw no one else at the pumps, so I figured it would be best to get this over with. I yanked down my pants and squatted behind the counter, pulling my cheeks apart so Cthulhu could see my gift. I felt something slither out, and it made crunching and slurping and smacking sounds, but then it zipped back inside me. When I turned around the sacrifice's head was gone, but why didn't my guest want the rest of him?

Unless he didn't like my offering.

What if Cthulhu is a picky eater?

Now I sit in my living room eating nachos I stole from Shell and drinking Canadian whiskey and watching a bukkake film festival, wondering how I can make it up to the god in my lower intestines. I have no one to give him because I don't love anybody, not even myself, so I can't offer up my own body, and besides, how would he eat me? If he eats my ass, then he eats himself, and that's just not possible.

After days of pondering it, I wonder if I can fit the whole world in my ass.

One way to find out.

I strip off my boxers, which are musky because I've been wearing them for so long, and it's like peeling the cellophane off a Kraft single and smells the same, and I can feel the seat rip off my ass, and it sounds like unrolling a swatch of duct tape, and I go naked outside. I see Harry staring at me as he gets in his car, and I wave bye to him because he's going to die soon—everyone's about to die—but he ignores me and starts talking on his cell phone because he's SO IMPORTANT.

I sit down in the grass and spread my asshole as far as I can.

Something presses against the inside of my anus, and I feel my turd-cutter stretch.

Cthulhu takes a bite out of the planet, and he goes back for seconds. Thirds. Fourths, and everyone is screaming and the earth is collapsing and everyone is dying and I am smiling.

Cthulhu is, too.

I am the end.

DIAL 9 FOR APOCALYPSE

Brad Johnson spiked his remote control like a football. It didn't shatter, but something inside it cracked and rattled. He'd reset his modem and gone through the setup process, and he *still* had no cable connection. He paid a ton a month for service, and every Sunday—right when the game was about to begin—it dropped.

He stomped to his bedroom/home office and went through his files until he found his last cable bill. He flipped through the thick bundle of tri-folded paper. Where the hell was the customer service number? You'd think it would be on the first page. He saw a website he could go to so he could chat with a rep, but no. For all he knew they were bots. He wanted a real person, preferably with an American accent. It was the weekend, though, so he didn't have high hopes.

There! Finally! Buried in a bunch of fine print! The customer service line. He put his finger on it—so he wouldn't lose it—and marched to the living room, to his cell phone.

Fury thrummed through him, and his hand shook. He forced himself to calm down before dialing out. The phone uttered a half-ring, and an automated system answered. Of course.

"Welcome to Cable Now, the finest in entertainment viewing. Please listen carefully as our menu options have changed."

Why do they *always* say that?

"If you're calling to upgrade your service, press one."

As if.

"To pay your bill, press two or go online to myservicecablenow.com/paymybill. To set up a payment—"

Oh for Christ's sake!

"—press three or go online—"

Stop!

"—to myservicecablenow.com/setupapayment. To hear your statement—"

He pressed zero.

"—press four. If you are a new customer, press five."

Brad reconsidered using the online chat.

"For anything else, press six."

He pressed six.

"For help paying your bill, press one."

Come on!

"If you are calling about your business account, press two."

Brad slumped into his easy chair. Anger dripped off him like sweat, and he felt tired.

"If you are calling about your personal account, press three."

He pressed three.

"If you are calling about your internet connection, press one. If you're calling about your cable, press two."

He pressed two.

"If your cable is down, press one."

He pressed one, feeling a bit hopeful this time.

"If you think you're special, press one."

What? No. He'd probably heard it wrong.

"If you think the customer is always right, press two."

What the fuck?

"If you accept that the customer is almost always wrong, press three. If you made this call in error, press four, or simply hang up your phone."

Brad stared at his cell, dumbstruck. What could he do? Well, he *did* believe the customer is always right, so he pressed two.

"To go fuck yourself, press one. To take a long walk off a short pier, press two. To commit suicide, press three, or simply shoot yourself in the head."

His anger burned more than ever. He'd play along, all right. He'll get a rep on the line and give them hell. He pressed one.

"On a scale of one to nine, one being the lowest and nine being the highest, how pissed off are you? Please select the number on your touchtone phone."

Brad pressed 9.

"Would you like to kill someone? Press one for yes, two for no."

Apoplectic, thinking of whoever came up with this IVR, he jammed his finger down on one.

"To kill your parents, press one. Other family, press two. Friends, press three. Strangers, press four. Celebrities, press five. My creators, press six. Yourself, press—"

Brad pressed six.

"If you thought that would work, press one. If you're just a dumb ass, press two. If you selected this in error, go home and fuck your mother."

Brad growled, and he didn't even realize it. He pressed one.

"What are you still doing here? I thought I told you to go fuck your mother."

Was that a *Goodfellas* reference?

"To end this call, please press one. To end this world, press two." No other options.

"Fuck! You!" Brad screamed. He jabbed down on two.

"Thank you for ending the world. Would you like to take an optional survey to let us know what you think of our service? If so, please press one."

Oh, someone was going to get an earful. He stabbed the one on his phone.

"Just kidding, loser. Kiss your ass goodbye. Thank you for using Cable Now. Fuck you." And it hung up.

"Fuck me? Fuck you!" He dialed them back, ready to cancel his service, but all he got was a busy tone.

Something bright flashed out his window, and the world shook. Looking out in the distance, he saw a mushroom cloud rising. A whistling sound came from above, and he looked up just in time to see a nuclear warhead falling toward him. It detonated in mid-air, but that was all he saw. He was too dead to see his own mushroom cloud.

BUTT CLUB

"Have you figured out a rating system for them yet?"

Ed turned to see a stranger walking next to him. This was his fourth week of commuting to the city, and despite the vast crowds he'd started recognizing quite a few regulars along his route. He'd never seen this guy before, though.

He looked normal. Short blond hair, skinny frame. Black-rimmed glasses like Buddy Holly. He looked like a hundred others around him, but for some reason he'd chosen to speak to Ed.

"Excuse me? Are you talking to me?"

"Yep. And you know exactly what I mean. You won't want to admit it at first, but you *do*. I've been watching you a long time. I don't know your name, but I know you're just like me."

Ed shook his head. "I really don't know what you're talking about."

The stranger smiled, and his face suddenly seemed savage. "You're looking at *butts*."

Ed felt a slight chill. He would never talk about it to anyone, especially in today's politically correct world, but he really enjoyed watching women's butts while walking from the train to the office and back. It was a miserably hot route, and it helped him survive. It helped keep him sane. He tried not to be a creep about it. It didn't even turn him on. Yet some women had butts that looked like works of art.

But how did this stranger know?

"I don't blame you. Summer in the city is a wonderful time. Ladies wearing next to nothing. Tight jeans, shorts, high skirts. There are a lot of beautiful butts on display. What heterosexual man wouldn't look? But you. You're special. And you don't get

159

caught. Takes one to know one, am I right?"

Ed didn't know what to say, so he said nothing.

"There's more like us. We formed a group. Butt Club. I think you're a prime candidate to join."

"Why would I want to join something called Butt Club?"

"Because you have no one to talk to about this. And you really, really want to talk about this."

True. How many times had Ed gotten together with friends, and it was on the tip of his tongue to talk about it? Sometimes he felt compelled to mention these butts on social media, but he knew it would result in a witch hunt. He liked his life and wanted to keep it intact. He liked having friends.

"No," he said. "That sounds too creepy. I don't want to do that."

"That's your prerogative. But first answer my question."

"What question?"

"Do you have a rating system yet?"

Ed had thought about that kind of thing, but it sounded too repulsive. He only counted the number of great butts he saw from the train to work and back. If he saw any before or after that period of time they didn't count. It cheered him up to get double digits, like maybe he'd accomplished something. Like the miserable commute had been worth it.

"I'm not into objectifying women."

"Come on. That's got to be the most hypocritical thing I've ever heard. Of course you objectify women. I've seen you watch butts, and when a really juicy one comes along your eyes lock on it for blocks on end."

How could someone he didn't even know know so much about him?

"I'm not interested. Please leave me alone."

The stranger whipped out a notebook. "Just look at this."

Ed didn't want to, but the notebook nearly slapped him in the face. He saw a lot of statistics, kind of like the back of a baseball card. He also saw illustrated butts. Lots of them. The stranger had talent, too. All of them looked very realistic. Each butt had two drawings: one clothed and the other of what the stranger thought it would look like unclothed.

They were *exquisite*!

The stranger's smile no longer seemed feral; it was warm.

Welcoming. He held out his hand. "Brad."

Ed took it. "Ed."

"Welcome to Butt Club."

At first it was just Ed and Brad. They walked together every morning and evening. Soon Ed had his own notebook. He couldn't draw butts, though. He described them to Brad, and he magically reproduced the butt like he was a police artist.

Near the end of the month Brad invited Ed to his first meeting of Butt Club at Brad's place. Ed was supposed to take his wife out to a movie, but this was too important to pass up. He canceled with Helena—had to work late, honey—and headed out to meet the other members.

There was Jared, who liked his butts big and black. He liked to imagine himself being able to put a drink on top and not have it fall off. He was a clay man. He could reproduce his findings pretty faithfully. He took pictures of the sculptures and showed them off to everyone. He also confessed to caressing them at night, hoping it would give him sex dreams.

Aday was a bit older than the rest. He had a thin spot of hair on the crown of his head and a few gray strands in his sideburns. He liked bubble butts—like Jen Salter and Kim Kardashian's—and he could ramble for hours about them. He didn't have any artistic talents, so he overcompensated by talking about butts. He recently tried composing poems about them, but he sucked as a writer. Still, he had fun. Ed remembered one of said poems being called "Skirt-Holding Weather."

A hot summer day

with a strong wind blowing.

Scantily clad ladies on their way to work.

Some wear short dresses or skirts

and they hold them down to stay decent.

This doesn't always work.

The wind kicks up the back of a woman's skirt.

She's wearing a black thong.

Her tan buttocks in all their muscular glory.

She grabs her skirt and pushes down,

161

accentuating the shape of her butt.
Thin cloth stretched out tight
Showing where her ass crack is.

Sometimes walking to work is worth it.

The last member was Paul. He was infatuated with shapely butts on skinny women. He'd been busted the most because he took too many risks trying to see boobs, too. He had to be constantly reminded that they weren't Boob Club. Paul didn't care, though.

All were married men except for Brad. He was in a long-term committed relationship with three women, all with wonderful butts. What did their significant others think of Butt Club? They had no idea what their men were up to.

Ed's first meeting started out awkward. Who wanted to talk about such a personal topic with a roomful of strangers? As he got to know them he relaxed. He felt more open about discussing butts, which he didn't feel comfortable even mentioning to Helena.

Aday mentioned something called VPL. Ed asked him what that meant, and everyone snickered. He felt too much like the new guy in that moment.

Brad grinned. It was the savage kind. "Visible Panty Line. The holiest thing we can see in Butt Club except for when a breeze comes along and lifts up a skirt. That's rare, but when it happens it's truly *magical*."

It made Ed feel good. He liked VPL a lot. Good to know that it had a phrase.

Future meetings were even better. He made sure to set the time aside for them, always careful to warn Helena that he was going to be working late. She took it well. It gave her more time to see her friends instead of just watching Netflix with Ed.

His fifth meeting was a game changer.

"Creep shots," Brad said.

"That's too dangerous," Paul said.

"Not if you don't try for boobs, you pervert," Aday said.

"Hey, I *need* boobs. We *all* do. There is no yin without yang."

Brad held up his hands. "Stop. Paul, *no* creep shots for boobs. Stay on point. If you get caught, the women might press charges.

You might be tempted to give the rest of us up to save yourself. Boobs are out of the question."

Paul frowned, but he didn't say anything more.

"So we need rules," Brad continued. "Don't do anything to betray your purpose. Remember that the target isn't the only person to be worried about. Other pedestrians might notice. Not all commuters are apathetic. They *will* call you on it."

There were more rules, and Ed took notes. He nearly drooled at the prospect of preserving the fleeting, yet great, butts he saw every day. Put them on the cloud, and they could live *forever*. It made him feel like the curator of a museum.

Paul, a website designer in his square life, came up with an excellent idea. "I'll build us an intranet site. We can upload our individual creep shots so we can all see what we've done."

Wow. Now Ed can see *even more* great butts! The world was well and truly a magical place!

But he had to be more careful. Helena and Ed were in the practice of being open with each other. He could no longer let her have access to his phone all the time. He put up a thumbprint security measure just to be safe.

Taking creep shots turned out to be easier than he expected. Everyone had their faces plugged into their cell phones. What difference did one more person make? Nobody checked his screen because they were too busy looking at their own.

After doing this for a week he went home to upload his findings to Butt Club's intranet site. Helena was home, so he went to the bathroom to upload while taking a leisurely shit.

It was impossible to do this in a timely manner. He paused to admire each picture, reliving the glorious butts of the day. He blew each one a kiss before finishing the upload.

Helena pounded on the door. "Hon? What's taking you so long? I gotta go."

"Sorry, babe. I'm taking . . . going number two."

"I swear, if you're in there just looking at your phone I will murder you. I will skin you. And I will get a St. Bernard just so I can make it wear you like a coat."

Ed was used to her outlandish threats. On their honeymoon she feared he might drop her on the way over the threshold. "If you do, I'll core out your skull. I'll shove roadkill into it. And I'll make you zombie-walk into a pit of vipers."

So he took his time. He didn't use the air freshener because he knew she would sniff. If she didn't smell poop she would at the least punch him in the shoulder. She could hit hard, so Ed wanted to avoid that.

He washed his hands and opened the door. Helena pushed past him and took a whiff of the air. She glanced sidelong at him, still suspicious. Then she relented, shooing him away.

Close call.

At the next meeting Jared had an interesting proposal.

"I just found some porn online about people who grope strangers in crowds. Usually they grab butts, but they're surrounded by masses of people, so most targets think it's just jostling."

"Yeah, I've seen that," Brad said. "A lot of guys rub their bare dicks on strangers' butts, too. There are cumshots and all. Sounds a bit risky."

"We don't have to do that other stuff," Jared said. "We grope a butt, what's the worst that can happen? They notice, and we apologize for an accident. At best we graze a wonderful ass, and no one's the wiser!"

"I don't think I could do that," Ed said. "I would feel too much like I was cheating on my wife."

"Me, too," Aday said.

"Let's forget it," Brad said. "Jared, I guess you'll have to stick to feeling up your sculptures."

The next night, while watching *Mike and Molly* with Helena, Ed decided to check his Facebook. He used his thumb on his phone's screen to open it up.

"What was that?" she asked.

"What was what?"

"You had your phone locked. You unlocked it with your thumbprint just now. You've never done that before. What's going on?"

Ed's brain kicked into high gear. Thankfully his time in Butt Club helped hone his reaction time. "I saw a news story at the train station. Identity thieves can steal your info if you don't lock your phone. Something to do with scanners. I have our bank accounts on this thing. Why take a chance? You should probably lock yours, too."

He knew right away that she thought something was wrong

with how he answered. She didn't say anything, but he knew she would file it away for later. He would probably have to play it safe until she forgot about it.

After some deliberation he decided not to go to the next two Butt Club meetings. She remained slightly cold to him for a week, but soon after she was back to her usual self.

When he returned to Butt Club he learned that during his absence Jared had been arrested. He was deathly afraid of having his wife bail him out, so he asked Brad to do it. As it turned out, Jared had tried groping. The first two times he pulled it off. The third time he grew bolder. His enthusiasm overcame him, and his grope turned into a full-on butt slap. The idiot was recording at the time, so the cops confiscated his phone. Thanks to all the creep shots, he was going on the sex crimes registry.

"Don't worry. I didn't give 'em anything on Butt Club."

Brad, Aday and Paul had a huge discussion about it. Jared had put them all at risk. Thankfully nothing came of it. They had to punish him, though. They couldn't kick him out of Butt Club. He might feel the need for revenge. Paul said he could cut Jared off from the intranet site. Brad liked that. They voted to ban him from Butt Club for a month. Jared grumbled, but he took it.

"I'm glad I missed that," Ed said. "I don't do well with confrontation."

The day before the next meeting, Ed's life changed forever. On the way to the office, walking up a flight of steps, he suddenly found the world's most spectacular butt nearly shoved in his face. He'd been looking at his phone, so he didn't notice it at first, not until he almost planted his face into its glory.

It was perfect. Curvy. Not too big. Not too small. *Just right*. At the top he could see two dimples he could easily see putting his thumbs in while grabbing her hips. The top of her crack began its slow descent just above the waistband. He could see it continue through the tight jean shorts, spreading each cheek out so they didn't look like they were attached. They wrestled with each other hypnotically. Glancing down he saw that the shorts were so short that the bottom curves of her butt showed clearly, enough so that he knew she either wore a thong underneath or nothing at all.

Ed was in such awe that he almost forgot to take a picture. Not caring what anyone else might see, he jerked his phone up. A last-minute decision entered his head, and he started recording this ass as it shuffled and undulated against itself.

She turned at the corner and walked away. Only then did he realize that he had a full rod in his pants. The front bulged really far, so he untucked his shirt for the rest of the walk.

Throughout the day he looked at the video whenever he had the chance. He got nothing done at work. He didn't even look at butts on the walk to the station. He had it on repeat the whole time on the train.

When he got home he was delighted that Helena wasn't there yet. He went to the bathroom and watched it again, this time with his hand on his dick. For the first time since he started questing for butts he jerked off thinking about it. It didn't last long. About a minute passed, and he panicked when he realized he didn't have anything to cum into. He jumped up, aimed his dick at the sink and fired off five strong, bullet-fast ropes.

He hadn't cum like this since high school. It made him feel young again. Powerful.

Still shaking, he uploaded the video to the intranet site. Only then did he clean up after himself. He took a shower so Helena wouldn't smell the orgasm on him.

When he got out he had four messages on his phone. Each came from a member of Butt Club.

He decided to call Brad first.

He did not bother to say hi. "Do you realize what you've found?"

"Oh yes," Ed said. "The greatest butt in history."

"That's just the tip of the iceberg. This is the butt you were born to find. Butt Club's Goddess. Generations of men like us will worship her until the end of time. Ed. How does it feel to have discovered a new deity?"

"Wow. I never thought of it like that. That's nice of you to say, Brad."

"This is the beginning of a new chapter. This changes *everything*. Don't miss tomorrow's meeting."

"Wouldn't dream of it." Ed hung up.

The other messages were not as impressive. Just eager congratulations. Aday decided to write a poem about it. Jared had already begun a sculpture of it. Paul wanted to know where the video was taken. He wanted to try and meet this one in person.

Ed decided against telling him for fear of another groping incident.

"Hon! I'm home!"

Ed shut his phone down. He got dressed and headed out to greet Helena. He found her setting her purse down and kicking out of her sneakers. Her face looked a bit flushed from her daily workout. He didn't say anything; he just swooped down and kissed her deeply.

Helena, used to mere pecks on the lips, luxuriated in this sudden passion. As they drew away from each other, she panted. "Where did *that* come from?"

"I just really wanted to do that," Ed said. "When was the last time we got crazy?"

She smiled. "It's been a while. And I've been feeling neglected lately. So . . ."

Ed squeezed his crotch, showing off a massive erection. Her eyes lit up when she saw it. He nodded his head toward the bedroom, and she led the way. Ed took the time to admire her butt. He would have definitely put it up on the intranet site if he'd seen it out in the wild. It bounced back and forth, and with each move his dick twitched.

He couldn't take it anymore. He grabbed her butt, pulling her to a stop. He kneaded her through her yoga pants. It felt wonderful. No wonder Jared liked groping so much!

Ed shoved his face into her butt, sinking his nose into her crack. She gasped and started laughing. He snorted, inhaling the sweat that still lingered from her exercise. It was slightly poopy, but he thought it enhanced the experience.

His fingers hooked in her waistband and pulled down. Then he yanked down her panties, burying his face into her bare butt. She moaned, and he licked. Not too dirty. Just the right amount of dirty.

They made wild animal love for more than an hour. Helena came five times, and Ed came three times, each as powerful and confident as the first orgasm in the bathroom. Sweaty, they fell asleep in each other's arms.

Ed dreamed of the world's greatest butt. Following it in the streets of the city. On the train. To his home. She turned around, and he saw it was his wife.

He woke up with morning wood that felt like a crowbar. It

nestled in Helena's butt crack, its head pushing into his belly button.

She must have sensed his sudden consciousness because she snapped awake and moaned, clenching her butt. "You want more? Christ, Ed. Did you down a bottle of Viagra?"

"Nope. Maybe we're in heat."

She looked at the clock. "We have twenty minutes before the alarm goes off."

She moved to her back, spreading her legs. Her vagina bloomed like a flower. Ed stung like a bee.

Later, on his walk to the office, Ed saw The Butt again. He couldn't believe his luck. This time it was clad in yoga pants so tight he didn't have to imagine what it looked like naked. If he could see the front he had no doubt that she would have camel toe. Deep camel toe. He could probably see each pussy lip in perfect clarity.

After a moment of appreciation he began recording again. Once more he showed up for work with a raging hard-on.

That night he eagerly showed up for the Butt Club meeting. Everyone sang his praises, and they stared in awe at the new video. Ed felt his face flush with shame when he realized he had an erection in a room full of men. But then he noticed that he wasn't alone. All of their pants were bulging. He didn't know how to feel about that.

"Holy shit," Paul said. "Ed's packing heat."

Everyone looked involuntarily. Aday said, "Jesus, Paul. You pervert." But he didn't look away.

"How big is it?" Paul asked Ed.

Ed didn't really know. Unlike other boys he'd never measured it. It looked like ten inches, so that was what he said.

"Can I see it?" Paul asked.

"Stop," Aday said. "I'm killing this conversation immediately."

"I've never seen one that big. In real life, I mean."

"You will shut the fuck up *now*," Aday said. "We're here for butts. Not penises."

This topic wilted everyone except for Paul. To get things back on track Ed uploaded the new video. They all watched it again on their own phones.

"We have to talk about this butt," Brad said. "Jared, how is the sculpture going?"

"It'll be done by next week."

"Good. We'll display it here." He pointed to a walk-in closet. "It will be our shrine. We will worship there."

"We need more information about her," Aday said. "If we're going to worship her butt, we should know her name. Where she lives, works. If she's with someone."

"If she's single, I'm all over that," Jared said.

"No," Brad said. "Butt Club is not about sex. It's about love. An appreciation of art. I will not have you sully our Goddess."

"We all had hard-ons looking at her," Jared said. "You, too. Don't deny it, you hypocrite."

"I can't control that anymore than you can. Hell, I get an erection just from riding the train sometimes."

"Except it wasn't a train that did it this time. Let's face it. You sexualized this butt. It gets you hard."

Ed felt panicked. His guts twisted like when he was eight and his parents fought. For a moment he feared that this was the end of Butt Club, and he had caused it. He wanted to shrink away to nothing.

Aday held up his hands. "Stop. Let's pull back on this. Brad's right. If we sexualize The Butt, we will destroy it. We can't let it drive us crazy. We have to keep our intentions to worship and nothing more."

"Besides," Ed said. His voice trembled. "I might never see The Butt again."

Everyone in that room knew he was wrong, even Ed himself. Sure enough, he saw The Butt almost every day for the next month. It was never clothed the same. The woman knew what she had and wore it proudly. Butt Club went mad with joy with every new upload. Brad started walking with Ed again so he could see The Butt in person. He didn't even take pictures. He only admired it, smiling.

Other members speculated about her. What her life was like. What she acted like. They gave her a life she had no idea she had. Somehow that appealed to them.

One night, while having dinner with Helena in the city, it happened. They settled down with an aperitif and some appetizers. As they ate they talked about their day. Helena's boss was a jerk. Yelled at her a lot. Blamed things on her. Sometimes even hit on her. Ed opened his mouth to respond when he saw The Butt.

It walked by their table, hugged by the tight skirt of a fancy outfit. The Butt bulged, trying desperately to escape. He didn't realize it, but he looked very silly with his mouth hanging open and his eyes popping from their sockets.

He'd never dreamed that he would see The Butt away from his commute. His pants filled up, and he moved to get his phone.

"Ed? You okay? You look like someone just punched you in the balls."

Fuck! Helena! His mind scrambled, trying to figure out a way to get a picture without Helena noticing. Despair overcame him as he realized it was impossible.

Helena turned so she could follow the path of his eyes. She caught it just in time as the woman sat down at a table with a young man. Helena whipped her head around so fast her hair jumped. Her eyes blazed.

"Were you looking at that woman's ass?"

"I, well, no."

"Don't bullshit me, Ed. I will rip your cock off. I'll use it to fuck the hole where it used to be. And I'll set your fucking asshole on fire."

Sweat bubbled up on Ed's forehead. This could earn him more than a punch on the shoulder. Nothing less than the truth would save him. "I . . . uh . . . yes."

Her eyes held him in place. They could have turned him to stone. She simmered, and then she looked down. "I can't believe you."

"Sorry, babe. It's not like I'm going to leave you for a stranger who has a nice butt. It just caught my eye, that's all."

"Don't call it a butt like you're being cute. Be an adult and call it an ass."

"Okay."

She stared a challenge at him, and he knew what would come next. "Does she have a better ass than me?"

"God no." Zero hesitation. "I'm in love with your b—ass. I swore to honor and cherish that ass until death do us part."

She smiled, and Ed thought—prayed—that it meant the end of this argument.

No such luck.

"That's sweet, hon. Now give me your phone."

Ed's insides iced over, and for a moment he thought he was having a heart attack.

"I know you're hiding something from me." Her tone could have frozen fire. "It has something to do with that phone. Give it to me. And unlock it first. Or I will scream. I will slap you. And I will throw your ass out." She held out her hand.

Like a robot Ed slowly gave her his phone. He pressed his thumb to the screen and closed his eyes. All the pictures he'd uploaded, he deleted . . . except for the ones involving The Butt. He couldn't bear to delete something so *holy*. He just hoped Helena wouldn't recognize it.

"What the fuck is this, Ed? Jesus Christ."

He couldn't answer her. He felt like crying.

"Open your fucking eyes and explain yourself!"

Gingerly he looked at her. He'd never seen such fury in her eyes, and it was mixed with a healthy dose of disgust.

"I've known you for seven years. I used to thank my lucky stars because I had myself a good man. You look my friends in the eyes, not the tits. You don't watch other women. I've never seen you watch porn. I was certain you never so much as jerked off. Mom told me every man is a pervert about at least one thing. But I defended you. *I defended you*. And now she's right. Creep shots, Ed? Of the *same ass*? Who is this woman? Does she know you're doing this? *Why* are you doing this? Do you know what a *violation* this is of her? It's almost rape, Ed. It's definitely stalking, and it's *not cool*."

He took it all in silence, daring not to speak for fear of breaking down.

"Talk to me, you sack of shit. At least try to explain yourself."

Ed sniffed, wiping at his eye. "I have no defense."

"That's what I fucking thought."

This was all he could take. The shame burning in his guts like a tire fire choked him, and he started crying. He tried to hide it behind a napkin.

"Oh Jesus Christ, Ed. You're crying? Like a bitch? I never thought you were a bitch. Wishy-washy, yes, but not a bitch."

He couldn't say anything. His guilt was too strong.

"You're making a scene. People are looking at us."

The thought horrified him, but he couldn't back down now,

and to run away would make him look even more like a bitch.

"Okay," Helena said. "Here's what we'll do. We'll go home. I'll have my brother come over. He'll help you pack up your things, and I'll give you a thousand dollars from our savings. That will get you a place to stay for a bit. And then you'll get divorce papers from my lawyer. You're going to sign them, or I'll . . . I'll . . . Shit. I don't know what I'll do to your pathetic ass. Now. Let's go."

He went, and he didn't dare look at anyone else on the way out.

The next three days were nothing short of miserable for Ed. The only thing that made him happy was butt hunting, in particular The Butt. When he got home—after uploading his day's findings—he felt lonely. Empty. He didn't know what to do with himself. Sometimes he just stared at a blank wall until it was time for bed. He tried turning to drink, and while it felt good at the time, the hangover nearly destroyed him. He almost called in sick, it was that bad. Never again.

Finally he did the only thing he could do: he went to Brad's and asked to see the shrine.

"It's ten o'clock, dude. Can it wait?"

"No," Ed said. "It has to be now."

Brad stepped aside and escorted him to the walk-in closet. "You need to be alone?"

"Yes."

Ed went in and closed the door. He pulled the hanging string, and a red light snapped to life above him. It illuminated the life-size sculpture and all the print-out photos of what it was based on taped all over the walls. He lowered himself to his knees so that he was face to Butt. He closed his eyes. He clasped both hands together and started praying. Praying for Helena. Praying for her to be by his side. Praying for her to love him again. He didn't want to feel this pain anymore.

Much to his surprise it made him feel better. He opened his eyes and gazed upon the glory before him. Just like the real thing. He caressed it, wishing it wasn't so hard and cold. He wanted it to feel like flesh. He wanted to touch the real Butt. It was the only thing in his life worth living for.

He gave it a gentle kiss and stood. Turned out the light. Opened the door. Brad stood a respectful distance away, waiting.

"Everything okay?"

Tears sprang up from Ed's eyes, and he wanted to break down. Maybe not in front of Brad, though. Men shouldn't cry in front of other men, or at least that's what his father always told him. He couldn't speak, not until he got control of himself.

Brad saw the tears. Wordlessly he guided Ed to a seat and put a glass of bourbon in his hand. "Tell me all about it."

Ed poured his sorrows out, and Brad listened intently. At the end he could only smile. "That's a horrible story, my friend, but there *is* a silver lining."

"If there is I don't see it."

"The Butt. Do you know the chances of running into it away from your commute? Getting struck by lightning twice is probably easier. This is significant. It means that *The Butt chose you.*"

Ed's stomach rose inside of him as if he'd forgotten to take the final step on a flight of stairs, thinking he was on solid ground. Brad's tone sounded so portentous, like maybe how Jesus would have sounded during his Sermon on the Mount.

The Butt chose me!

Ed practically floated home. Everything was right in the world.

He told his story at the next Butt Club meeting, including the part about how The Butt chose him. Jared liked that a lot.

"I think I'm riding the same path, Ed. My wife thought my artistic outlet was cute. She even posed for me once. But she's seen me make a few sculptures of The Butt, and she does *not* like my new obsession."

"Anyone else having trouble at home?" Brad asked. Aday and Paul remained silent. "I am. My favorite girlfriend has started noticing my appreciation of butts. It might be time to put Butt Club on hiatus."

"No," Ed said. "We can't. The Butt is too important. It *chose* me. We can't back away from something like that!"

"I agree," Paul said. "We need to ramp things up. Take it to the next level." He paused. "We need to kidnap The Butt. Worship it like it was meant to be."

Ed breathed so hard he nearly panted.

"Out of the question," Brad said. "Butt Club started as something questionable but legal. With the creepshots we were on the border. Cases have gone to trial, but none of them have won so far. Kidnapping is something different. It's one hundred percent illegal. I won't be party to it. Anyone attempting to do so will be banned from Butt Club for life."

"You said it yourself," Ed said. "The Butt chose me. This is bigger than us. Bigger than the law."

"This is about religion," Jared said.

"The Butt is all I have to live for," Ed said.

Brad stared out at his fellow butt aficionados, unbelieving. Perhaps God Himself had looked like this upon realizing the lunacy of His own creation, humanity. Startled he shook his head like a gymnast regaining balance. "Butt Club is canceled for the next month. Paul, I want you to cancel everyone's access to the intranet site, even mine. No more butt watching on your commute. Think about other things. Calm down. Let's get the idea of Butt Club as a cult out of your head. Meeting's over."

Everyone glanced at each other, uncomprehending. Butt Club canceled? Impossible! Silence reigned. Not even a nervous cough could be heard.

"In case you didn't hear me," Brad said, "get out of my home."

They stood uncertainly and shuffled toward the door. They all went their separate ways without so much as saying goodbye.

Ed couldn't do it. He couldn't ignore the wonderful butts on his commute. He restrained himself from taking creep shots, but he couldn't *not* look. Might as well have asked him not to breathe. It didn't bring him as much joy as it once did, though.

He prayed for The Butt, and it never came. The world seemed drab. His food had no taste. Everything seemed sterile. Without the intranet site his home life had no meaning. How had he survived before he'd joined Butt Club? He was a different person back then. Butt Club was the difference between BC and AD.

On the third night his phone rang. It was Paul.

"Were you telling the truth at the last meeting? About The Butt being the only thing making your life worthwhile?"

"God yes," Ed said. "I'm going crazy without it. Without Butt Club."

"Jared feels the same. Where do you stand on having The Butt for ourselves?"

Ed paused. Kidnapping was wrong. He knew this. But The

174

Butt wasn't really a person; it was the personification of an idea. Besides, he was the chosen one. The Butt was his by right.

"I'm for it," he said.

"Good. Meet us tomorrow night at eight. We'll be at my place. And don't tell Brad or Aday. We're starting our own Butt Club."

Ed smiled. Everything was right with the world again.

The next day Ed received a link to the new Butt Club intranet site with his login and password. He resumed taking creep shots that morning. All he could think about was the new Butt Club meeting tonight. He'd miss Brad and Aday. Without them Ed wouldn't be the man he was today. But Butt Club had to go on.

Paul's place wasn't as nice as Brad's. The wife and kids were out of town and weren't expected back until tomorrow. They had no sculpture to worship, but Jared brought one more suitable for travel. All in all, not bad.

"We need to know more about The Butt," Paul said. "Ed's closest to it. I say we take time off work to go with Ed on his commute. When we see it we can track it. Maybe get some front pictures. Maybe we can even figure out its owner's name, and if we get that? We have *her*."

The next few days were thrilling. Ed liked having Paul and Jared with him, and the way they coordinated with each other made him feel like he was on a military operation. Or better yet, in a spy movie. Jared went into her office building, and at great risk he managed to learn her name: Marla Genovese. With that Paul was able to research her online. Within two days he had everything on her from her Facebook page to her Social Security number.

"She's not married, but she's seeing three guys. Nothing serious. She's a fashion model, but no nudes, unfortunately. She makes seventy-five thousand a year, but I bet she'll do better next year. She likes to party. Mostly vodka and cocaine. And I even have her address. She lives in the northern 'burbs. Very nice neighborhood."

Ed didn't know how he felt about knowing all of this information. Before it was fun because it was The Butt. Now it felt creepy. He didn't want The Butt to be a part of a person with a life and personality and loved ones. He wanted the object. The idea.

"How are we going to get her?" Jared asked. "We can't

exactly take her off the street in broad daylight during rush hour."

"We do it at night," Paul said. "From her home. She doesn't live with anyone except for a cat. We just have to make sure she's not entertaining any of her boyfriends."

"That's still a crazy thing to pull off. Do you have a specific plan?"

"I'm working on it." Paul then started describing what he had so far. Forget military ops or spy movies; now Ed felt like he was planning a heist. It was actually a pretty good plan with very little violence and practically no chance of getting caught. Too bad Brad and Aday were too scared for this.

Over the next few hours they tweaked the plan, and by the time they all left for home they'd decided to kidnap The Butt on Thursday night. They all put in for Friday off from work.

Two days. Two! And Butt Club would never be the same.

On the night of the kidnapping they all met at Jared's place. It was the closest to The Butt, and his wife had left him, so they didn't need to sneak around. Upon success they would hold The Butt here, in Jared's basement.

They donned black clothes and black skull caps. They painted their faces black. The black gloves were the final touch. They then got into Paul's black van and headed out. Thirty-five minutes later they parked in the shadows around the corner from her house. Ed sneaked out into her backyard. No one saw him. He kept to the wall, observing everything he could. The house was dark and silent. He knew that Jared remained behind as the getaway driver. Paul would be approaching the front door with a key he'd made from a putty imprint he'd sneaked at her office when she was away from her desk.

If either one of them ran into trouble they were to dial the other. Their phones were set on vibrate. The receiver would acknowledge by rejecting the call.

The door clicked, and Paul waved him in. Ed didn't close the door all the way for fear of making a sound. He then followed Paul up the stairs, both keeping their feet to the sides so they wouldn't cause any of them to creak. Paul had showed them the blueprints, so they knew where The Butt's bedroom was. They moved close to the walls, making no noise at all.

The bedroom door was wide open. She lived alone; why

bother to close doors? Ed and Paul peeked in and saw Marla in bed, her eyes closed, her blanket up to her neck. The cat lay sleeping at her feet. They saw this by the light of her charging phone and the power button on her cable box.

Paul produced a bottle of chloroform and a handkerchief. As quietly as he could he unscrewed the cap. It made a tiny scratching noise.

It was enough to wake the cat. It regarded them curiously, eyes shimmering in the near dark. Ed had expressed some concern about dealing with the cat, but Paul had brushed it off. "Cats don't flip out like dogs. I'll bet if we don't make any sudden movements it'll just watch as we kidnap its owner."

Paul folded the handkerchief and held it to the neck of the bottle, saturating it. They approached, Ed watching the cat. Its nose wrinkled when it smelled the chloroform, and it stood, alert, not liking the odor.

Paul stood over Marla's face, and when he bent over, the cat hissed, its ears back, fangs bared.

Marla's eyes opened.

Paul panicked and tried to slap the handkerchief down on her mouth. Before Ed could grab the cat, it leaped at Paul, nails slashing at his arms. It gave Marla just enough time to roll out of the way. The handkerchief hit her ear, doing no harm.

Paul screamed as the cat climbed his chest, sinking its claws in and biting his face. Blood seeped from twenty thin burning wounds. All thoughts of The Butt were gone, and he tried to pull the animal off of him. He got it away from his face, but now it tore his already savaged arms to ribbons.

Ed watched the whole thing in utter horror . . . until he noticed Marla. She flipped on the lamp on her night table as she rolled out of bed like a trained commando. He saw that she was completely naked. His mind couldn't stress it enough: *that's what The Butt looks like naked!* He stared, mouth agape, as she sprang from a crouch to a standing position. The Butt ululated just like it did when walking in the city, except now it bared its glory to Ed. He felt truly chosen indeed.

"Ed! Help me!"

Ed heard Paul's frantic request, but he couldn't decipher the words. He *couldn't*. The Butt occupied every ounce of his consciousness. It bunched up as Marla crouched again, and he marveled at the thick shapely muscles constricting. He hadn't been aware of the boner trying to bust his zipper, and he didn't even notice it when he came, nearly soaking through the entire front of his pants. It was the greatest orgasm he'd ever had, and he missed it because he was so lost in The Butt.

"Ed! Goddammit! Help!"

He didn't see *why* she'd crouched down or where she'd done it. He didn't see the safe and the dance her fingers performed on its numbers. He didn't see the gun she drew from inside.

He only came back to himself when she turned toward him, The Butt no longer visible. Her breasts were amazing. Her vagina was shaved bare, and he could see every detail of the front of that wonderful cleft, but none of it was as impressive and awe-inspiring as The Butt.

Marla pointed the gun at Ed first, and when she knew he was frozen in place she turned it on Paul, who still struggled with the cat. She whistled, and the cat unhooked its claws, dropping to the floor. It calmly walked away, standing next to Marla. Paul, gasping and groaning, collapsed to the floor, eyes wild, trying to assess the damage.

She aimed at Ed again. "Who are you assholes, and what are you doing in my home?"

Ed didn't understand. The Butt should be his. Why was the previous owner pointing a gun at him? None of this made sense.

"Are you robbers? Sex criminals? What?"

Ed tried to speak, but his mouth was too dry. He coughed. "Would you please . . . turn around?" His voice trembled and sounded squeaky.

"No, I will not fucking turn around. Answer my question."

"Don't," Paul said. "We're going to be arrested. Plead the Fifth."

Ed didn't hear him. The only thing that took command of his mind was his need to see The Naked Butt again. "Please?"

Her eyes narrowed. "Don't I know you?"

"Yes! Your Butt chose me! I'm here to finally claim it!"

"Oh Jesus." She sighed. "You're the guy who checks me out on my commute. What the fuck do you think you're doing here? This is insane."

"It was meant to be." Ed raised his arms out and started moving toward her. Toward The Butt. Ready to be embraced.

Her jaw clenched. "Don't fucking move."

Ed took another step.

"Ed! Stop! She'll do it! Just let her call the cops!"

Ed took another step.

"I'm warning you. I see you as a threat. If you get any closer I will shoot you, and I will shoot to kill."

Ed took another step. One more, and he'd be four feet from her.

She fired twice. Double tap, center mass. Both bullets ripped Ed's heart to pieces. He crumpled in a pile and died with a beatific smile on his face and his pants full of cum.

Paul held up his bloodied hands. "Please! Don't shoot me!"

She didn't, but she aimed the gun at him while she called 911. Only when the cops arrived did she put it down.

—

ONE YEAR LATER.

Brad lounged on a bench, watching the morning commuters go by. There was one guy in particular whom he saw every day. Amateur butt gazer. He'd just graduated to creep shots. And so history repeats itself.

He missed Ed. Ed was a good guy at heart, and he'd started down the wrong path. He'd lost the plot. His obsession destroyed Butt Club. Maybe that was for the best.

Brad still saw The Butt every once in a while, but he kept his distance. While his appreciation remained pure, he didn't want to make the same bad decisions Ed had.

Paul went to prison, sentenced to five years. Jared, who had driven away as soon as he heard gunshots, got caught groping in public twice more before getting sent to prison, too. Aday went on to become a semi-famous slam poet, haunting local coffee shops.

And Brad got married. No more Butt Club or anything like it. He missed the thrill of the hunt, but his life felt so much more satisfying now.

"Hey! Did you just take a picture of my ass?!"

"Uh . . ."

Brad watched the dumb kid flounder. Nope. He decided that he didn't really miss it. Not at all.

THE PATH

He gazed down the path lined with gnarled, dead trees and wondered if anything had ever survived here. There was an occasional weed, but the grass was wilted and brown. Not even moss grew between the ancient blocks of stone, set by the pilgrims when the Wild West meant Ohio. Why anyone would blaze a trail through such a waste land was beyond Scott Emmett. Even as a child he didn't care to know where the path led. His father had once warned him it was dangerous down there, not that young Scott ever intended to test the theory. Some told him there were bears, others haunts, and Scott continued not to care.

Except now it was *his* land, and if he was ever going to sell it —which was his intention, since the property was worth at least a couple million—he needed to see what he owned.

The inheritance had come as a complete surprise, as Scott was of the opinion that his father was too mean a bastard to die. He bore many scars that had been beaten into him by the old man, to say nothing of the undoubtedly true rumors of how his father had murdered his dear wife.

And now, much to Scott's pleasure, Edward Bradley Emmett was six feet under. Sleeping the Big Sleep. Worm chow. Chia corpse. The ground hogs were bringing him his mail. All these phrases, though old, brought a smile to Scott's face. Cancer, normally a hideous way to go, was amusing and ironic when it came to Old Mr. Emmett. He was a man who spent a good portion of his life sucking his supposed loved ones dry, and then his own body had devoured itself. Scott had a good long laugh over that one.

His humor was quickly killed by the hassle of dealing with

lawyers, even if they'd already been paid for. Scott hadn't known how much red tape was involved when it came to dead folks, but he was starting to feel like he was wrapped in it, a disgruntled crimson mummy. There was supposed to be a government agent coming to evaluate the land, but Scott wanted to see everything first, so there would be no surprises.

He glanced back at the house behind him. The Emmetts had been living there since they'd built it in 1699, and it resembled the castle they'd owned in England before moving to the colonies in a successful attempt to take advantage of the overseas demand for tobacco. The family had already been rich, but now they were walking moneybags, wealth built on the broken backs of countless slaves. Scott didn't mind the money, but the slaves sickened him. The idea that his ancestors owned human beings made him shiver and wonder what might be lurking in his own blood. Most times he tried to ignore it. It wasn't as if *he* had done anything. And he'd never liked his family, anyway. But still, he felt guilty.

This was one of the reasons he hadn't even considered taking up residence at 517 Pawgnasauket Avenue. Looking at the artifice, one couldn't doubt its haunted nature, and if slaves had died here, they would make fearsome wraiths.

But there were also memories, none of which Scott felt like reliving.

(They found her, dead and naked, in Farmer Brown's pond.)

He took the first step down the decrepit path and marveled at how well the stones had been placed. Certainly there were cracks, but for the most part the blocks were level. The going was easy; not once did he stumble as he walked down the slight hill into a small muddy valley where a pond sometimes grew in the spring. His father had told him frogs hibernated in the ground until the water would come back, but Scott had never seen evidence of their existence, even after some digging committed when he was eight. It was the farthest he'd ever come down the path.

Until now. He crested the upward slope and found a forgotten forest, nothing but hollow fallen logs and stumps. No animals frolicked, not even birds.

He continued down the path, wishing the sun would come out from behind the thick gray clouds above. The weatherman hadn't predicted rain, but the skies threatened with a storm nonetheless. He doubted Apollo's bright gaze would make anything down here appear cheerful, anyway.

Beyond the trees, farther than he could have imagined, was the boundary of the Emmett land: a pair of rocky hills, beyond which was a severe drop to the roiling sea seventy feet below. Scott had seen them on a map but never in person. They resembled a woman's legs, their peaks her knees, and between them a cave.

When his father had kicked him out at age eighteen, Scott had moved to the city, where he'd stayed until now. Given his urban lifestyle he'd never seen a cave before and had come to believe such things were created by pulp writers, despite pictures he'd seen in school books and on TV when he was a kid. As a result, he at once didn't believe his eyes, and suddenly desired to examine it closely. It was Something New and Mysterious. He wanted to know what was down there, and he truly hoped it was treasure. It looked like the kind of place a pirate would hide his booty, and it explained why his father had never wanted him to go down the path, as there were no dangerous animals around. The old man had been hiding his riches in the middle of nowhere, so the IRS couldn't find it.

The sudden curiosity was so strong he'd set foot inside the cave before practical questions came to him. It was dark, so why didn't he go back to get a flashlight? What about rope? Surely there were pitfalls. Maybe he needed to acquire a companion, as this wasn't a one-man job. And what if something bad happened? What if the ceiling were to collapse and trap him?

(The autopsy said she drowned. Her lungs were full of water.)

Then he saw the torch. It had burned recently. His father? Most likely. Scott reached into his shirt pocket and removed a pack of Camels and a lighter. He was trying to quit, but he found it a lot more difficult than he'd expected. He lit the cigarette first, then the torch. As the former burned slowly and provided a mere glow, the latter flamed brightly, illuminating the depths before him. The steady flicker revealed a set of natural stairs leading slightly downward. He heard a trickle of water from below, but the only thing he saw was rock, and a lot of it.

(They didn't know to check what kind of water it was, but it didn't matter; the neighbors knew what kind of man Mr. Emmett was, and they started the rumors accordingly.)

Scott started down, holding the torch in front of him just in case a step had become too eroded to hold him up. *Wouldn't that be peachy?* he thought. *I'd break my neck and no one would ever find me.* His friends would ask questions, but he was certain they'd never discover him in time.

This thought did not deter him as he continued forward, eager for a flash of treasure or whatever his father had hidden down here.

After what seemed like a half an hour, Scott reached the bottom and soon wished he hadn't.

The floor was smooth, as if someone had sanded out any abrasions, sleek as the floor of the Capitol building. Several cold dead torches lined the walls, and scattered about were contraptions made of splintered wood and dull metal. He cast his light among these things and was shocked to comprehend what they were.

(There were marks on her body, but they were not fatal. They knew Mr. Emmett's nature.)

A stretch rack. An iron maiden. A chair of spikes. Thumbscrews. Too many torture devices to notice at once, and they were not the tools of a dilettante dominatrix; they belonged in the days of the Inquisition.

Something tickled the back of Scott's mind. It felt like a forgotten memory trying to birth itself back into understanding, but it wouldn't come. Not yet.

Scott wasn't sure he wanted to remember.

He ran his fingers over the spiked seat to find every point still sharp but coated with flaking rust, or at least that's what he hoped it was. Nearby, shackles hung on the wall, showing a thick film on the inside of the manacles.

(Flesh was missing from her wrists, but interviews proved she'd always been that way.)

Scott's breath became heavier, and his heart beat faster, building its speed slowly like a well-rehearsed orchestra. The iceberg's tip was showing, and the rest was slowly coming to light.

Next to the shackles he noticed a strange shape on the wall. It was black and lumpen, like nothing he'd ever seen before. The thought occurred to him it might be a large bat, but he knew it wasn't so. He'd watched many hours of Animal Planet with his friends and a bong, and he knew what a bat looked like.

When he got closer he recognized it as some kind of cloak. He was about to reach out and grab it when it moved. Scott let out a gasp as he stumbled, striking the back of the spiked chair. It was bolted to the floor, so it didn't give an inch, forcing Scott forward to his knees. The torch slipped from his hands but did not go far. Fear drove him forward to scoop up the fire, and he pushed it out like a sword as the cloak fell away, showing a face both terrifying and familiar.

And it came to him.

He killed her. I know it because I watched it happen.

Scott remembered the fight. They'd thought he was in bed, but really he was in his father's library, reading a book of stories by some guy named Lovecraft. He'd heard them arguing in subdued tones, probably about money, which was usually the main topic of discussion. Their sounds instantly ceased with a *clang!* that reverberated throughout the house. Even as a child he knew what it had meant, and he eased out toward the parlor, where he saw his father hovering with a frying pan over his unconscious mother. The old man giggled and dropped the utensil so he could take Mrs. Emmett up into his arms.

He took her down the path to the cave, and little Scott had followed. His treacherous mind had spliced it out like a damaged piece of film, and he'd never noticed the edit before. He *had* been down here, and because of the repression he didn't know well enough not to come back.

Not to come back, and not to look once more into his father's pale, empty face.

"You're dead," Scott said. Though his fear was quite real, he felt silly saying it. The line belonged in a *Tales from the Crypt* comic book, except one where the moral didn't exist. What had he done to be placed helplessly in the hands of this lunatic again?

The face glared down at him, unmoving, like a statue made of flesh, but Scott knew it was a person. The eyes gleamed in the firelight, and the torso pumped with breath.

"I saw you in your coffin."

Still nothing, which was somehow worse than if Mr. Emmett had responded.

"What do you want?" Scott wailed.

Mr. Emmett stood silently, eyes blazing intently at his son.

"I'm not afraid of you!" His voice sounded false even to himself, not that it mattered. His words still had no effect.

Scott willed himself not to shake. He was almost forty years old, far too old to fear his father. Too old to fear *anyone*. Gritting his teeth, he roared and pushed himself to his feet, lurching forward. With great satisfaction, he jammed the flames into his father's gut.

But it passed through him.

The torch hit the wall behind Mr. Emmett and splintered almost enough to extinguish. Panic flushed through Scott's system, but he quickly became calm as he realized what this meant: his father was a ghost, and years of reading old horror stories told him that ghosts could harm no one unless the person in question had a heart condition.

Now that he was composed, Scott took down a fresh torch and lit it off the remains of the old one. He lifted it to the figure of his father and was unsettled to see the old man was still looking at him.

Can ghosts see the living? he wondered.

Finally Mr. Emmett moved. He stepped forward among his torture devices, and a rich laugh emanated from his spectral vocal cords. It was soon overcome by a brittle shriek.

Scott saw his mother kneeling on the floor, naked, just like she was on that night so many years ago. Her arms were extended to the thumbscrews where she was held in place. Her flabby, scarred breasts trembled as she watched her husband approach, holding a whip.

Scott wanted to turn away, but it felt like an external force was making him watch as his father lashed out at her time and again, her blood slapping the ceiling every time he drew back for another blow. She screamed, but no one could help her. The past was already written and could only echo throughout the eons.

Their ghostly images blinked out and reappeared at the rack. She was laid out and longer than she should have been. Bright pink stretch marks adorned her body, and in her mouth was a dirty metal funnel. Standing over her, legs spread, was her husband, and he was urinating into the cone. Her throat worked madly as she tried to swallow his waste rather than drown in it. When he was done, and she was still breathing, he laughed, jumping to the floor.

"My great-great-grandfather killed witches," Mr. Emmett said. "I've never met one, but if I ever did, I'd bring her here. For now, I'll have to be sated with a money-grubbing whore."

A lugubrious moan escaped from the funnel, but there was nothing that could be done. Mr. Emmett lifted a bucket and began to pour water down her esophagus. By the bottom of the stairs, Scott could see the image of a young boy, watching. It took him a moment to realize he was looking at his own ghost.

All the torches suddenly flared up, bathing the cave in light bright enough to have been provided by electricity. One by one, ghosts popped up at each torture device, and they were all the same. Scott remembered his father finding him. He remembered the rage. He remembered the pain.

At every different apparatus, all at the same time, he could see the torturer and the victim, his father and himself. Scott on the stretch rack where his mother had died. Scott in the iron maiden. Scott under the ever-dripping spout for days. Scott with weights crushing his legs. Scott with splinters under his fingernails. Scott inside a cage, in which it was too short to stand and too slender to sit. And more. So much more.

"No," he muttered. Memories unfolded like nocturnal flowers. All his life he remembered being beaten by his father, but never like this, yet it seemed right. This *really* happened to him, and it continued happening to the ghost of his childhood in this long-forgotten cave.

Scott could take it no longer; he fled up the stone steps and burst out the opening only to be confronted by yet another image of Edward Bradley Emmett. Scott's feet halted before the rest of him, and for a brief terrifying moment, he thought he'd topple into this new haunt, but he managed to maintain his balance.

The ghost of his father never faltered; he remained as stoic in death as he had been in life. Even when torturing, killing and laughing, he was dull and empty.

Scott struggled for something to say, some invective to spit, or maybe a desperate plea for an apology that would never mean a thing. His tongue remained dry, though, and only a pant came forth.

"You can't leave, Scott," his dead father told him. "You're here with me forever."

These words broke Scott's paralysis. With a courageous yelp

he rushed forward to slip around his father. The old man/ghost put up a hand in his son's path, but it appeared to be a half-hearted attempt. Scott was forced to pass through it, as if the figure was only mist.

The weird sensation did not stop his flight. As he stumbled up the trail he heard his father utter a laugh, amused by his son's fear.

It was only as he approached the house, exhausted and out of breath, that he realized he was still clutching the torch. Shaky, he brought the flames close to his face and blew them out with a tremendous breath.

For the next few days he remained indoors, locked away from the world by TV he didn't care about and radio-broadcasted baseball games he couldn't pay attention to. His thoughts constantly revolved around the cave. At first he thought he would simply never go down the path again and eventually the memory would fade, but time was Swiss-cheesing this theory until he knew in his heart it would never work. He considered hiring some guys from the city to seal the cave shut, and he'd almost called them several times, but something within him prevented this from happening.

On the seventh da, he figured out what this internal force was. For as long as he could remember, Scott felt like he was isolated from everyone else. Without love. Trapped in a purgatory of emptiness. His existence was meaningless. He was *soulless*.

He'd thought his life had been stolen by his father's abuses, but he'd considered it only figuratively. Now he knew how literal reality was. His soul—his *ghost*—was being held captive in that cave, and to ignore it was to surrender any chance of happiness. The apparition of his father was right: he couldn't leave the cave. Not yet.

How could he free his innocence? An exorcist? Or will any man of God do? Scott didn't think so, as he'd never been a believer, and his father had never acknowledged a power higher than himself. He thought perhaps the occult could offer a spell, only that sounded too ridiculous to pursue.

There was a small part of him that constantly reminded him only crazy people saw ghosts, and maybe this was a problem for a shrink, one with a generous prescription pad. This voice, however, sounded false; in his heart of hearts, he *knew* the cave was truly haunted.

It then occurred to him that there were things on earth that *could not* have a soul. What if he destroyed the torture devices? Would it not seem that without those dread contraptions, the ghosts could not continue their never-ending cycle? The wooden parts would be easy to eliminate, but would it be enough to dent the metal bits?

The next day Scott armed himself with a torch, a lighter and fluid and a sledgehammer, and he proceeded down the path to end this once and for all. It was a sunless day, but the clouds weren't thick enough for rain. The wasteland was barren of life, as usual, but near the opening of the cave he found a dandelion he hadn't noticed before. It wasn't the ideal life form, but it was something.

He leaned the sledgehammer against the hill so he could light the torch. When he was ready to descend he gathered his equipment and entered the cave, for good or ill. As soon as he reached the bottom, he started lighting all the torches on the wall, expecting to see his father at every corner of the torture chamber.

The old man didn't show his face.

It was difficult to choose which device to destroy first, but as soon as he decided on the iron maiden, he didn't hesitate. Scott opened the case and brought the hammer down on each spike, one at a time. When the inside was rendered useless, he pounded the outside until it was an unidentifiable lump.

Next he broke out the wooden pieces of the spiked chair and threw them in a corner, where he would later use a torch to burn them. The rest, he pounded until it was just as ineffective as the iron maiden.

He moved from device to device, and still there was no sign of his father. Scott had expected resistance of *some* kind, but he had no trouble in breaking every single piece of equipment beyond repair. He stood, panting, watching the splintered pile of wood burn, still gripping the scuffed sledgehammer in both hands, trying to remember if he'd forgotten anything.

It came to him in a flash as bright as a mushroom cloud. *The shackles.* He whirled so quickly the sledgehammer dropped from his fingers and thumped to the floor. At first he went to scramble for it, but then he noticed how futile that would be.

Hanging from a pair of manacles was the transparent form of a young Scott Emmett. Standing next to him was his father, and he held the one instrument Scott had overlooked: the old man's fists. Mr. Emmett wrapped a hand around the child's throat.

"You thought you were being clever," his father said. "Not a bad plan. But torture devices don't kill people. People kill people."

"Don't do that," Scott said. "I'm begging you."

The old man smiled, but his eyes were blank. "I know. How does it feel to be a big, strong adult and still be at my mercy?"

"Just let me go. Please."

Edward squeezed suddenly and savagely. The child-ghost screamed, and Scott felt pain shoot through his throat. He fell to his knees, clutching the hurt spot, hoping to subdue the agony.

When he started flaking away, Scott knew there was no winning. His father was too cruel and ruthless, and pain like this never went away. Chips of Scott rained down from his writhing body and littered the floor like a layer of snow. His thoughts began fragmenting until he couldn't hold a cogent idea together. As his face opened he felt his consciousness pour out like water from a broken jug. By the time his adult body had been reduced to dust, he was looking out from the eyes of his child-ghost.

"Welcome home, son," his father said. With a powerful twist, he turned Scott's head around as easily as twisting the top off a jar.

Edward left his son's corpse hanging from the wall as he took a torch and started up the steps back to the real world. Before he reached the path he carelessly stepped on the dandelion, severing the last life form of the wasteland from the ground without a thought. There it wilted, and soon it was gone.

STORY NOTES

"Attitude Adjustment": I have a group of short stories that I like to call my Office Horror cycle. This is one of them. It was brought on by this change that I've seen over the years of corporate jobs. This anti-confrontation thing. Maybe it comes from a good place, but sometimes it just doesn't make sense. You know those evil-is-when-a-good-person-does-nothing situations? That's the kind of thing I'm talking about. Now you're punished for doing the right thing, and it drives me crazy. It's also an excellent way to control people's minds . . .

"Monster Cock 2": How the fuck could I have made a sequel to "Monster Cock" when I ended the world in that one? Well, here's another cycle of mine. The Monster Cock cycle. How many ways can I end the world with man's obsession about dick size? So far, the answer is two. I've been doing some thinking, though.

"Daisy, Jeppke, and the Kid": This is kinda-sorta based on a true story. I'd read about a couple of junkies who tried to sell their baby in a Target parking lot. I tried to think of what kind of people would do that, and this story came to me. I tried everything in my power to think how they would think. No one is the villain of their own story.

"Snipe Hunt": This is another kinda-sorta true story. It happened when I was at one of my father-son camping trips with the Cub Scouts. We pulled the trick, but we set the bag up like the rattlesnake eggs trick. It scared the hell out of the adults, which made me so happy.

"Holliday Steps Out": I have a lifelong fascination with Wyatt Earp and Doc Holliday. Yet there was something odd about Wyatt during his final years. He ran a bunch of shady businesses, and this was after Doc's death. He also said some very kind things about Doc in those days. What if they'd switched bodies at the end?

"Party's Over": I had this dream about an aging rock star who is dying, but he doesn't know it. All of a sudden he hallucinates himself and all of his closest friends from his heyday, but as they looked back then. I woke up and thought it would be a better idea if they were actually aliens late to the party. And why not throw some subversion in there, too?

"Clyde Nebbins Meets the Devil": I wanted to write a quick story about someone who wanted to sell his soul to be the best at something really fucking stupid. Something no sane person would ever want. I thought about paper hangers and garbagemen and all sorts of silly things, but I settled on crossing guard. It made a lot of sense to me, and I'm glad I was able to get some drama out of it.

"JESUS WAS DEAD FOR THREE DAYS! CLICK HERE TO SEE HOW HE CAME BACK!": I like time travel stories, but sometimes I just get sick of the usual things, like people afraid to step on a butterfly or not running into your past self or any of that stuff. There are too many rules. I wanted to do one that had no rules so I could play fast and loose with everything. I think that if time travel existed, the Crucifixion would probably be the number one tourist spot. One thing led to another led to this story.

"Captain Meth-Mouth on the High Seas of Chicago": I started out thinking I would write a story about one of the guys who has to work on a theme park adventure thing like Pirates of the Caribbean, about how unfulfilled he felt with his life. Then I decided to add zombies because why not have a pirate situation in the zombie apocalypse. Once I had that idea, the rest just exploded out of my head almost full-formed. This one was a lot of fun to write, and sometimes I think maybe I could do an entire book about these guys. Perhaps some day.

"The Last of His Kind": I like to write about lonely people. Not just people who mutter about never going out, I mean people who flat-out have no friends. Loners. People seeking more from life and never finding it. Sometimes they imagine things like friendships with soap opera characters. This guy just happens to think that the last vampire in the world is talking to him. Poor bastard.

"Going Down": This one came from an angry place. (No shit, right?) It was written when I was suffering from a horrible bout of pancreatitis. The doctors originally thought I was going to die, so they loaded me down with Dilaudid. By this time, they decided I was going to live, and I was trapped in the hospital with mind-numbing TV shows. I started getting sick of how everyone could not stop talking about themselves all the time. ME! they all screamed. ME! ME! ME! We're a narcissistic lot, aren't we? What could be more narcissistic than filming one's self sucking one's own dick? At least at first. Then the twist comes in. All this guy wants is fame for bullshit, and what does he get for his efforts? Drowned in his own blood and genitals. On a side note, my very first reading was of this story at a comic book store in Chicago. I utterly horrified everyone, and that made me very happy.

"Rumble in the Retirement Home": Wrestlers don't often live long enough to make it to the retirement home. Obviously these characters are based on Hulk Hogan and Rowdy Roddy Piper. I thought it would be pretty funny for rival wrestlers who have both gone senile to battle each other in such an environment, thinking they were younger versions of themselves. I was actually kind of surprised when I got a bit of drama out of it. There's a moment where I teared up a bit while writing this one. I hope you know what I'm talking about.

"Late Start": This is 100% based on a dream I had once. Yes, Andy and Barney were in black and white while the rest of the world was in color. And yes, Barney really did threaten to rape me. I have no idea where this ridiculous dream came from.

"Piety": The monster came first. I had this horrible thought of a beast that hungered on male genitals. The trouble was finding a character to inflict it upon. Why not a God-fearing man who led his life by the Good Book?

"Black Friday": I am utterly and thoroughly disgusted by the madness created by the very concept of Black Friday. Having worked in retail, I recoil in horror at the thought of having to face all those customers, especially the ones frothing at the mouth to save what? Five bucks off on a TV? I refuse to go out on Black Friday. I won't give in to the unrelenting greed. So naturally I wrote an exaggerated story about it. But it's not too exaggerated, if you ask me.

"The Worm": I wrote this one strictly for the gross out. A friend told me this story once about how he knew a woman who didn't eat the worm. She shoved it up inside of her. One horrible thought led to another, and here we are. I have to say, I'm glad I affected a *Fangoria* reviewer enough to be mentioned in the review.

"Dream Quest for Dope": I have a policy of never writing a story just to be sent to a specifically themed anthology. What happens if it's rejected? Are you going to find another anthology with that exact same theme? And if you rewrite it a bit, any editor worth their salt would be able to figure out who it was originally written for. I made an exception for GG Allin. He was just such a fascinating guy. I decided I'd send him to Leng for some super heroin. I was surprised to learn later that I was the only one to combine Allin with Lovecraft. I thought that would have been a natural thing to do. Much to my pleasant surprise, I made it into the anthology.

"I Am the End": I'm a huge fan of rant songs, but the Dead Milkmen did it better than anyone. I wanted to give it a try with the most absurd concept I could think of. I think I did a pretty good job, with apologies to Cliff from *Cheers*.

"Dial 9 for Apocalypse": My square job is in telecom. As you would expect, I spend a lot of time dealing with IVRs. None of them are straight forward, and they will all, instead of bringing you to where you need to go, suggest going to their website instead. And the URL is always fucking long. This story came from a place of frustration. A frustration, I suspect, that will never die.

"Butt Club": When I got a new job in the heart of Chicago, I noticed something I never really saw working in the suburbs. There are a lot of attractive women in the city, and there are a lot of men who will stop in their tracks and turn around to watch the women walk away. Some men glance, which you can see in the 'burbs, but most of them came to a full stop to admire the view. Sometimes to just stare. I got the eerie idea that maybe they all belonged to the same underground secret society, and so Butt Club was born.

John Bruni

"The Path": As one who suffered abuse as a child, I think about it a lot. I think about the things that are taken away as a result, opportunities that one might not get in the future, the way it changes the victim. The idea of a childhood held captive by a ghost kind of fucked with me. This story comes from that darkness.

About the Author

John Bruni is the author of several books, most recently AND JESUS CAME BACK from Rooster Republic Press. His short fiction has appeared in a variety of publications, such as A HACKED-UP HOLIDAY MASSACRE (from Pill Hill Press, edited by Shane McKenzie) and SHROUD MAGAZINE. He edited STRANGE SEX 3 for StrangeHouse Books. He lives in Elmhurst, IL, where he promises he's not as violent as you would think. He's only ever punched two people over the course of forty years.